THE LOST AND THE SCARRED

T. MARIE ALEXANDER

Mom,

Life hasn't always been white picket fences and roses, but you've been there through it all without too much complaining. This is for you.

WARNING

Although this novel features a young adult main character in high school, it is a dark contemporary romance and is not suitable for younger teens due to mature content and language. The recommended age is eighteen+. Some scenes in this book may be triggering.

PROLOGUE

ROX

Twelve Years Ago . . .

"I'm taking her!" My daddy's slurred voice booms throughout the house. "She's my daughter!"

"You will not touch that little girl again! Do you hear me, James?" Ms. Wells spits back at my daddy with just as much venom.

Ms. Wells has been my nanny since my mommy and brother died last year. At first, Daddy said that he needed time and that Ms. Wells would be like a new mommy. He didn't lie. Ms. Wells is the best. She makes me grilled cheese sandwiches even though Daddy tells her not to, and she tells me stories of faraway lands for kids like me where they never grow old and mean. She tells me I can be a lost girl just like Wendy and explore lost places. But as much as I love hearing her stories and dreaming of my own Neverland, not even she or the stories can stop Daddy when he gets like this. No one can.

All Daddy do now is yell. Ms. Wells used to didn't say anything back, but as Daddy's words got meaner, she had to speak. He called her the 'n' word. Ms. Wells says we never call people that. I feel bad for her though. It's all my fault that Daddy is now mean to her too. I do things that make him mad.

When a loud boom lands on my door, I bring my quivering small hands up to my ears, trying to drown out what I know is to come. I move deeper into my closet, rocking back and forth. Daddy never finds me in here, tucked away in my closet behind princess dresses that he buys me as apologies. They buy me a couple of hours until Daddy is asleep, but in the mornings, nothing can conceal me.

"Roxanna!" Daddy yells through the door. "Unlock this damn door!"

I hear him jiggle the knob again, but when it doesn't budge, he pounds on the door. I press my hands harder into my ears, but the pounding doesn't stop. Not in my head. Not against my door. Not in my heart. Silent tears roll down my cheeks, and I swiftly swipe them away. I can't cry. If Daddy do get in here and see the tears, it will be worse. Much, much worse.

"James, stop this!" Ms. Wells hollers at him.

My daddy doesn't say anything and the pounding on my door stops. I stay behind the dresses for a moment until

I hear the all too familiar clumping footsteps of my daddy walking away. Crawling from behind the princess dresses, I race over to my bed and grab my one-eyed brown rabbit that Mommy gave me before she died. The rabbit isn't as nice as the dolls Daddy gives me, but I love this rabbit. Curling up with the stuffed animal, I finally exhale. It's over. At least for tonight.

I look out my window to the second star on the right. That's where Peter Pan lives. Ms. Wells says if I follow that star, it will lead me to him. She said that it led her people to their Neverland too. Just as I start to close my eyes and try to enter my beautiful Neverland, a scream sends me bolting upright on my bed. A loud bang, like on those black-and-white movies Daddy like to watch, has me covering my ears again. It does nothing to cover the next boom, which sounds louder, or Ms. Wells' cries.

I get up from my bed and walk over to the door. I know I shouldn't. Daddy is on the other side of the door. But Ms. Wells cried. When I cry, she comes. Doing my best to be as quiet as possible, I crack the door open and stare out. My free hand goes to my mouth as I see Ms. Wells on the floor and Daddy pointing a gun at her. I didn't even know Daddy had a gun. He told me once before while watching one of his black-and-white shows that only bad people had them. The side of Ms. Wells' pretty blue dress is tinted dark.

Her eyes dart to my door but quickly move back to Daddy. He didn't miss her small move, though, and whirls around. My body freezes, and I stare at him with wide eyes.

I should have stayed in my bed. I should have stayed in my closet till morning. Daddy drops the gun and charges at my door. I scream as my body finally moves, sprinting back to my corner, but it's no use. He's bigger and faster than me.

Daddy grabs my arm and I try to pull away, tears streaming down my cheeks.

"Please, Daddy! Please don't!" I say through heavy sobs. My cries don't stop him. They never do.

He picks me up off the floor and tugs at one of my pigtails. I watch as my daddy's hand balls into a fist as he looks at me. Like he hates what he sees and is punishing me for it.

"You look like her," he slurs.

My eyes widen as I try to pull back. He said the words—the words that always bring pain. I brace myself, seeing his hand twitch in my hair. He draws it back and I squeeze my eyes closed.

"Put her down, now," I hear Ms. Wells say through her own sobs.

Daddy twirls around and I open my eyes. Ms. Wells has Daddy's gun in one hand as she points it at him now.

"She's my daughter," my daddy shouts in response, dropping me to the hard, wooden floor. "I will do whatever I please with the brat."

Ms. Wells watch me for a long time, before saying, "Run."

I run over to where she lays on the floor, one hand holding her side and the gun raised at my daddy in the other.

She shakes her head at me and tells me to run again. I look back at my room and then at the door leading outside. Daddy takes a step forward, and the gun in Ms. Wells' hand goes off. A scream leaves me as Daddy drops to the floor, holding his leg and repeating "shit" over and over and over. Turning back to my nanny, she shakes her head again and says, "run." She wants me to leave.

Turning back toward my room, I run inside and head over to my bookshelf, finding my Peter Pan book and then grabbing my rabbit off the bed. Leaving everything else, I go back out the room. Daddy is too busy with his leg to even care about me running. I stop in front of Ms. Wells and place a kiss on her cheek. I'm going to miss her. And her grilled cheese sandwiches and her stories about Peter Pan.

"Run, my lost girl," she whispers. "Run and don't stop until you are far, far away from here in your own Never-land."

I nod, and with my rabbit and book in hand, I run.

Following the second star to the right.

CHAPTER 1

WRAN

Twelve years ago . . .

"Go help your brother shovel the snow," my father says, never taking his eyes from the television and sipping down his third beer.

"Like hell I will. He can do the shit by himself," I grumble back at my father. There's no way I'm helping him. He gets out of doing his chores because he's older. They want me to learn discipline and respect—things I already know, just choose not to use. They're pointless anyways.

"Get off your sorry ass and do as I say boy," my father shouts.

Ignoring him, I stomp back to my room and slump down on my bed, pulling my headphones back over my ears. My father might be a drunk lately, but his words are weak.

He never does anything. Just sits in his chair and drinks himself into a stupor. It wasn't always like this. My father was one of my buds, but a few months back, he lost his job working at some hotshot law firm. One of the owners was arrested for second-degree murder. He was all over the news. I will never forget what he looks like. Because of him, my father is like this. They were searching for the man's daughter, but it came to a stop after a few months of no results. The firm was closed down too. No one in their right mind would hire them. Hence, why we're in this situation.

I will never understand how someone can kill someone else without any reverence for life. It's despicable. It's evil. And I will never forgive the son of a bastard for ruining my family. We were doing just fine before all this stuff. We had enough money to hire someone to shovel the snow. And my brother wasn't trying to make up for my father's lacking by killing himself with two jobs and school. No fourteen-year-old should have to pretend to be sixteen just so the damn water won't get cut off. I might not be old enough to get a job, but I do know that Josh shouldn't be doing all the work. Our father should be more of a man.

I slap my hand over my face and groan.

And I'm making Josh shovel snow by himself on his day off.

Removing the headphones, I toss them to the end of my bed. I'm just as bad as our father, making Josh do everything. I get up from the bed and head over to where my snow boots lie on the floor. I slide them on and secure the straps before grabbing my coat and heading out front.

Josh looks up from his shoveling and removes the forest green scarf covering his mouth and nose. "Hey, kiddo. You here to help?"

I hate when he calls me that. Do I look like a kid? I haven't even entered my teens and I dwarf him, yet I'm the kid. Those words don't leave my mouth, though. My brother has enough on his plate without me smart-mouthing him and being a burden. So instead I simply nod. If becoming a popsicle will help him out, then I guess I'm braving this frigid snow and becoming a popsicle.

"There's another shovel 'round back." Josh searches the remaining patch of the drive. "There's not much left."

I nod again and turn to go but stop in my tracks. I look over my shoulder to where my brother has gone back to shoveling and say, "Sorry, bro."

Josh looks up, and for the first time since that shit of a man ruined my life, my brother smiles. He doesn't say anything, but it's his time to nod. He knows what I'm apologizing for. I don't have to say more.

Shoving my hair from my face, I turn away and head around back. The stupid neighbor's dog has been barking all morning. That's another reason my father is in an even grumpier mood than usual. That dog would make anyone's head burst. We should be used to it, but this morning it's worse. They must have forgotten to feed 'im or somethin'. Coming to a stop, I glare at the thing, willing it to stop the barking. It doesn't. Just stays in place, nose against the metal fence, looking over behind our house and barking. I turn to the pile of snow that's holding the dog's interest and frown. There's an odd lump on it, and I have to squint to get a better look. My eyes go wide when I make out a body. A small body.

It's a kid.

I take a step forward when it coughs and shivers. Gulping, I dart over to it and ignore the dog. I bend down to turn the kid over, but before I can, it does so on its own. My eyes widen at the person before me. It's an angel. A beautiful, beautiful angel. I pull my hand back as I look her over. Her eyes remain on me for a second before they close, and her head falls back against the snow. She must have been here since last night. It snowed again last night, and she's practically covered in it. I rake the snow from her body and hair. I nearly flinch away when I see what the snow veils. She's so tiny. So frail. She's wearing what I guess used to be a white dress with flowers all over it. It hangs on her as if too big, but something tells me it wasn't too big when she put it on. Her hair is so matted you can't see its true length. Her lips are cracked, and her face is sunken. And her skin . . . it's so, so white. Abnormally pale. One would think she was an angelic corpse if she hadn't just moved. God, she looks like she's starving.

Turning her over to see her full on, I do flinch back this time, accidentally dropping her. I know her. I've seen her. On the TV. On the news. She may look different now, but it's her:

the girl whose father did this to my family. I rummage my brain for her name but can't remember. I don't care though. Her and her murdering father did all this to us. They took our life. She deserves to freeze. She deserves to be buried. I don't care how much of an angel she appears. I hate her. I hate her father. And they can both rot in hell for all I care.

I get to my feet, ready to leave her, praying that it snows again so that no one finds her, when she coughs again. I glare down at the unmoving girl. The cops have stopped their search for her. Her father is in prison. Would anyone even miss this girl? She rolls slightly over, and for the first time I notice the book and ugly torn stuffed animal in her bony arms. Her eyes flutter open, and my breath hitches. Why does she look like an angel? If she didn't, I could just leave her here to wither away. She deserves it, right? She deserves to feel what it's like for your whole life to be uprooted.

Even as I think it, I know my mother would be scolding me for thinking it if she was here. I can't leave this girl to freeze. And from the looks of it, she's been freezing for a couple of months now. The winters here in Kingston aren't pretty. They're not super bad, but this winter has been dreadful and longer than normal.

With uncertain resolve, I bend down and pick her up. Man, she's tiny. She groans in my arms as I settle her head against my shoulder. At that moment, I hear my name coming from the front. Crap. I'm supposed to be helping Josh finish the driveway. I look at the tiny girl in my arms. As much as I hate her, she needs me. She needs someone.

I yell up front to my brother, "Be there in a minute."

I glance over at the old cellar doors. No one has been down there since my mother passed away. All her things are down there. I suck in a breath before going over to it. That's the only place to hide this girl. I know if Josh finds her, he'll send her away. Call the police. That's probably the right thing to do, but she's not going anywhere. I remember the news. Her mother is dead too. She has no family. They'll send her to foster care. I've heard stories about those places. And if anyone is going to have the luxury of torturing this angelic corpse, it's going to be me. Readjusting her a little, I open the cellar doors and walk down the narrow stairs, letting the door slam on our descent. The floors creak, and when I reach the bottom of them, I turn on the lights and stop dead in my tracks. It looks exactly like it did when I was five. Except for the boxes labeled with my mother's things, it's all the same. Granted, there's enough dust on everything to grow a garden, but it's the same.

Going over to the couch, I lay the girl down. She shivers and balls up, never relenting her hold on the Peter Pan book and the rabbit. Taking off my coat, I drape it over her. I doubt the coat will make any difference. She looks like she will be forever frozen. When she stops shaking, I smile down at her. When I realize I'm smiling, I scold myself. Just because she has a pretty face doesn't mean she's not the enemy. She will forever be the reason for all the pain in my life.

"Wran?" I hear again my brother yell again. "The drive is done. Thanks a lot, bro. Thanks a lot."

I sigh at the irritated tone in Josh's voice. I had every intention of helping him. He does so much for me, for this family, and I've been a punk lately. It's not Josh's fault that this girl and her father ruined us. And I don't want him to think I'm mad at him. He's my brother. He's my only brother. I apologized for everything moments ago, and then let him down. But watching the sleeping girl before me, I can't bring myself to be upset with myself. She needed my help more than my brother, and as much as helping her felt like ice in my veins, something in me wouldn't let me walk away.

It's been hours since I found the girl. She hasn't stirred once from her sleep. Every couple of minutes, she unconsciously pulls my coat tighter, like she can't find heat in her dreams. She looked like she hadn't eaten in forever, so I made her a grilled cheese. At eleven, it's the only thing I know how to make. Well, that and ramen noodles—but I ate the last pack of noodles.

My brother left for work an hour ago without saying anything to me. I feel like shit. I really didn't mean to disappoint him. That was a no-win situation. I could have left the girl in the snow. I could have let her freeze that pretty little face off. Josh would have been mad at that too if he found her and knew I knew she was there. Freezing.

A low whimper leaves her, and I lean over to make sure she's okay. Her eyes are wide open, but she has them trained on the back of the sofa. I raise my hand to touch her and she flinches. The pain that contorts on her face is like nothing I have ever seen. This angel is already in agony.

I pick up the half-eaten grilled cheese. I might have gotten hungry again while watching her sleep, but at least there is a half left.

"Hungry?" I ask her, placing the sandwich in the small space between her body and the back of the sofa.

She stares at the sandwich for what seems like forever. If she wasn't going to eat it, I could have eaten the whole thing. At least I thought about her. That's more than the daughter of a murderer deserves. She should be grateful. She turns and looks at me and then back at the sandwich. I suppose she thinks it's safe because she picks it up and slams it into her mouth. The whole half thing. In one bite. If I didn't hate her so much, that would be impressive. I don't think any of my friends at school could have eaten a whole half grilled cheese in one bite. She picks up the plate and licks at the bit of cheese that oozed from the sandwich. Geez.

"Still hungry?" I ask, watching her lick the plate, even though there is nothing on it now.

She gives me a shy nod and nothing more. I get up from the couch and watch her frantically start to shake her head. She just said she was hungry. Why is she shaking her head?

"I'm going to make you another one." I point at the plate. "You do want another one, right?"

She nods again. "You will come back?"

I inhale again as my eyes turn to saucers. That's the first time she's talked. And if I thought she was an angel before, her voice confirms it now. She sounds like a song. Like bells chiming in a church tower. And I hate it. It's just another thing that makes me look past what she did. I don't want to look past what she did. She needs to hurt too. She needs to hurt more.

"Then stop shaking your stupid head and let me make it," I yell at her.

She draws her book and rabbit to her chest and looks away from me. She doesn't nod. She doesn't speak. She doesn't cry. I want her to cry.

Leaning forward, I grab her face so she must look at me. "You are not my friend. You are an ugly little girl with weird purple eyes and a head too big for your body. You are dirty and foul and the only reason you are alive is because God doesn't want you in heaven to ruin it."

I grab her ridiculous bunny and panic rises on her face. She goes back to shaking her head, reaching for her little toy. I hold it so she can't reach it, which isn't that hard. I'm tall for an eleven-year-old boy—the tallest in my class. I wait for the tears to come, but they don't. She doesn't cry, and I don't understand why. I insulted her. I took her bunny, which obviously means a lot to her. I called her ugly. I might not think she's ugly. And her purple eyes are weird but in a good way. Things like that are supposed to make girls cry. She's supposed to be crying!

Anger rolls off me as she continues to reach for the stuffed animal. I throw it in the corner as she stumbles to her feet. I push her back down on the couch and wait. She stares at the corner but makes no attempt to move again. The tears I want finally come. And I hate it. I'm supposed to be happy with her tears. They are supposed to make me feel better about what she did. Seeing tears on an angel's face seems wrong, though. And they make me feel like a jerk.

I stomp over to the corner and retrieve the rabbit. I go back to her and hand it over. She takes it with shaky hands.

"I'll go get you something to eat. Stay here."

She nods and I leave. Stomping through the snow to the house, I can't help but think about how pretty she is. Even dirty, she's pretty. How do I bring myself to punish her when I can't even see tears on her face? It's not fair! I'm handed this opportunity, a chance to make up for all the hurt my family has gone through these last couple of months. And I freaking like her. It's not fair!

I throw the door open and head toward the kitchen. We don't have any more cheese left but I'm sure there is something here I don't have to cook to feed her. She's too tiny, and I am positive, after seeing her eat the grilled cheese, that it's not by choice. I rummage through our cabinets. There're some chips and a few snack cakes. I grab them and set them on the counter then open the fridge. Josh cooked chicken and mashed potatoes last night. My dad didn't eat and his plate is still untouched. I grab it and pile on the chips and cakes.

As I make my way back toward the door, my father yells, "Where you goin', boy?"

I stop and look over my shoulder to where he hasn't moved, beer bottles littered around him. I shake my head at the sight. My father was once a great lawyer. I could brag to the guys about him. Now, he's an embarrassment. Instead of finding another job, he felt sorry for himself and turned into this—a drunk letting his eleven and fourteen-year-old sons do the work to survive. He once told me that Belmonts didn't back down from anything. That we are survivors. I guess he didn't mean himself.

"To Luke's." I lie and walk out the door before my father can ask more.

The girl is still on the sofa when I reenter the cellar. She stares at the plate with wide eyes and a parted mouth. I sit it down beside her and she immediately grabs the cake that's on top. She shoves it down without even chewing. I find myself wondering what happened to her. The news said that they found her father injured and a woman dead. She was nowhere. Everyone assumed she was dead. But she's sitting here in my cellar starving. How has she gone four months without no one seeing her around? I'm pretty sure if I saw an angel walking down the street in a white dress with flowers, I would remember her.

I don't say anything to her until the plate is empty. There's not an ounce of anything left. If not for the crumbs and chocolate lining her mouth and hands, you would think I'd brought her back an empty plate.

"You must have been really hungry," I say to her. "When was the last time you ate?"

She shrugs and begins licking her fingers. It's actually cute, but she won't be hearing me say that.

"What's your name?" I continue to ask.

She pulls her fingers from her mouth and stares at me. Then her eyes dip and she looks around the cellar as if she has no clue what her name is. I'm sure she does. It's not a hard question to answer.

I'm just about to ask her again when she lifts the book she's been holding near her. "Lost girl."

I look from her to the book, not understanding. I know her name isn't Lost Girl. "Well, Lost Girl, I'm Peter Pan."

The corner of her mouth turns up and she yawns. "My real name is Roxanna."

She lies down on the couch and balls tightly into my coat. I look around the room and spot an electric heater. I go over to it and drag it across the room to where she lies. Plugging it in, I turn it on and sit back down beside her.

"I'm Wran."

She nods, but I don't think she heard me, because the next thing I know, soft snores leave the only place that is not pale white on her body.

CHAPTER 2

ROX

Present

Three years.
Three months.
Eleven days.
And roughly seventeen hours.
That's how long he has been gone.
But who's counting?
Not me. . .
Okay, so maybe I have been counting. Sue me. But you can't possibly understand how long three years, three months, eleven days, and seventeen hours feel when you're missing someone. Especially someone you don't know will return.

I had just turned fifteen when he left—too young to accept what was happening, but old enough to understand what going away meant. The only thing he left me with was a kiss on the forehead, a credit card in case I needed anything, and the apartment we already shared. I cherished the kiss, but the credit card didn't make up for the lonesomeness and heartbreak.

Heartbreak. Yeah, not something people would think a teenager would understand. But I did. I loved him and he left to protect our country. It was his duty, he said, even though in the past he had made countless insults toward the very entity he was joining. I didn't understand it. I still don't, but I did respect his decision. Okay, so I respected it once I was done being mad. Wran never made a decision without reason. But at the end of the day, he left. He left me alone.

I sigh and tap the bell. "Order's up!" I yell to the front of the house. I've been working at Aunt May's since my eighteenth birthday—so, a week. I couldn't wait to get my own job and stop using the stupid credit card he left me with. Granted, it does come in handy when I want to go shopping or to see a movie. Okay, complaining is lame. I don't have to pay a bill, and I can use it to my heart's content. Somehow the balance is always paid in full every month, even though Wran sends all his checks home.

"Rox!" a voice calls.

I turn around to find a frustrated Sharon nearly growling at me with both hands on her hips.

"I've been callin' your name forever. Whatever's on your mind, forget it and pay a-fuckin'-tention."

"Sorry," I apologize. "Is there an order I need to get? Doesn't look like anyone new has come in."

"You would know that if you weren't busy day-dreamin'," she huffs. "There's someone out back for you. Someone hot."

My stomach flutters and a stupid grin spread across my face. I told Cade to meet me here on my break. I've had a crush on Cade since sophomore year. He hadn't noticed me then though; the artsy type of people wasn't on his radar. And without Wran here, I sort of let myself drift into the background. I didn't care about wearing pretty dresses or doing my makeup anymore. Those things were always meant for him, and there was no one else I cared to impress except for Wran. Well, no one until Cade.

For some reason, Cade decided today was the day to take notice of me. He ate lunch with me outside, even though it was freezing cold. Then asked to see me again. You can't imagine how shocked I was. Cade not only sat with me in the common area and suffered through Kingston's crazy winter weather, but I made enough of an impression for him to ask me out. It was unreal. I couldn't even bring myself to give him an answer at lunch, so I wrote "yes" on his hand in a freaking pink Sharpie.

I take off my apron and hand it over to Sharon. Running my fingers through my hair, I go over to the back exit and take a deep breath. I can't believe he actually showed up. I push open the door and my giddiness dissolves. Cade stands there with his hands in his pockets and mouth drawn down, looking utterly lost. He's not alone. Claire and her bandits stand in front of him with smirks placed happily across their flawless faces. I glance at Cade, but he doesn't meet my eyes. I start to retreat when snickers come from the girls. Wran taught me that Belmonts don't back down. I might not be a Belmont, but he made sure to teach me to never let people make me feel inferior. To never run again. I forget the exit and stand my ground. It's only Claire, and I've suffered far worse than she can dish out.

My eyes narrow, and I frown at each of the three girls. "What do you want? I'm working."

They full-on laugh at my attempted bravado, but I don't back down. Normally, this would be something to avoid. I don't need any more conflict in my life. But Cade is here, and I don't want to appear weak in front of him. Besides, if Claire has to treat people like trash, it's because someone else is threatening her and she's helpless to do anything about it. Claire pulls her hands from behind her back, the rest following in her lead. Before I know it, cups of Aunt May's homemade banana pudding smoothie come flying at me. There's no time to duck before it lands splat in my face. And as if that isn't bad enough, one of them throws scalding coffee at my shirt. I scream as the hot liquid makes contact with my already scarred skin, and I can't stop the tears from falling. The girls continue their marathon of laughter, whereas Cade does nothing—just stands there looking dumbly at the ground. He has every right to look that way. He brought them here. If he wanted to humiliate me, to hurt me, all he had to do was reject me. That would have been painful enough. I stare at each one of them before I retreat into the diner, their laughter echoing in my ears.

I thought, when I ran so many years ago, the torture would stop. But running, finding Wran, him making me go to school, that has all been its own torture. A different kind, but torture no less. I don't know what was going through Wran's head when he told Josh about me hiding in his cellar. When they both made me go to school. Everyone knew what my father had done. Everyone but me. I hadn't known that Ms. Wells had died. I hadn't known that my father killed three police officers when they came to take him away. And everyone punished me for his wrongdoings, as if I alone could have stopped him. Up until Wran and Josh ended my stint in homeschooling, I was dead to the world. Times like this, I wished I still was.

I go to the sink and shrug out of the fleece-lined flannel, wincing as I do so. The coffee is going to leave marks. No big deal. They'll blend in with the rest. I wipe away the salty tears and begin to pull away the wet shirt when a hand lands on my shoulder. I look over my shoulder at Aunt May. The pity in her eyes breaks me more than the coffee. I hate when people pity me.

"Why don't you go on home, darlin'? It's slow tonight," she says, and I grind my molars at the sound of her voice. I'm fine. It's just coffee and smoothie. I've gone through worse. This is nothing.

"That's okay, Aunt May. I have an extra shirt in the back. I'm going to put that one on," I say as I pick bits of banana from my hair. I groan; this is going to take forever to get from my hair.

"It wasn't a request. Go home, Roxanna."

***I turn around, dumbfounded. She's sending me home for something I had no hand in. Okay, so maybe I shouldn't have told Cade to meet me here when I went on break, but I never thought he would bring Claire. This isn't my fault, and I don't want to go home. "Aunt May, please, I need this job."

"But—"

She waves away my plea. "No buts. Go home and clean yourself up. Be back here tomorrow."

Defeated, I nod and pull my flannel back on.

"Oh, and tell Wran I said hello."

My eyes snap to her and there's a smug smile on her face. If Wran was back from his tour, I would know. Then again, I was in school all day and came straight here afterward. Aunt May has probably heard more town news than I have by now. "What do you mean?"

Aunt May laughs and walks off. If Wran's back, then something must have happened. He hasn't called, texted, emailed, or anything since the day he walked out of our apartment after telling me he was joining the army and needed some space before his training began. That was three years, three months, eleven days, and now eighteen hours ago.

Forgetting about work, I race out the back door, nearly slipping in the coffee and smoothie, and run through the slush all the way to the apartment. Not even the cold chipping at my bones slows me down. All I can think about is seeing him again, after so much time has past. I've seen him change so much since I was six, but the one thing that always remained the same was his shaggy black hair. I know he had to cut it when he went into the military. At least, I think that's still a requirement. Maybe it has grown back. If not, he's still probably just as jaw-dropping with a buzz cut.

I remember when I first saw him. He was so tall. The tallest boy I had ever seen. Granted, I hadn't seen many boys after my mom and brother died in that plane crash. Dad pulled me out of my private kindergarten, and I was home-schooled with Ms. Wells until I ran. But when I saw Wran, it was like I had found my Neverland. He was mean and cruel to me for a long time at first. Or at least he pretended to be. I could see beneath that streak. I saw beneath the cruelty the night he fed me and then bathed me and brushed the tangles from my hair. He said he only did it to make me look less pathetic, and he didn't want to ruin his mother's sofa with my grubbiness. I'm sure the second half of his statement was true, but I think he would have done it even if I wasn't sleeping on his mother's sofa.

Coming to a stop in front of my complex, I feel my pulse race even more at the sight of a light on in my apartment. A little squeal slips from my lips as I race up the stairs. He's home. He's finally home! It's about freaking time. Wran has a lot of explaining to do. Like why I haven't heard from him in three years. The military might be rigid and meant for the merciless, but they still get to contact their family. Opening the door, I come to a stop in the frame and frown at the person sitting before me.

Josh.

Not Wran.

Josh.

"What are you doing here?" I ask, closing the door. Glancing around the space, I frown deeper when I notice no sign of Wran. No bag. No suit. No nothing. "Where's Wran?"

Josh pats the couch beside him as he examines me. Yeah, I'm a banana-covered mess. So what? "Come sit. We need to talk."

My brows dip. Something must be awfully wrong if Josh wants to talk to me. Josh isn't a huge fan of mine. He claims I made Wran grow up too fast. At first I believed him. I actually ran away to make things easier on them, but Wran came after me. Wran and Josh have been at odds since that day. That also happens to be the day that Wran scolded and told me that Belmonts didn't run. He made me an official part of his family that day. I feel bad about the brothers clashing, truly, but I can't control how either brother feels. I can only control the variables I add to the situation.

"Please tell me he's okay, Josh. I can't lose him." I hate how pathetic I sound. Like a child pining for a toy. I look over to the bookshelf where my old rabbit sits. For the first time in years, I feel like holding it. Something in me tells me that Wran is not okay. Something must have happened while he was away. Captured, maybe. Killed in action. I shake my head. No. Wran is too stubborn to allow either of those things to happen to him. It must be something else.

Josh pats the cushion again. "Just sit and we'll talk."

With heavy feet, I walk over to the couch and sag down beside him, doing my best not to get the sofa dirty. "What happened? Is he . . . is he dead?"

Josh turns to me so fast, I almost jump from the couch. "God, no! Why would you think that?"

"He's not here, and you are. You don't particularly like me."

"Maybe not, but my reasons for disliking you have nothing to do with you personally."

I glance at the rabbit again. "So?"

Josh rakes his long black hair away from his face. Their hair is the only thing the brothers share. While Wran has striking brown eyes with flakes of gold, Josh has gray ones. Like his father, like a raging storm. And where Josh is soft, Wran has always been sharp and hard. Don't get me wrong, Josh is a heartbreaker too: lean features, a soft boyish face that makes him look much younger than he is.

When he was a kid, people thought he was older than he was. He took care of his family, me included. I can't see how the people who hired him thought he was old enough to work when he clearly didn't look so. Then again, we live in Kingston. Everyone within Kingston city limits knows everyone, even though we're a divided community with the wealthy on one side of the railroad and the less privileged on the other. They probably handed him the job because they knew it would be the only way either of the boys would eat.

"Wran is fine. He went out looking for you when you weren't here. He asked me to stay in case you showed up."

"Why didn't you just tell him I was at work?" I ask.

"I don't want my head chewed off any more than you."

Right. Me working is not something Wran would be pleased with. He's been sending all his checks home to me. And I have the credit card. The one thing he requested when he left me was that I finish high school and keep my grades up so I could get into a good college. He wanted me to pursue something with my art. But little does he know, I haven't painted anything since the day he abandoned me.

"So, what did you want to talk about?" If Wran's out looking for me, he's fine. Josh can't want to talk about him.

"That night," is all Josh says.

I shake my head and get up from the couch. I know exactly what night he's talking about, and we are not talking about that night. We agreed to never speak of it again. Why is he bringing it up now? It was nearly three years ago. "No."

"Roxanna." He gets up from the couch and grabs my arm, face stern, reminding me so much of Wran. They both can be protective and controlling when they want to be.

I yank away from him. "Don't call me that. And we are not speaking of it."

"Rox, then. He needs to know."

"I don't even remember it. How can I tell him something I don't even remember?"

"I remember. I remember every detail and the events that followed. I'm positive you haven't forgotten her. Kind of hard to do that."

No, but the things that led up to that night have been cleared from my mind much like what happened to me as a child. The therapist I was seeing told me that the human brain wipes away things that may be too painful for us to remember. It's a safety net and one that many people need. My only reply to that was my net had a huge hole in it. The nightmares of the day I ran from my dad never stopped.

"No. Please, Josh, don't." I can practically hear the sobs in my voice. I don't want Wran finding out about that night or about her right now. It's too soon. He doesn't need to know I fell apart when he left. He doesn't need to know something that I can't even remember doing. And since he's home early from his tour, he doesn't need more to stress over.

"Fine, Rox, we won't tell him tonight, but we're telling him first thing tomorrow. We've both already ruined him; the least we can do is be honest with him."

"But—"

"No buts," he cuts me off. "This is my decision. You're not gonna change my mind."

I nod and slump back down on the couch. Why would Josh do this to me? I know he doesn't like me. I'm sure he hates me after what happened. But he knows Wran is the only person I have. Why would he want to take that from me?

You know why; you took something from him.

When the front door jiggles, my eyes shoot to the door. I jump up just as the door opens, and all thoughts of Josh and that night vanish. Wran walks in and my chest flutters. I look him over and exhale. His hair is still short, but not buzz-cut short. It's shaved into a fade on the sides, but the top is longer. It looks nice on him. Other than that and the obviously hurt arm in the sling, he looks fine. He looks like my Wran. He closes the door with his good arm as I come to a stop in front of him. His eyes roam over me, searching every inch of me. His Adam's apple bobs up and down as his eyes go back to my head. When he left, I had brunette locks that met my waist—mainly because he wouldn't let me cut it. I needed a change after he walked away, so I cut it into a bob and bleached it blue.

With his good arm, he reaches out and fingers a longer piece of my hair that hangs around my face. I can't read his expression. That's new. I've always been good at reading Wran. The military must have bettered his poker face.

"Nice. It doesn't suit you, but it's nice," he says, and I frown.

We haven't seen each other in three years and that's what he has to say? That my hair doesn't suit me? What the fuck? His ridiculous hairstyle isn't what I'm used to seeing on him either, but I'm not complaining. "That's it?" My voice sounds every bit as frustrated as me.

"What do you want me to say, Rox?" he asks, looking past me and at his brother.

I turn around to where Josh stands, trying to be oblivious. It's not working. With the way these brothers fight, I'm sure Wran noticed him the moment he stepped foot into this apartment.

"I'll be going. See you later." Josh walks over to us and leans down to me. "We'll talk in the morning. Have your phone on."

I nod and he leaves. The small apartment grows silent. Deadly silent. I swear I can hear the gears turning in Wran's head. He has that look on his face where you can tell he's gnawing his cheek, and his head is tilted. I try to ignore the look on his face by focusing on the messy clothes I'm in. I really should be showering. The smoothie seeping into my flesh isn't comfortable, but I don't want to walk away. If I walk away, Wran might disappear. I might wake up crying again from a dream that's not real. I can't handle him not being real this time. Not after the Cade thing.

Wran must finally notice my grunginess because his face becomes stone. It's an expression I know all too well, an expression that seemed to follow us whenever we were together. He was much lighter when he was with his friends.

He motions to my wet, messy clothes. "What happened?"

I shrug, not wanting to tell him about Cade. My crush for Cade didn't manifest until after I was forced to give up Wran. Knowing Wran, he wouldn't be too happy knowing I had a crush on someone. Cade can drown a thousand times now, for all I care. "Nothing."

"Go clean yourself up. You look disgusting."

I stare at him with narrow eyes. First, he insults my hair, and now the way I look. Yeah, I look filthy, I feel it, but we haven't seen each other in forever and that is all he has to say to me? I roll my eyes at him and turn around, stomping toward our small bathroom. Getting this gunk off me will be nice. And as much as I like bananas, smelling like baby food is something I want to avoid at all costs. I start up the shower and peel off the flannel, tossing it on the white tile floor. The rest of my clothes follow, and I test out the water. When it's hot enough, I step inside and let the water mix with my now spilling hot tears. How could he not miss me? We've been a part of each other's lives since the day he found me in the snow. And now he's indifferent.

I choke on a sob as I grab my favorite soap and begin to scrub at my skin. I scrub until pink tints my normally pale surface. The soap slips from my hold and I bend down to retrieve it, more tears mixing with the water. I try to keep the sobs at bay, but they don't stop. Wran has been my whole world. The best friend I've ever had. Yeah, we bicker and fuss. Yeah, we've kissed and made up on multiple occasions.

But nothing we've ever said or did to one another has taken him from me. Whatever happened to him over the past few years is taking him from me, and it feels like someone is hammering a thousand nails into my heart.

When I no longer feel the water washing my tears away, I look up.

Wran looks down at me, frowning.

I wrap my arms around myself, scowling at him. "What are you doing?"

CHAPTER 3

WRAN

I step into the shower with her and turn the water back on. Rox had it scalding, the evidence of it streaking her perfect porcelain skin. I leave it cold 'cause God knows I need it. I didn't think it was possible for her to get any more beautiful. When I left, she was my angel, sent from heaven to torture me and destroy everything I had ever vowed. Now, she looks like a fallen angel. A pixie. Tinkerbell with blue hair. Sexy as hell. I think she even got shorter. The way she looked at me, though, when I walked through that door, with complete unbroken love, needed to be crushed.

Josh once said that I was a sadistic bastard. He knows about my tricks. All the pain I've caused. Josh knows that I love to make this beautiful girl before me cry, yet her tears break me in two. It's my curse: to forever love what I loathe.

"What are you doing?" she asks again, more force behind her words. Like my father, her words are weak. Rox can act like she doesn't like me seeing her, but we both know it's a lie. A part of her wants to be modest around me because that's what I taught her to be, but she can't. I can see her urges beneath the surface. It's all in the way her bottom lip quivers and she can't keep her eyes from roaming over me. Bet if I leaned over and kissed her, she would let me.

Replacing my frown with the cocky grin I know she can't resist, I bend down in front of her, letting the water cascade over me. "You act as if I haven't seen your body a million times before."

She gasps as if shocked by my words, her mouth agape. My gaze immediately falls to her pink lips, the only part of her that has ever held color. "That . . . that was b–before."

Her voice comes out low and broken. Her words paint a vivid picture of what my leaving did to her. At the time, leaving seemed like a good idea. We were getting too complicated. I started to care too much, and my plans were falling apart. I fell in love with her. I'm not ashamed to admit that. I loved Rox. I loved the girl whose father ruined my family. Whose father is still ruining my family. I had to find a way to be away from her yet still take care of her. The military was my answer to both.

The army also saved me from jail.

Rox was fifteen when I left. Still under the age of consent. I had turned twenty the day I left her. If I had a choice, I probably wouldn't have left. Yeah, I wanted distance, but I wanted her more. Josh gave me no choice. My brother and I will never see eye to eye. He hates my lost girl. Said she was ruining my life. He would have done anything to break us apart—save me, as he claims—including getting me arrested for being with a minor.

If Rox knew that tidbit about my dear older brother, she wouldn't have been sitting on our couch talking to him. Yeah, I asked Josh to stay here if she came home, but I'm damn well sure I made it clear he was to leave the moment she stepped foot through our door. And what the fuck did he mean by he'd be calling her?

Grabbing her arm, I pull Rox up and cage her in against the shower wall, doing my best to ignore the water running down her tiny frame. I suppose cold showers don't work when you're fully clothed and as far gone as me. "Why is Josh calling you in the morning?"

Her brows dip and her cheeks turn nearly as pink as her abused skin. She should not be blushing at my brother's name. "It's nothing."

The fact that she doesn't look me in the eye tells me she's lying through her teeth. We've always been open with each other. Well, she's always been open with me; I haven't exactly bestowed the same courtesy upon her. Either way, she hasn't lied to me before. "You sleepin' with him?"

Her head shoots up and her brows meet her hairline. "Of course not," she seethes. "Don't insult me like that."

"I've said far worse to you." Which I have. "Why are you taking calls from him?"

She starts to look away again, but I grab her pretty little face and force her to look at me. She bites down on her lip and her eyes fill with more tears. I haven't even been home an hour and I've made my girl cry twice. I wipe at her eyes, not wanting to see the tears spill over. I turn around and turn the water off, just to make sure I don't confuse waterdrops and tears.

Rox shakes her head, eyes glued to the shower floor. "It really is nothing."

Now I really am getting angry. This is the second time she's lied to me. Deliberately. Before I left, she would have never done that. "Twelve years, and you're gonna act like I don't know when you're lying to me?"

Her eyes snap to mine and her modesty is forgotten. She jabs her finger into my chest and says, "Twelve years and all you have to say after not seeing me for three is that my hair doesn't suit me?"

I want to laugh at that, but I refrain from doing so. "Really? You're crying 'bout that?"

She shoves me back with a force I don't expect. I have to catch hold of the shower door to keep from slipping and looking like an incompetent idiot.

"Did you even miss me? Even a little? I know we left things not so good, but Wran—"

I lean down and crush my lips to hers before she can finish. I can't believe she's worried about me missing her. She's my life. My world. Whether she knows it or not. My missing her is obvious. To me, at least. We might have left things unresolved, but not one day has gone by that I haven't thought about her. Two weeks before my brother's ultimatum, Rox and I made love for the first time. It was the absolute best day of my life. But then I told her she sucked in bed and that she shouldn't have been so frigid over the years. Maybe that way she would have known how to handle a man. I didn't mean a word I said that day. Like my brother said, I'm a sadistic bastard, and I know it. We didn't talk for a week. She stayed in her room and I stayed in mine.

Pulling away from her, I give a small smile. Not the cocky one that makes her giddy, but a genuine smile. "Of course I missed you, Rox. Don't ever worry about that."

She stares up at me, disbelief filling those gorgeous violet eyes. "Why didn't you call? Or text? Or email?"

I don't know what to say to that. I could have called or texted a million times. There must have been so many times when I wanted to hear her voice that I picked up the phone and listened to her voicemails. I listened to them every night. I remember the very last one she sent me. It came about eight months after I left. The hurt I heard through her tears still haunts me to this day. *Wran, I know you don't want to talk to me, but I need you. S–something happened. I did something bad. I–I don't know what to do. I'm scared. Please, please call me. Text me. Anything, please. I just need to hear you.* I didn't call her or text her. And she stopped trying.

"I'm sorry," spills out of me. "I wanted to. I tried to, but I couldn't bring myself to do it." I glance away from her as breathing becomes hard. Suddenly this bathroom seems too small, and all I want to do is get out of this shower. We really need to upgrade. I know for a fact that Rox didn't touch the checks I sent home. Grabbing the towel hanging on the railing, I wrap it around her, doing my damnedest not to face her. Why didn't I call her? Josh never made that part of his demands. I could have called her. "I'm sorry," I say again, all the dread and regret I've felt over the last few years filling those two words. Who knew going without your girl for so long would make you feel like you'd gotten hit with a wrecking ball? Who knew seeing her again would be even worse?

I leave the bathroom so she can dress, and I can get out of these wet clothes. Once in my room and in something dry, I slump down on my bed. This is all a mess. I don't know what I expected when I decided to come back. That she'd magically forget that I left? That I ignored her for three years? That we'd kiss, fuck, and make up? I. Left. Her. An apology isn't going to fix that. For all I know, she has moved on.

Grunting into my hands, I lie back on the bed and look up at the stars on my ceiling. They were left here by the pre-vious tenants, but I couldn't bring myself to take them down. Rox said they gave her hope. She used to talk all the time about how they represented finding a place where we both could be happy and free, where we're no longer lost. She was young at the time, and I didn't have the heart to tell her there was no such luck in this world. We have to live the life we've been dealt. And for us, that means a life of misery. A life where she will forever be known as a murderer's daughter, and I will forever want revenge on said murderer's daughter even though I love her to pieces. In her world, though, we'd be the perfect couple. We'd live in a condo that overlooks our town, because it reminds her of a treehouse. And we'd spend every night stargazing after she cooked dinner. We'd go on dates and pretend our age difference didn't matter, all the while ignoring the gossip around town.

We live in Kingston. Stuff like that doesn't fly.

I groan again. Why am I even thinking about this? I know it's never gonna happen. Rox should know that it's never gonna happen. We're not kids anymore. So why can't I bring myself to let go of her fantasies of us? Why can't I bring myself to let her go?

A knock on my door makes me abandon my thoughts. They were useless thoughts anyway. I turn to my bedroom door to see Rox standing in one of my old Star Wars T-shirts that is still too big for her. I remember when we first got that shirt. Peter Pan was playing at some swanky theatre at the same time Comic Con was going on. It was a win-win for us both. We had to sneak away for the week to attend both, and stayed at some dump motel I found online. I complained the entire week, blaming our accommodations on her when I had picked the place. She was just happy to be away from school with me.

"May I come in?" she asks, her voice sounding shy even though we both know she's far from that.

I sit up on the bed and nod. She sashays over to the bed, and I have to bite down on my jaw to keep myself calm. If she knew how good she looked in my shirt, she wouldn't be in my room. Rox was a string when I left. She ain't so stringy anymore. She has boobs. And hips. And legs that go on forever, even though she's like five feet. She smirks at me and I realize she knows exactly how much three years have changed her body.

She stops in front of me, hands on her hips. "You're sorry? Am I supposed to accept that?"

"Yeah." I rise from the bed and circle my arms around her waist. "You were also supposed to be in my bed when I came back instead of sitting up making plans with my brother."

Her body goes rigid in my arms, and I tilt her face up to see a pained expression lining her soft features. "I wasn't making plans with him. I hate him!" The fire in her voice makes me sit back down. She and my brother have never gotten along, but she has never said she hated anyone. And there have been a lot of people she should have probably said that to—myself included.

"What did he do to you?"

"Nothing. Forget it."

"No. What the fuck did Josh do? He's dead if he laid a hand on you."

She flinches at my words. I forgot how serious she takes threats like that. I suppose I would too if my father did what hers did. "Look, I didn't come in here for that. I missed you. I don't want to fight. If you don't want to tell me why you completely cut me out, fine. I won't bring it up again, but I want my best friend back. I want my Wran back."

God. If only she knew that her Wran was the cause of all the pain in her life, she wouldn't be saying that. I wish I could tell her that all the bullying, all the shunning, was my fault. I wish more than anything that when she looked at me with those big hopeful eyes of hers, I didn't feel guilt for her unhappiness. But I know the moment I reveal all my secrets, she'll be out the door so fast, she'd make the Flash look slow. I can't deal with that. I can't lose her.

Slowly, I rise and place a chaste kiss on her sweet lips. "One day, I will tell you everything. When you are ready."

"I'm ready now," she begs.

"No, you're not, my lost girl." She'll never be ready.

"Fine, whatever. Can I stay in here with you tonight?"

My eyes narrow at her. The last time she asked to sleep with me, before we were actually dating, was when she was having nightmares of her father. From the look on her face, I know that's exactly why she is asking now. I thought she had stopped having those. I give Rox a nod before pulling her down onto the bed. "You never have to ask. My bed is your bed." No matter why you're in it.

"Thanks."

I kiss the top of her head. I wish I could kiss more, but I know with me having just shown up, that is a no-go. I've got to regain her trust, even if I don't deserve it. "Don't thank me for that. Ever. Just get some sleep. It's late. I'm tired. You look tired, and you have school in the morning."

A soft sigh leaves her as her shoulders drop. "I could always stay home with you. Maybe make you breakfast. Just for one day."

I shake my head at her. As much as I want her to stay, she needs to be in school. I graduated, and I'll be damned if she doesn't. Her art is the most beautiful work I've seen. Dark at times, but beautiful. She needs to do something with it. I don't want her to have to depend on some man, even if it is me, to take care of her when she has all the ability in the world. Speaking of her art, where are all her canvases and easels? I suppose they could be in her room, but before I left there were paintings and easels everywhere. Not one inch of this apartment went without a little Roxanna.

"What happened to all your artwork?" I ask, looking around my room. She used to make sure to have something in here. I didn't notice the bare walls until now, and I don't like them. This room feels empty without them crowding my walls.

Her eyes drop, and she rolls over to her side of the bed without another word. I'll let that go for tonight. I've had a long day, and right now I just want to hold her in my arms. There'll be plenty of time to bug her about it later.

CHAPTER 4

WRAN

It's early when I wake. The sun hasn't yet risen, and my tense muscles are begging me to climb back into bed with Rox. If I was a normal guy I would give in, but I'm not. And there are a few things I need to handle before Rox heads to school.

I glance over at her, balled up and clutching her pillow for dear life. Leaning over, I place a kiss on her cheek. She turns over, faces me, and her body immediately relaxes. I shake my head at how predictable this girl is. She's had nightmares for as long as I've known her. She never wanted to talk about them, but I had thought they stopped. Suppose not now.

I start toward the bedroom door when a beeping catches my attention. I look to the nightstand where Rox placed her phone last night and snatch it up. Josh's name flashes across the screen, and for a second I think about throwing the thing against the wall. He basically threatened me to keep me away from her, yet here he is messaging my angel at five in the morning. The phone buzzes when I slide the arrow across the screen. So, she finally got smart and password protected the thing. No biggie. There's more than one way to find out what the hell my brother wants with her. I pocket her phone and head toward the living room where I left my phone last night. I yank it off the wire without any regard to it, quickly sending my brother a message to let him know I'm on my way. Whatever is going on between them ends now. I'm back, and I'm not leaving again.

Shoving my own phone in my pocket, I yank open the door to our small apartment and bolt down the rusting metal stairs. If he so much as tells me he looked at my angel with anything other than brotherly love, I really will be headed to jail.

I insert the key in the ignition and slam the door. Without giving the car time to warm up in this chilly February weather, I swerve out of the lot. My own fucking brother has been going after her. I can't believe it. I don't want to believe it. Josh and I have our differences, sure, but never did I expect him to go after Roxanna.

"She's too young for me, and quite frankly I don't have time for the quiet ones." He told me that when I asked him about her around my seventeenth birthday. He wasn't close to her by any means back then, but the way he watched her unsettled me, and I needed to know his intentions with her. I should have pushed for answers back then.

Flooring it, I speed past all the stop signs and the one traffic light that leads downtown and across the tracks to their side of town. I need answers and I need them now. As I pull to a stop at Josh's place, my phone chimes. I grab it and laugh at the message splattered across the screen.

JOSH: No need to show up here.

Yeah right. I ignore it and hop out of the car. It doesn't take a minute before I'm up the pavement and bashing my fist into the wooden door like a madman. I suppose she does turn me into a madman, but I'm fine with that. The door is yanked open, and I come face to face with a Glock 40. What the hell he is doing with a gun is beyond my worries. Not giving him time to lower the weapon, which I'm sure he has no clue how to use by the way he has it aimed, I shove past him and into the house that once belonged to my pops. Once Dad gave up on trying, Josh decided he would rather live here than give up Mom's house. Keeping this place is the only thing we've agreed upon in a long time. This house has been in my mother's family for a while. In fact, it belonged to her grandmother and her grandmother before that. No way was I letting something as mediocre as Pops not paying the taxes take this place away from us. Mom put too much work into it for us to lose it.

The door closes and Josh places the gun down on a side table. He crosses the distance and looks me up and down as if searching for something and then asks, "How'd you get over here so fast?"

I shake my head at his question. "Traffic laws are the least of my problems, sheriff."

Josh bypasses me and turns on a small lamp in the entry hallway. My eyes move from him to a small table that's been there since before Mom died. A picture of all of us sits up top it with a small candy dish beside it. Mom is holding me, while Josh stands in front of her and Dad with his arms crossed, pouting. My parents appear happy, smiling at each other and all that shit. It looks fake to me. My dad hasn't smiled like that in I don't know how long. Way before the firm incident.

"Why are you here?" Josh's voice pulls my attention away from the photo and back to him. I pull out Rox's phone and shove it in his face.

He flips the phone over and that stupid grin we both share appears on his face. "I didn't know you were into pink now."

"Drop the bullshit," I say, and walk past him to the living room. The sameness of the area stops me, and I look around the space. Dad didn't change anything after Mom's passing. And Josh hasn't changed anything after kicking Dad out and putting him in an income-based apartment where he can drink and wallow in despair without worrying about rent. Must be nice not to have responsibilities. Oh right, he does. He just doesn't give a crap.

I plop down on the tan linen couch and put my feet up on the coffee table. Without glancing down, I run my hand along the cigarette burns; I know line each and every cushion. Josh might only be a cop, but I'm sure he can replace the linen. It's not like it's in the condition Mom left it in.

"What are you doing here?" he asks again as he tosses Rox's phone back to me and sits down in the leather chair Dad frequented.

"Why are you texting her at five in the morning?" I demand. He knows exactly why I'm here.

"Because we need to talk."

"What about?" My voice rises.

Josh throws his head back against the chair and laughs. "I'm sure you bombarded her with that question last night. What did she tell you?"

"You know exactly what she said. Now drop the act, Josh, and answer me."

Folding his arms behind his head, Josh just stares at me with a grin on his face.

I get up from the couch and walk around to the fireplace, trying to calm my nerves. I'm here for answers. Busting a cap in his head isn't gonna get me the answers I need. And if he truly is screwing Rox, hurting Josh isn't gonna sway her in my direction. No, that will only anger her and make me look like the bad guy.

"I think we need scotch," my brother says, and gets up from the chair.

I watch as he disappears around a corner, only to come back a minute later with a half-empty bottle of single malt. He takes a swig and then hands it over to me. I down it before he realizes he is giving alcohol to me. I'm far from being a minor, but we both know I've never handled my liquor well. Granted, that has never stopped me from drinking before. Although I can't say the same about my brother. Before this moment, I'd never seen him drink.

I set the nearly empty bottle on the fireplace and turn back to Josh. "Just answer one question. Are you fucking her?"

He chuckles again and my hand flinches toward the bottle. I see nothing hilarious about this situation. Josh knows how I feel about her. He knows she's mine. Before I have time to smack some sense into him, the laughing fades and he's staring at me as if I'm the one auditioning for a part in The Lion King Broadway musical as a hyena.

"No," Josh says, and takes his seat again. "I'm not the one into little girls."

I go back to the couch and slump down. That's something, I guess. Although, I wouldn't call Rox a little girl. But if he's not messing around with her, then what was last night and this morning about? She says nothing, but it doesn't sound like nothing. Something is going on between them. "Then what is going on between you two? And if you say nothing, that bottle"—I point to the one on the fireplace—"will be against your head."

"Geez, little brother, did the military make you that hardcore?" he jokes, but I'm not joking.

"No. Dad did that."

"You weren't like this before you left."

My palms dig into the already ruined sofa. "And last I checked, that wasn't my choice."

Josh crosses his legs. "It was for the best. She was fifteen years old. You shouldn't have been messing around with her. Besides, she ruined you. The brother I remember was never as hell-bent on revenge as she makes you."

"That doesn't matter."

My brother leans forward and rests his arms on his legs. "I beg to differ, and I'm positive Rox would too if she knew all the things you did."

My hands clench into the couch's material more. I breathe in and then out, like my anger management advisor told me to do, before turning toward my brother. Josh has never been one to tolerate my rage. I highly doubt three years has changed that.

"Look, I just need to know what I missed. I don't need any surprises when it concerns her. Please, brother, tell me nothing is going on with her."

"Nothing is going on with her, Wran. I've never felt that way 'bout her. You know that. Besides, she's in high school for crying out loud, and I'm the sheriff. Those two things don't go hand in hand. You do still need to stay away from her though. That girl is not good for you. Never has been."

I let out a deep sigh. Here we go again. "I don't care if she's good for me or not. I love her."

"You don't love her," my brother says. "I've seen love, and your mind games are not it. She may think it is love, but she's a kid. Everything she knows has been molded by you and her father. And you, little brother, have been molded by her father's actions. That's not love."

"Whatever." I know how I feel about her. I may hate her father with a passion that rivals an addict's need for drugs, but that doesn't change how I feel. It only changes my course of action.

"Wran!" Josh yells across the small distance. "I'm being serious. Stay away. For your own good. Keep paying for the apartment but go back to the military. Go anywhere she's not. I can't threaten jail time again, but I'm hoping those years away taught you something."

I'm on my feet so fast that Josh visually flinches. "You made me leave her once before, but you're out of your mind if you think I'll ever leave her again. She's mine!"

Josh crosses his arms and rises from the leather chair, stepping so we're shoulder to shoulder. His eyes never waver from mine. "You sure she's just not another one of your toys? We both know how you love to break them and then put them back together."

Before I know it, a sickening crunch rings out and Josh is falling over the leather chair. I move around the chair and glare down at my older brother. He looks up at me, blood trickling from his right nostril. Wiping it away with his bare arm, he uses the arm of the chair to get up.

He points toward the main entrance. "Get the fuck out, Wran."

Gulping, I run my hand over the back of my neck but don't move. "Man, I didn't mean to do that."

"Don't make me say it again."

I step back, knowing when not to push him. "Whatever. We'll discuss this more later."

"No, we won't. I have nothing to say about Rox. What I need to discuss with her is an A and B conversation—you can see yourself out of it and out of my house."

I don't make the correction that it's our house.

He knows anything that has to do with her has to do with me, but I'm not going to push. Josh wants secrets, fine. I'll figure out what's going on one way or another. We live in a small town; people talk. Someone will know something about what my brother is hiding.

Turning, I head back toward the foyer and out of the house. Within the minute, my car roars to life and I'm speeding down the gravel road. I glance at the dashboard to my clock, and grunt. It's not even six a.m. and the need to drown out everything is already very prominent. I should have raided my brother's pantry for more scotch.

By the time my car comes to a complete stop, a blinking neon sign greets me. It spells out L-I-Q-U-O instead of liquor. And even though I know this is the last place I should be, I go inside. Like my brother, I've never been a huge drinker—mainly because I had to watch my pops drink himself into a stupor every day for the last twelve years. That didn't stop me from drinking—only limited me. Coming here, though, has always been a type of fucked-up therapy for me, and not due to the booze. My senior year in high school was particularly difficult. It was the year Rox became more than my charge. Sure, she's always been more, but before then I'd never laid a hand on her in any way that wasn't meant to destroy her or protect her.

I stumbled in here one night after a party, high as the Empire State Building, and drunk. One thing led to another and before realizing it, I was spilling my guts to a cashier a few years my elder. Janice, her name was. She was the opposite of Rox in every way imaginable, and she wasn't gonna put me on a pedestal to become a savior and lead her to fucking Neverland.

Janice is exactly who I need right now.

I glance around the small store that mainly carries beer and hard liquor until my eyes land on a woman with unruly blond hair with pink streaks, and makeup so thick you'd think she belonged on a street corner instead. For all I know she does that as well. There are plenty of men on the other side of town that would pay for her. She would never tell me what her other part-time job was, though. As I walk over toward her, she smiles and leans forward, letting her elbows rest on the counter.

"Well, if it ain't Wran Belmont," she says in her overly suggestive voice. "Long time, no see."

"Same," I say, stopping in front of her. "I didn't expect you here this early."

"I didn't expect you at all. What is the occasion?" She twirls a pink strand around her boney painted finger, somehow leaning in closer, her ample chest pressed up to her chin.

"Rox turned eighteen about a week ago. Last night was my homecoming."

Her brows shoot up and she straightens. Janice sits down on the leather stool, no longer smiling. "The infamous Roxanna. Why aren't you home with your sweetheart? You do somethin' already?"

Running my hand over my cropped hair, I let out a hard laugh and shake my head. "Nah, I found her with Josh last night, and then woke to him messaging her."

"When you say 'with Josh,' do you mean with Josh?"

I tilt my head at her and raise a brow. Besides Rox, this woman knows me better than anyone. Is she really asking that question?

She shakes her head as if realizing what she just voiced. "Of course not. He'd be termite food if that was the case."

"Precisely," I retort. "But something is going on with them. Maybe you might have some gossip for me about her."

"There hasn't been any news about her and the sheriff recently, but right after you—"

The bell dings, indicating a new arrival, and I peek back. The last thing I need is a run-in with my pops this early in the morning. I wouldn't put it past him to show up this early for a 40. Not unless he's already passed out somewhere. Turning back to Janice, I tell her to continue.

"She fell off the wagon after you left. Partying. Drinking. Drugs. Girl was a hot mess. If anything happened between them, it was during that time. He was always hanging around, although it seemed more protective than anything to me."

I frown at that. Of course I had known Rox would be hurt—she's the most emotional person I know—but I never expected her to turn to that poison. I don't know if I believe it, mainly for the same reason I don't do it: our fathers. Rox has never told me all about her life before I found her in a pile of snow and ice, but she did mention he used to drink a lot. And if the bastard can murder people, I'm pretty damn sure he can hurt a child. Secondly, this is coming from Janice. She might be nice to talk to from time to time, but I don't know how factual her gossip is. For all I know, it's just that—gossip.

Janice looks over my shoulder as the customer behind me clears her throat. I ignore her.

"Thanks for the info," I tell Janice. "I should be getting back to Rox before she wakes."

Janice leans forward again, licking her lips. "Alright. If you need anything else, phone me. No matter what time of day. And if you decide to move on from little Rox, I'm sure I can teach you some things."

I laugh at her and shake my head, stepping back so the irritated customer behind me can make their purchase.

Woman's been sayin' that since the first time I stumbled in here, even knowing my answer is forever the same. She's not Rox, and tormenting her wouldn't be the same.

CHAPTER 5

ROX

I hate him.

I hate him.

I hate him!

How dare he leave like that? After years of being gone, Wran left this morning without a word. He didn't even have the dignity to leave a note or anything. Not to mention I woke up late because my phone is missing. And now the lady taking the orders is as slow as Methuselah. Having been working in the service industry for a week, I can understand that mornings require more work, but I have school and I really, really need my caffeine fix. Especially since last night's sleeping arrangements did little to ward off the nightmares. Correction: memories—because the things that happened in those dreams happened in real life too. I just only seem to think about them when my eyes are closed.

Sleeping with Wran helped before he decided to go away, but I suppose it's going to take more than him showing up again for that to be a solution.

"I can get you," a man says as he steps up to the second register, grinning like it's not 7:30 in the morning on a Friday.

Quickly, I switch lines before anyone can go to him, and place my order. "A venti Americano with three shots of espresso and a splash of soymilk. Thanks."

I hand the man a ten and tell him to keep the change.

My coffee comes in record time, and I don't hesitate to gulp down a mouthful, ignoring the blissful steam and letting the caffeine engulf me completely. As a child, I hated the smell of coffee. It was my father's go-to drink when he needed a clear mind and alcohol was off the table. It seemed to have had the same effect on him as the whiskey. It would sober him out for a few hours, but then he was right back to the monster I hid in closets to get away from. When I first began drinking coffee, I was terrified I would end up like that man, but caffeine apparently has the opposite effect on me. Yeah, it gets me wired, but it also puts me at peace. Strange how something that's meant to provide energy just makes me happy instead of jittery.

Catching sight of the clock, I turn and leave Starbucks. It's a good thing this place is only a seven-minute walk from the high school. I don't think I can bear a longer walk in the cold. It's not freezing by any means, and Kingston has suffered far harsher winters, but walking in forty-five-degree weather is still not something I want to do.

I make it to school with time to spare; the first bell hasn't rung yet. However, nothing can keep the disdain off my face when I round the corner to my locker—not even coffee. Resting against my locker, with his legs crossed at the ankles and his hands in his pockets, is Cade. The guy from last night. Any other time, the sight of him would have made me swoon in my shoes. My heart would speed up and I'd break out in a cold sweat. Now, it does nothing. If anything, the sight of him makes the coffee in my stomach churn. After the stunt he pulled last night, I want nothing to do with him. I can't believe he brought them to my job to humiliate me. I suppose I'm lucky that Aunt May took a liking to me and Wran years ago. If that's all Cade wanted with me, he could have kept ignoring me and let me think he was a cool guy.

Cade straightens as I come to a stop in front of my locker. My eyes roam the hall instead of giving him my attention. He has wasted enough of my time—time that shouldn't have even been taken out on for a guy. My life can't support boys right now.

"Hi," he says, but my eyes still don't find their way to him. What did he think showing up at my locker would do? That I would magically forget that he let girls basically assault me while he did nothing but stand and watch?

As if!

"Umm." I see his shoes take a step closer to me, and I step back. "I kinda wanted to apologize for last night."

"Kinda?" I finally give him some attention. "You kinda want to apologize?"

He grins, and my hand tightens around the still hot coffee cup in my grip. "I haven't heard you say that much for as long as I've known you."

"You don't know me. I highly doubt talking to me yesterday for the first time in five years gives you the right to say that."

He takes a step back, as if I offended him. "You're right, but that doesn't change the fact that I need to apologize. I didn't know they were going to do that. And it was only a shake and some cold coffee. No serious harm, right?"

Cold coffee!

Before I can stop myself, my coffee is spilling in his face. How's that for cold coffee? "I hope that leaves third-degree burns! But if not, no serious harm, right?" I huff out and storm off without grabbing my things for first period. Really, what kind of apology was that? No, it didn't cause any serious harm, but what kind of person stands by and watches another get tormented? One that is just as bad. Those types of people have no place in my life. I would say no place in this world, but I'm not like them.

I stomp into class and drop my bag on the floor. Sitting in my assigned seat, I lower my head to the desk. Today can't get any worse. A tapping on my shoulder has me reopening my eyes. A loud whimper escapes me, drawing the eyes of my teacher. I give her a reassuring smile before glancing up at Claire. She flips her long, straight blond hair over her shoulder and smiles. We both know it's fake. Her smiles haven't been truly genuine toward me since the seventh grade.

We used to be friends—best friends, actually. I ruined that when I told her there was no way Wran would go for someone like her and to stay away from him. He wasn't exactly mine then—I was only thirteen—but it felt like it, and I didn't want my only friend trying to take something that I wanted. Not to mention I already had to suffer through Wran's actual girlfriends. That in itself was a nightmare. But Claire didn't heed my warning. She made a move on Wran. He turned her down but still . . . friends don't do that. We've been on the outs since, and everyone in this school knows why. I believe that's the reason they all either ignore me or torture me. I broke the girl code. She did too, but no one seems to realize that.

It doesn't bother me now. If anything, it made me even more aware of people. I became too comfortable with the Belmonts. I never wanted for anything during my adolescence. I'm afraid to say that I forgot how I even ended up there. Claire reminded me that my father is not the only bad person in the world. She reminded me that there are different forms of torture, and that I can't overlook people just because they don't fit the profile of a murderer or sociopath.

I roll my eyes and sit up straighter in my desk. "What do you want, Claire?"

She flicks a strand of my hair. "Have fun getting the banana out of your hair?"

Crossing my arms, I smile through gritted teeth. "Actually, yeah. And it left my hair smelling fantastic. Thanks so much, but in the future I would much rather you try it on yourself."

"What is your problem, Roxy?"

No one's called me that in a while. It's usually just Rox or Roxanna. "Nothing, Clairey." My eyes roam around the room to see a few students staring at me. None of these students have heard me talk much in the past three years. I'm pretty sure most of them thought I was a mute. "You haven't spoken to me in four years. What's your deal now?"

Claire leans in closer to me. "You staked claims on the Belmont brothers, so I'm staking claims on Cade. Stay. Away. From. Him."

I staked my claims on one Belmont brother! One! Besides, it's not like her daddy would let her anywhere near Wran. Claire is one of them. Her father probably already has it in mind who she's going to marry. And I bet it will have everything to do with him bettering his little carwash company. Bet she hates that.

"I want nothing to do with him."

She let out a hoarse laugh. "I saw you yesterday with him. He's mine, and if I have to make myself clear, sullied clothes will be the least of your problems."

"I have ninety-nine problems, but you aren't one, Claire."

The bells rings and she jerks away from me, heading to her seat at the back of the room. Turning toward the board, I watch Mrs. Garner's eyes flickering back and forth between us as if she would like to ask what just happened. She won't though, because that's the type of teacher she is. Here at Kingston High, we have two types of teachers: ones that actually care about their students but stay out of our angsty quarrels, and the others, that couldn't care less about us. There are plenty of the first where it concerns me.

I roll my eyes and look at the clock on the wall. Today is going to be a long freaking day.

By the time the lunch bell rings, everyone is back to ignoring me, which is how I like it. I swiftly grab my bag from the floor and exit calculus, heading down the hall toward the front of the building where my locker is located. I stop a few lockers away and stare at the guy standing next to mine in a long-sleeved navy polo and slacks. Seems like my locker is the hot spot today. Tilting my head against the wall of lockers, I watch as he makes conversation with everyone around him. Wran has always been a people person, whether he likes to consider himself one or not. I would be terrified if all those people came up and just started talking to me. But he seems at ease.

A locker a little way down slams, and I turn around to Claire. Her gaze is on Wran, even though just hours ago she told me to stay away from Cade. I roll my eyes and make my way to Wran. My claim is still staked, even though we are not back together. Just because he missed me doesn't change the fact that he abandoned me years ago without a word. I didn't know if he was alive or dead. Okay, that's a lie. I knew he was alive or else the checks would have stopped coming. But still...

I tap Wran on the shoulder and he turns around to me.

He smiles, leans down, and kisses me. On the mouth. At school. For everyone to see. I pull back and arch a brow at him. We haven't even had a chance to discuss anything, and now he's kissing me. The shower was one thing, but I'm not ready to forgive him just yet. And I don't think a school hallway where gossiping teens and teachers are standing around is the place to hash it out.

"What are you doing here?" I ask as I take a step back and lean against the locker.

"I thought I could take my girl out for lunch." He says it oh–so–confidently.

"Umm, Wran—" I'm not your girl.

He looks past me and down the hall. I follow his gaze to where Claire stands, her skirt looking a little bit shorter than it was before. "If you don't want to go, she looks like she does." Wran's eyes find mine again. "Little Claire is looking mighty grown up these days, and since last night didn't exactly go as I planned . . ."

He trails off, leaving me to finish his sentence. "Don't be a pig. You're better than that. Besides, she's only seventeen.

You wouldn't go there." Not even if he went there with me. We're different.

His body stiffens at my words and the playfulness that was gracing his face is gone. "According to Josh, I'm a grade A pedophile."

What?

Why would Josh even call him that?

Before I have time to reassure him that Josh is talking a load of BS, he grabs my books and bag and heads toward the school's exit. I trail behind him until we reach his green car. He hops inside and throws my belongings in the back. I sigh and get in the car.

"I thought you wanted to have lunch with someone that could get you off," I gripe as he puts the car in reverse.

"I might be taking you back to the apartment so we can recreate last night's shower event. Except this time, you know where you belong."

"I'm not going to have sex with you." My eyes stay trained on the moving scenery outside the window. The last time we did that, he left, and my world got turned upside down. Sex has been the last thing on my mind in these last three years. And I really don't want to hear him tell me I'm doing it wrong. Especially since my experience hasn't grown since the first time. I don't want him to know I spent most of this time pining for a ghost. It's pathetic and it makes me look pathetic. If I've learned anything living with the Belmonts, it's that they hate weak people. That's one of the main reasons Wran stopped visiting his father: Mr.

Belmont turned into the person he taught his children to despise.

When the trees are no longer a blur, I turn to Wran. He puts the car in park on side of the road across from the church and turns around to face me. "We have three years to make up for. No time like the present to start, sweetheart."

I glance up at the church and Wran turns around in his seat to follow my gaze. "You really want to do this here?"

He nods and swivels back to me. "I'm sure the big man upstairs will understand."

I cross my arms and shake my head. "You don't get to leave for that long, come back, and act like nothing's changed. I've changed."

He points to my shortened hairdo. "I can tell. I miss the waist-length black hair. You're taking your Tinkerbell fascination to a whole new level."

"I like my hair like this!" I exclaim. There is nothing wrong with a girl having shorter hair. Besides, I think I look better this way. My face isn't so hidden.

"You look like a boy. And I don't like it," he yells back. "I did not raise you to look like a wimpy-ass boy."

It's not that short.

"You didn't raise me! Geez, you're only five years older!"

I slump back against the car door and run my hands through my hair. One day. That's all I wanted. One day where things with us were back to normal. But things are never going to be that way again. Not after he left. If he couldn't give me one day to figure out how I felt and to come to some sort of conclusion without his snarky input, what are the next few months going to be like? Especially with us living under the same roof.

"Maybe you should take me back to school."

"Yeah, maybe I should. I actually want to be with someone my brother hasn't fucked."

My hand shoots out fast, but it doesn't connect with Wran's face. He catches hold of my wrist and slams it against the window. I wince and do my best to pull away from him.

"Try that again and I will break it." His voice comes out hard and chipped, and for the first time I believe him. Wran has made threats in the past, but they have always been lighthearted, or at least I thought they were. This doesn't sound so light. He has had problems controlling his rage in the past, but it has never been directed at me before. Not in a physical way, at least.

Wran must see the fear on my face because he drops my wrist and moves back over to his side of the car. "I'm sorry. I didn't mean to do that."

"What happened to you? You . . . that . . . You have never laid a hand on me before." I struggle to get the words out. Even during our minuscule fights over the years, he never hurt me. He let me do the hitting. He would take most of the pain. His retaliations only ever included harsh words. Harsh words I can take from him.

"Nothing happened. I miss you. Tons. I know last night didn't seem like it, but now it seems like you've moved on. I'm just trying to figure out where I stand with you now that I'm back."

"Would it be so bad if I did? Move on, that is?" I question him. In no universe have I moved on. I can't, but I need to understand his feelings more if I'm going to make a decision about mine.

He gives me a pointed look, the same look I've seen Josh give him over and over again. "I don't want anyone else to have you. So yeah, it would be bad."

I look away from him. Even if I wanted to move on from him, I don't know if I could. Granted, I've never really wanted to be with anyone else. Not in the way I was with him. It would feel like a betrayal, and I don't think I could handle the emotions that come with loving someone as wholehearted as I loved—love—Wran.

Cade doesn't count...

Not after his stunt last night.

Plus, I never loved him.

"I've never been with Josh. Please don't say it again," I tell him.

"Never? Not even when I left?"

I shake my head. "No. I was a complete mess when you vanished, but I didn't betray you. Josh was there for me when I needed someone to talk or cry to. It never went farther than that. I promise you."

"Then why won't you or he tell me what he wants to talk about? I'm a grown-ass man. I can handle whatever it is."

I arch a brow at him. Grown-ass men don't throw tantrums when they don't get their way.

"It's not about you. It's about me and something I did. I'm not ready to tell you about the worst mistake of my life. It'll come out eventually, but when I'm ready. So please, please don't ask about it again."

Wran moves back over toward me and pulls me against his chest. "Fine. You win. This time." He grabs my wrist and brings it to his lips. "Sorry 'bout this. Didn't mean to hurt you."

I smile at him and run a hand over his head. He has the softest hair I've ever felt. "I know. I trust you with my life."

"And I'll protect you with mine." He lets go of me and slides across the seat, starting the car up again. "Now, should we go get lunch—or would you rather go back to school?"

I think about that for a moment. As hungry as I am, I don't trust myself not to throw myself at him if we're alone. Yes, Wran is my best friend, but he's also the man I love. Or rather used to love. I'm not sure if I'm still in love with him anymore. But I've never been able to deny him anything, and if he so much as gives me that stupid smirk, I'll be jelly in his hands.

"School," I finally say. "I need to find a book in the library, and I have a meeting with my counselor. College stuff." It's a lie. That meeting was yesterday, and it didn't go well. Since the start of high school, all I've ever told my counselors is that I want to go to art school. Yesterday, when Tasha asked why I was planning on going to community college instead of an art school, she didn't like the answer I gave.

He tilts his head to the side. "I was meaning to ask you about that. What happened to all your paintings? There was never an empty surface and now the walls are barer than the Sahara Desert."

"I grew out of thinking drawing was a reliable option for a career," I answer. If he knew the real reason why I stopped drawing, he would throw a fit. "I figure I need to do something more realistic with my time. I don't want to have to die before my work makes any money."

"What would you do?"

"I want to help kids. Protect them. I don't want anyone to go through what I went through."

"Three years away and you turn all noble on me. Something like that will be good for you. Although I think you should continue with the art too. You're too talented to waste such a gift."

I simply smile at him. There is nothing noble in my reasoning at all. It's merely a way to keep hiding from everything else until I can escape this place and go to a place where anything is possible. As much as Wran has made Kingston a home, I want to explore outside of these city limits. Maybe out there the world isn't so cut and dry.

CHAPTER 6

ROX

The short ride back to school is awkward. Neither Wran nor I say anything. It never used to be this weird between us. I miss that. It hasn't even been a full twenty-four hours since he's been home, so maybe it'll get better. We simply need to get used to being around one another again. Once that happens, we'll be completely fine. I roll my eyes to myself as he comes to a stop at the curb of the school. We are so not getting back to normal. Not after what I've done, and most certainly not when he thinks I've moved on to his brother. Ugh!

I reach for the door at the same time I feel Wran's hand brush against the soft side of my other hand. I glance over my shoulder at him but am at a loss as to what to say. Instead, a small smile rises to my lips and I hop out the car, immediately retrieving my belongings from the back seat.

"Hold up!" Wran shouts at me. He leans across the seat and opens the glove compartment. Pulling out my phone, he tosses it to me.

Awkwardly, I catch it and curse under my breath. He had my phone this entire time! He's the reason I was almost late for school and didn't get to enjoy my coffee! Not to mention he didn't even bother to leave me any this morning before he left.

Before I have time to yell at him, Wran gives me a wicked grin and speeds away. One of these days, the sheriff isn't going to be so lenient.

Turning around, I immediately stop in my tracks before climbing the stairs that lead to the school's entrance. Cade is standing there. In fresh clothes, I might add. There doesn't look to be any scars or bruises on his face, which I suppose is good. Getting suspended for bullying would be so ironic. He beckons me forward. I look behind me to make sure Claire or someone else isn't there. In no universe does it make sense for a person to want to talk to someone that threw hot coffee in their face hours ago. Okay, so it most likely wasn't that hot after I had been sipping on it the entire walk from the coffee shop.

When I make no show of moving, Cade pushes through the door and literally jumps the five stairs to where I'm standing. He flashes that gorgeous smile that had me crushing on him before, but I step away from him. Something must be seriously wrong with him if he's smiling at me after I dumped coffee on him. And if nothing is wrong, then I don't want to know what cruel joke he's about to play on me now. For the last three years I've been relatively bully free. No pranks. No rumors. No crying myself to sleep because of them. Yeah, there were a few outliers, but nothing major. I don't want to go back to that place.

"Sorry!" I blurt out before he can say anything. "About the coffee. You don't have to retaliate. I will steer clear of you."

"No need to be sorry about that. I deserved it for last night and this morning."

I shake my head at him, trying to get him to understand. "It wasn't your fault. You did nothing wrong, and I shouldn't have taken out my anger on you. Can we call a truce?"

"Only if you'll stop talking and let me talk."

I nod my head and remain silent. This guy could literally ruin my senior year. There is no way I am regressing back to my freshman self where I hid behind Wran's reputation.

Cade brings his backpack around and unzips it. He pulls out a sandwich and hands it to me. "I didn't see you in the cafeteria and thought you might be hungry. You sorta threw your breakfast on me."

A giggle bubbles up out of me and I hate it. I should so not be laughing at that, but at least he can make light of it. Maybe he won't seek vengeance.

"I really am sorry about that. For the first time in my life, I wasn't thinking."

He takes a seat on the bottom stair and pats the spot beside him. "I like when you don't think. It feels more you. You definitely have more spunk than I thought yesterday."

"And 'spunk' is good?"

He nods, and I'm left baffled. My dad didn't think spunk was good. I'm pretty sure I would be buried six feet under if I had even tried something like that with him. And Wran, well, I don't think he likes spunk. He likes sweet and innocent. Although there have been times when I've been spirited around him. He's never said if he likes that or not.

"Aren't you gonna eat the sandwich, or did your boyfriend take you to lunch? That was Wran Belmont, right?"

I nod. "Yeah, that was him. We were supposed to get lunch but that didn't happen. And he's not my boyfriend."

I unwrap the sandwich and look through it. I remove the tomatoes, biting into the salami and pepperoni.

"Huh. Most girls would have taken off all the meat and cheese and bread."

My nose scrunches up at his statement. That's not much of a sandwich. "I like food."

"You don't look like you eat enough."

"I work at a diner. What do you think I do all night when it's slow?"

He stretches his legs out and crosses them at the ankle while I continue the last of my lunch. "With you, I would have guessed homework. You're always making the rest of us look bad with your A++ in every class. Guess I figured you would be somewhere with your nose in a book or covered in paint."

I wrap up the remainder of the sandwich and hand it to him. "I haven't been covered in paint in a really long while. And I do have hobbies, thank you very much."

"Really?" He grins at me. "What do you like to do?"

"I like to watch the stars."

"Why?"

I bite down on my lip, not sure how to explain the reason behind that. I can't possibly tell him the real reason. It took all middle school to get these kids to forget about what my father did—not that they really forgot. I don't need to remind them of the terrible man that spawned me.

"No particular reason. I just think they are beautiful and fascinating."

Before he speaks, the first bell dismissing lunch rings. I grab my bag and books and rise from the steps. Cade gets up as well, tossing my half-eaten sandwich down the sidewalk to the nearest can.

"Score!" he yells when he makes a hole in one.

I giggle again and turn to leave.

"Hey, wait up!" he says as I reach the door. He leaps up the stairs and pulls open the door, gesturing for me to venture in before him.

I do and make my way through the warm bodies lining the hall without gaining any attention from unwanted peers. I always hated that Claire's locker was right down the hall from mine.

Opening my locker, I shove my books and bag inside and retrieve a sketchbook. My next period is study hall, and afterward, art. Art was the only elective that didn't require me to put in some serious brain power. Also, the teacher gives me credit just for showing up and helping her teach the class. Teaching in this case means handing out paper and markers and any other supplies that might be needed. Like I said, a complete blow-off class.

"So, um, can I drive you home after school?" Cade asks out of nowhere.

I honestly thought he would have gone his separate way after we reentered the school.

My mind immediately goes back to Claire's threat. She made it clear this morning that she wants Cade, and that I need to avoid him like the plague. This might make me a giant wimp, but I don't want her wrath upon me again. Not to mention Wran is back. It was one thing to crush on Cade when Wran was away, but now, I don't know. I don't know where Wran and I stand. And I don't want to give Cade hope when there's none now. Even before Wran's arrival, we wouldn't have worked. Crushing on Cade was simply a fantasy that I indulged in for one afternoon. It wouldn't have gone any farther.

"I don't think that's a good idea," I finally answer him.

"Why not?" he asks, shifting the weight of this backpack to his other shoulder.

"Well, I'm pretty sure Claire already called dibs."

"She's not the one I asked out yesterday or right now. You sure this has nothing to do with that Belmont guy being back in town?"

"No, of course not! Why would you think that?"

"We live in a small town. People talk—but you know that, Rox. Let me drive you home after school."

Yeah, I do. "I'll think about it and give you an answer by the end of school."

Cade smiles at me, and I feel that smile in my toes. I lean against my locker to keep myself upright. I guess Wran's homecoming can't change the fact that I'm a girl, and no girl is immune to that smile.

Slowly, oh so very slowly, Cade backs away from me. "I have a feeling you'll be saying yes."

I gaze after him as he makes his way down the hall. It's official: Cade Michaels is insane. No sane guy would be asking a girl out who purposefully doused them in semi-hot liquid for revenge. I shake my head and walk toward my study hall, letting all fantasies of Cade go. There's no way I'm letting him drive me home. And there's no way I'm going to get sucked into his world. I like being a nobody. It's safe, and after the life I've lived, I want to be safe. Not to mention it keeps my secrets hidden.

By the time I make it to my study hall and the final bell has rung, all the seats are taken except for the one in the back. I usually sit to the right of the class upfront, so I can see out the window, but apparently my lateness made someone think the seat was open. No biggie. I don't need to watch the passing cars to forget about everything.

Making my way through the throng of yapping students on cellphones, I plop down in the only vacant seat and pull out my sketchbook. Although my next class is art and I usually do nothing in there, Ms. Lane wants me to do the assignment for this week. She said that it wasn't a requirement, but she looked like she really wanted me to participate. I didn't think a self-portrait would be hard, especially since it doesn't have to be a direct representation, but it is. The only thing I've been able to draw is a lonely young girl looking out a window at the moon and stars as if they hold the answers to everything. As if she's searching for a way to escape. I have no clue why that's the only thing I can draw. I've been drawing for as long as I can remember, and the fact that I can't seem to draw anything other than this girl is really bugging me out.

I open my sketchbook to a clean page and just stare at it. After ten minutes of staring with nothing coming to mind, I sigh and close the book, resting my head against the cool desktop.

Before I know it, the bell ending the period is ringing. A yawn escapes me as I sit up straight in my chair. Darn it. I fell asleep again. That's been the pattern all week, ever since I saw the news about my father. I haven't been sleeping at night. At least not very well. No one here, though, has put two and two together, which I'm grateful for. Wran made sure when I started at this school that my past wasn't a topic of discussion. Not even the teachers seem to care. That might have something to do with Josh registering me with the Belmont name, even though everyone knows very well who I am. According to the guys, my face was on every local news network when this all went down twelve years ago. Why the school officials haven't informed anyone about me is beyond me, but I'm sure it has something to do with Josh being the sheriff.

The rest of school goes pretty much like study hall. I make up for my lack of sleep in my elective classes. None of my teachers say anything, but I see the concerned expression they give me, especially Ms. Lane. The nightmares don't seem to plague me here. Although it's weird, I get much needed sleep.

I walk down the checkered-floored hall toward my locker, frowning at the figure standing in front of it again. My eyes drift to Claire glowering at my locker as I bypass her and grumble. Great. I'm going to have to deal with the consequences of Cade's choice to stalk my locker. Ignoring him completely, I open it and place my drama book inside. I slam the door and wait an excruciating minute before turning around to meet Cade's preppy, smug face.

"I guess the rain means you'll be taking me up on that ride?" He points to the double doors leading out of the school.

My head jerks to the doors and I let out some very audible expletives. If it's raining, it's more than likely going to turn to snow. I don't recall snow being in the forecast.

Then again, I didn't have my phone to even check the news. No wonder he was so sure I would say yes.

Arrogant bastard.

"Don't you have something better to do than stalk a locker? It's getting weird," I bark at him and pull my phone from my pocket.

I pull up Wran's number and debate on whether it's a good idea to ask him to come get me. After the lunch debacle I'm not even sure he would come. Besides, this isn't the first time I've had to walk in the rain. I've had years of crappy weather without Wran to drive me anywhere.

"I still don't need a ride. Besides, I think your number one fan over there"—I point down the hall to where Claire is now standing with her friends, watching me and Cade as if they now have elephant ears that will allow them to hear our conversation—"will be a bit angry if you take me home."

Cade glances to where I pointed and frowns. He gives Claire a little wave before turning his attention back to me. "Maybe I'm tired of fans. Maybe I want the attention of a genuine girl that doesn't see all the college scouts hanging around our fields and gyms."

It's on the tip of my tongue to tell him that this town is too small to have that many scouts hanging around, but I have seen a few. And I get his point. "You're right. I don't see you that way, but before yesterday, you didn't see me at all. I've been here since seventh grade and yesterday was the first time you've spoken to me. It's not a stretch for me to think there's an ulterior motive behind this."

Cade takes my bag and begins walking toward the school's exit. I take one last look at the steamy expression gracing my enemy's face, then follow Cade. Before exiting the building, he takes off his heather gray wool coat and drapes it over me. I gulp and accidentally inhale the scent of fresh pine and sweat. He must have gym last period. He should not be giving me his coat. I am going to be dead on Monday when school resumes. If I'm lucky, Claire won't think to show up at my job again.

I take a step back from him, already regretting my lapse in judgment. This can't happen. I don't want this to happen. Being invisible for the last few years has been good for me. There have been no pranks. No teasing. Going out that door with this guy will change that. I'm pretty sure it's already been changed, but maybe I can put a stop to it before it worsens.

Cade grabs my hand before I can bolt and pulls me out into the crying cold world. We travel around to student parking and end up at a red Ford truck. I don't know what I was expecting Cade to drive, but this is not it. Maybe some type of muscle car like Wran. They seem more alike than I previously thought. Too bossy for their own good.

He unlocks the doors and I struggle to climb inside. I wipe my plastered hair back and turned to Cade. "You know, I didn't say yes to this ride."

He starts the truck before answering. "I saw the indecision on your face when you thought about calling the boyfriend. Besides, you did just climb inside. Didn't your daddy tell you not to get in strange boys' cars?"

I roll my eyes at him.

Yes. Yes, he did.

"Wran's not my boyfriend," I say to him, but I'm sure neither one of us truly believes that.

"If that's so, then go out with me. Just one date. Let me prove that I have no nefarious motives."

I run my hands through my wet hair and look out the window. He's asking a lot. Claire is already going to skin me alive for talking to him after staking her claim. When I don't respond to his invite, he pulls out of the parking lot and heads down the street that leads to my apartment. I don't know how he knows where I live, but it probably has something to do with Wran. They run in the same circle-ish. I wouldn't be surprised at all if Cade had worshipped Wran when he was a student. Every wannabe jock did. It was the natural order of things.

The next fifteen minutes, because that's how long it takes to get to my place, is awkward. I'm not sure if "awkward in a good way" is a thing. From my peripheral, I can tell that Cade keeps watching me when he should be watching the street. I do my best not to look at him and keep my eyes trained directly in front of me, watching downtown pass by. Granted, there's not much to downtown other than a few closed businesses, a church that looks more like a convent, a barbershop, and town hall. Oh, and the diner that I work at. We're lucky we got Starbucks, but I'm guessing that's only because people here love their coffee. Everything worthwhile is in Arlington. That's the town I used to live in. If you want McDonald's, you're driving the hour to get it. When I first came to Wran after the travesty, he asked me how I ended up in Kingston. I didn't answer him because I didn't know. I just ran.

We come to a stop outside my complex. I live on the second floor, and from the rusting staircase and downtown look of the building, you wouldn't believe that these are the nice apartments in town. Far nicer than most of the run-down houses on this side of town. They are red brick with big flashy windows and glass doors. I'm still convinced that they were supposed to be an office building when they were first built, but since this town isn't bringing in the executive types, they market them as luxury apartments. Luxury apartments on the wrong side of town. It's laughable, but this little apartment has been my home since I was twelve. It's not the best—I prefer the house—but Wran made this work.

Cade turns to me with a grin. "I really would like to take you out. I know you don't know me very well, and I'm competing with Belmont, but I'm not a bad guy."

I know he is not a bad guy. There's no way I would crush on someone I thought was bad. But I don't fit in with his people. He probably has one of the fantasy houses from the Stanford community in the opposite direction of this place. He probably goes to church every Sunday to appease his parents. Scouts are looking to sign him. He has options for his future. While I know Wran would give me his left leg to get me those options, we both know it's not really a reality for me. Only one I make up in my head. I don't think it would be healthy for me to date someone like Cade. Even if it's only one outing.

"Can I think about it and get back with you?" I ask him.

He nods, grabbing my phone. "You need my number for that. Just remember, getting to know people is a two-way street."

"Huh?"

"Back at school, you said I never spoke to you before yesterday. Well, you've never spoken to me either. Or anybody, for that matter, after he graduated."

I stare at him, mouth agape. Somehow, I've never thought of it that way.

Cade hands me my phone back, and I tuck it in my pocket and shrug off his coat. I guess letting people in does require some participation on my part. But then again, that's not really what I want. I don't want people to notice me, because if they do, they'll notice my past. My past is the last thing I need people questioning.

"I'll call you, but I should get in there."

He gives me a curt nod, and I dart out of the truck.

CHAPTER 7

WRAN

The rich, earthly smell of the punching bag slams into me as it swings back my way. With my eyes trained on the crack-ing leather, my fists collide with the weighted bag once more. I've been at the gym since I left Rox at school. When taking her to lunch didn't exactly go as planned, I came here. At least at the gym, I can control the elements around me. Most importantly, I won't get arrested for socking something or someone.

I send blow after blow into the bag until all I can focus on is the thump, thump, thump of my rapidly beating heart. When a hand reaches out and stops the punching bag, I turn with no regard for the person and send my fist into a new target. The sound of crunching bone rings through my ears before I realize what just happened.

"What the fuck, Belmont?" Luke yells at me as he holds his nose. There's no blood, so that's a good thing. Means it's not broken. Bad news: I wasn't hitting hard enough.

I haven't seen Luke Vibes since our senior year of high school. He knocked up some privileged girl in Arlington. Next thing I know, the dude's talking about dropping out of school and becoming a family man. He always said he wanted a big family, but neither one of us thought it'd be so young.

"Geez, Luke, don't sneak up on people like that."

"I'll keep that in mind next time I think of coming to holla atcha."

I shrug at him. "I was in the zone."

"You've been in your zone for hours. What's up, man?"

Luke releases his nose and eases down to the mat. It's only red. His nose will be fine in an hour or so. I drop to the floor beside my belongings and grab hold of the water bottle. I chug the entire thing and throw it aside.

"I should be asking you that. Last time I saw you, you were raving about a girl named Jenny and becoming a daddy."

Luke kicks my leg down from its raised position. "Don't say it like that. My life's good. I'm not the one trying to bury tanned cow skin."

I tilt my head in acknowledgment. Man has a point. "True."

"So, what's up, dude? What got you cracking knuckles?" He points to my hands.

For the first time, I notice the small scrapes and blood. So maybe I was hitting hard enough. A grin spreads across my lips as I wipe the traces of blood on my sweats.

Sighing, I lean back on the mat and stare up at the crappy fluorescent lights. "I didn't think it would be so hard coming back here after being gone for so long. Rox isn't the Rox I left. Josh is the Josh I left. Everything seems wrong. Off somehow."

"Right, right. Mr. Military-is-for-Weak-Men actually decided to serve after talking crap about the army."

I chuckle. I still believe the army is for weak men—even more so after hearing some of the reasons why they signed up. They get to leave all their problems behind. Delay taking responsibility for anything for a little while longer. They don't have to make the hard decisions that those who don't serve have to make. Sure, they are probably hurting someone by joining the military, but if they truly cared how said person felt, they wouldn't have joined in the first place. They would have stayed home, joined the workforce or gone to college instead of blindly following orders from power-hungry men that make no damn sense whatsoever. I can say that now with one hundred percent certainty. Some of the things my commanding officer had me do were plain stupid. Something to pass the time and give him an ego boost. If you asked me, he just needed to get laid. Being around mainly men isn't healthy.

Another snicker comes from me. I was one of them.

"I had no choice," I confess to Luke. "None at all."

"There's always a choice, man. And I'm sure things with Rox will work themselves out. If I'm recalling correctly, that girl worshipped you. Like got down on her knees and prayed."

"Ha, ha. It wasn't like that."

Luke bumps his leg against mine and raises his brows. "Sure, it wasn't. I would have let her praise me too if I wasn't afraid you'd kick my ass. Girl was hot for a seventh grader."

I'm just about to tell him to shut the fuck up talking about things he doesn't get when his phone chimes with "It's the wife calling. Don't pick up!" I roll my eyes and get up from the floor, as do he.

"Good life, huh?" I ask him. Doesn't sound like it from that ring.

He just smiles and says, "Yup." Then he's answering the phone and walking away.

I grab my own phone from the gym bag and check the time. It has been hours. Rox will be home soon. I grab my bag and discarded water bottle from the mat and race toward the exit of the gym. I wasn't planning on being here all day, and I most certainly wasn't planning on Rox beating me home. We need to finish our conversation. Or rather start the conversation I intended to begin when asking her to lunch.

As much as I hate to admit it, I want my girl back. Three years away didn't change how I feel about her whatsoever. I think Josh thought it would, but nope. I still love her. I still want to control her. I still want to destroy her. But above all, I really want to feel her again. Despite her having that ridiculous haircut now and there being hardly anything to pull, I want to feel those strands in my hands. She knew I was bluffing about Claire. I hate being transparent to her even after all this time. She knows I haven't touched another girl since she turned fifteen years old. It's crap really. Complete and utter crap. No one tells guys when they're young that one little girl holding a deformed stuffed rabbit and a stupid Peter Pan book will be the end of them. No one tells guys that falling for your enemy will feel like gutting yourself every single time you think of them.

Opening the door to my car, I throw my belonging to the passenger side and race out of the parking lot. My town doesn't have a gym, so I had to drive an hour just to come here. That means an hour to get home. I grab my phone and look at the time again, my eyes moving back and forth between the road and the screen. 2:42 p.m. Dammit! I toss the phone aside and step on the gas. I need to get home before her. If I know Rox, she's gonna lock herself in her room for most of the night playing ratchet music while doing her homework. She has all weekend to do that. I want to talk to her. I want to see her. I want to feel her.

Thirty minutes later, I'm parking my car in one of three slots available. I do a quick search of the area before glancing up to my shared apartment. All the lights are off, and there doesn't seem to be any sign of life up there. I sprint from the car and race through the heavy rain up the slick stairs. The bitter smell of over-roasted coffee slams into me as I open the door, and my eyes find the flashing green light of my coffee pot. I figured Rox would have turned it off before school.

Note to self: don't count on Rox to turn off coffee pots anymore.

That's obviously too much for her to do now. I'm just about to head to the small kitchen when a roaring from outside catches my attention. Pulling back the curtains, I search the parking lot. Seconds later, a red pickup truck with black stripes pulls up to the curb. Squinting my eyes, I try to make out who's inside. I know for a fact that no one around here owns a truck like that. No one around here needs their trucks to be their muscle, and that's all that truck is—some guy's catcall.

When the door to the truck finally opens, I drop the curtains from my hand.

"What the hell?" I seethe.

I pull back the curtains again to make sure I'm not seeing things. I'm not. My fist slams into the wall beside the window as I watch Rox get out the truck. A guy's truck. She should not be in a guy's truck. Least of all, his truck. If she needed a ride home, all she had to do was pick up the phone and call. Not get in some random guy's truck.

Okay, so he's not so random. I've seen him around. He's one of *them*: the well-off of our little community. When I was a kid, I used to be one of *them*. Never gave a shit about anything. Thought I was better than everyone. Only my mom could bring me down from my high horse. Or so I thought. Dad losing his job brought me down really fast. All my friends from that crowd stayed away, and I found myself a new crowd—one that didn't give a crap about prestige and power.

The door handle jiggles and my eyes instantly go to it. It seems like minutes before Rox comes in, even though it's only seconds. She stops in the doorway, hair plastered to her face and staring at me beside the window. I see her slowly take in my appearance before her eyes shift quickly back toward the outdoors. Inhaling, she shuts the door and rushes down the hall to her room. I follow. There's no way she's getting away without explaining why she came home in one of their trucks. She knows how I feel about them. Even with me gone, she shouldn't resort to help from one of them. They use people and they will use her. Spit her out and then laugh at her misfortunes. That's why I fled that side of town as soon as I was old enough to sign a lease.

She shuts the door behind her but I catch it and go inside without an invitation. It's my apartment after all. Rox drops her bag on her bed and slowly turns around. My jaw clenches at the sight of the nonchalant expression painting her pixie-like face.

"Can I help you with something?" she asks.

I stalk over to her and glare down at her petite frame. Rox has never been stupid; she doesn't need me to spell it out. She looks up at me. Her eyes meet my glare head-on. We stand like that for a good five minutes before she steps back, relenting. She knows who's in control here.

"Who the hell was that?" My voice comes out in a sharp yell, and I can see her cringe. Only just a little, but a little fear is better than no fear in my book.

"No one," she mumbles. "No one you need to be concerned with."

"Don't give me that crap, Roxanna! If it's not Josh, is it him? That guy the reason you're having second thoughts about us?"

She turns on me so fast, and before I know it, she's in my face. Her fist lands a nice clean punch against my jaw, and I wince. What the hell? She goes in for a second hit, but I grab her and spin her around so her back is against me. God, she feels good against me. She wiggles in my hold, making a certain body part stiffen. Fuck! Now is not the time to be responding like this. My arms tighten around her to keep her still, and when that doesn't work, I ease us down on the plush pink carpet I helped lay out when she was fifteen.

"Stop it!" I hiss in her ear. "All you have to do is tell me who that was and I'll be out of your hair. What remains of it, anyways."

Something wet slides down my arm, and I turn her around in my hold. Tears roll down her face, and I let her go. Confusion clouds my mind, and I inch away from the crying girl a little. We've had plenty of fights—not that I would consider this a fight—and she didn't cry. She never cries. Not in the twelve years I've known her. Something most certainly happened during my time away. Something changed my lost girl. I don't like it.

"No." She wipes at the tears, but they keep coming. "You have no right to come back into my life and demand anything. He or any other guy I choose to be with is none of your concern."

"Like hell. You're mine. You know that."

She scoots away from me, putting even more distance between us. "I don't belong to you! You just happened to find me in freezing snow and did the right thing. I never asked you to keep me!"

I can't believe she said that. Of all the things . . . "What the hell is wrong with you?"

"You left!"

I move back to her. It all comes back to a decision I had no choice in. I left. Like hell. I was forced to leave, but voicing that won't change anything. I wasn't here for three years. Plenty of things can happen in that time. I can attest to that personally. Never did it cross my mind that she'd stop loving me. I always assumed she'd be waiting for me. Never did I think she would move on to one of them. All Rox has ever done is wait on me. Even when I was being a dick and bringing home whatever I could get my hands on, she waited.

I get to my feet and barge over to her door. I yank it open and stomp out without another glance back at her. I go to my room and throw myself down on the bed. This is bullshit. Josh ruined everything. If he hadn't felt the need to get all brotherly and concerned out of nowhere, my girl would be right here in my arms and not getting out of one of their trucks. I wouldn't be lying here with a raging hard-on with the one person able to fix it out of reach.

Sitting up, I run my hand over my head. Who am I kidding? I could have fought. Girl has every right to want to gut me. I did leave her. She gave me her virginity, and a week later I was gone without informing her. That doesn't mean I'm going to let her walk away.

Exhaling, I rise from the bed. It takes forever for my feet to take a step toward the door, but eventually I force them to get to walking. Soft whimpering from inside Rox's room keeps me from barging inside and demanding what I want. Instead, I ease her door open to find her in a ball where I left her minutes prior.

I go over and ease myself down to the floor. Without hesitation, I reach over and cup her face, lifting it so I can see those big sad purple eyes fully. I don't know why, but those eyes have always been my kryptonite.

She yanks her face from me and sobs out, "Please don't."

"I'm sorry," I mumble to her and pull her over into my arms where she fits perfectly. If only she realized she fit that way . . . "I know I've been an ass since last night, and I wish I could explain it away, but I can't. I'm just an ass and you know that."

Rox tilts her head up a little at that. "Yeah, I do." I barely hear her response.

"If I tell you why I left, can things go back to normal? Can I have my Roxy back?"

She squints up at me and shakes her head. Of course no would be her answer. Me telling her the truth isn't going to erase the last couple of years for her. "You can tell me because I deserve to know why I was left alone."

I ignore her reasoning. "You weren't alone. You had Josh and all the students at the school. Hell, you could have even visited my pops. No one made you isolate yourself."

"Wran . . ."

"Okay, okay!" I let out a deep breath. "I had sex with a fifteen-year-old."

"So?"

I bite down on the corner of my lip. I hate to think of Rox's and my relationship as anything other than the innocent joy that it was. Yeah, I had my moments of jerkery, but at the end of the day I knew what I truly wanted, and that has been Rox since the day I found her.

"You were fifteen and I was turning twenty. It was illegal, and I was . . . am your predator. Josh warned me to stay away from you, and when I didn't, he threatened to have me registered as a sex offender. The options were to go away or stay and risk never seeing you again."

My eyes don't meet hers as I degrade everything we ever had together. It was wrong, yes, but it's not like I was forty and physically abusing her. That didn't matter though. One night with her and Josh finally had a way to break us. I don't know how he figured it out, but nevertheless, he put it together.

Rox pulls out of my hold and races out of her bedroom. She just left—like gone gone. I listen to the stomping of her tiny feet in complete shock. I just told her everything and she leaves like it is nothing. When I hear the front door slam, I leap to my feet and run after her. She's down the stairs and yanking on my car door by the time I open the apartment's entrance. I stare at her as she continues pulling on the handle, my blood boiling underneath my skin. Three fucking years and she turns into a coward that can't handle the damn truth. If that's all I came back here for then she should leave. A girl that can't handle the truth is a girl I don't need in my life. There're plenty of truths Rox needs to know, and if this one has her running scared, then I know she can't handle the rest.

The engine roars to life and I race out into the pouring rain before she can drive off. Fuck, I'm whipped. She's not leaving here until we talk this out. And if she still can't handle it, she can leave. Run away and freeze again. I grab the door handle just as she starts to back away. The car stops instantly and she jerks forward in the seat.

Rolling down the window, she glares at me as if I've killed her baby. "You can't stop me."

Say what now? "Get out of the car, Rox. We can discuss this like adults."

"I don't want to! And if you try to stop me, I will run you over."

Fuck this. I yank open the car door and push her aside. I climb in and slam the door, flinching at the jarring impact.

My poor car. "Grow up! I told you the truth because I thought you could handle it. When did you turn into this girl?"

"What are you talking about?" Rox shouts back at me. "I am handling it. I'm about to handle it as soon as you get out."

"What are you talking about?" I asked, confused. Rox has some serious problems.

"Josh. What did you think I was talking about?"

My hands tighten around the steering wheel. I'm not letting her confront Josh. "No. Just go back inside."

"No," she spits out. "He does not get to ruin my life and not pay for it."

I roll my eyes at her remark. Yes, he does. This is one thing that he's getting away with. I'm not sure when my brother turned into such a spiteful man—maybe around the same time I turned into such a vengeful one—but I'm not giving him another reason to tear me away from Rox. This might be news for her, but this has been my reality for years. Josh is a wanker and he will do what he pleases. I'm not going to let that affect Rox anymore.

Putting the car in park and easing my grip off the steering wheel, I turn to face her. "Look, I know you want to kill him. I do too, but I've decided I want you more."

"Really?" She goes to run her hand through her hair but stops. "Even with the short hair?"

I smirk at her. "Rox, I'm a guy. I couldn't care less about your hair."

She grins, but it doesn't last long. Her eyes dip and she bites the corner of her mouth like she always does when she wants to say or ask something that will piss me off. When her eyes meet mine again, I don't give her the opportunity to say anything I won't take well. Grabbing her leg that's propped on the car seat, I slide her across to me and gently kiss her. She needs gentle right now. She needs the guy that took care of her. That's the only way I'm getting her back after all this time. I might not know what happened, but I know it changed her. She's not the hard girl she once was. I can handle that. I will handle that, because nothing is taking her from me a second time.

When I pull back, I search her face for the blush that should be present. It's not. Instead, she looks like she's seen a ghost—skin so white that I swear she's frozen. She opens her mouth, but I place my hand over it. I already know what words are going to leave her lips and I'm not letting them. Time. That's all we need. And I'm going to give us that time.

"Don't say anything right now, Rox. You don't have to decide tonight or tomorrow night or even this year. Hell, I'll wait three years if that will keep you from saying what I know you were going to say."

In a small whisper, she asks, "How do you know what I was going to say?"

"I raised you."

She shakes her head. "For goodness sake, stop saying that! You did not raise me, and when I think of it like that, our being together is kinda creepy. So stop."

I snort at her reasoning. "Whatever you say. As long as you agree to go on one date with me."

"Wran," she whines.

"It's one date. Nothing more. We need to get reconnected. We live together, after all."

A high-pitched squeal that sounds like a rooster crowing blasts throughout the car. Rox rises a little and retrieves the phone that's in her back pocket. She silences the phone and frowns before looking up at me. "I have to go."

"Where?"

She bites down on her lip before peeking up at me. "I have a job."

"Wait, what?" Why does she need a job? I've given her everything she could possibly need.

"I started working at Aunt May's a week ago."

I frown at her but keep my mouth shut. Once she agrees to go out with me, I'll work on getting her out of that hellhole. She shouldn't be working a dead-end job that's going to confine her. "Fine, but what about the date?"

She shakes her head, and I'm tempted to run my hand over her hair like a dog. "Let me think about it."

"Does that have to do with the guy that dropped you off?"

Rox squirms in her seat and looks away from me. "No. It has everything to do with us."

Sure, it does. Because her squirming doesn't give crap away. "Okay. Go get ready for work."

Without even a second thought, she's out of the car, and I'm left watching her ascend the stairs to what used to be our safe haven.

CHAPTER 8

ROX

I rush inside the diner and head toward the back booth where the workers are usually lounging until their shift starts. There's an actual lounge for us, but for some reason this booth seems to be more useful. Lucky for me, it's empty. Sliding into the booth, I lower my head to the table. Feeling something moist and sticky, I yank my head up and grunt at the dried red sauce. Someone had the buffalo wings. Only Mercedes sits back here and eats those before a shift. Great, I'm working with her. Just as I turn in the booth, Aunt May saunters over to where I sit dressed in her signature pink apron adorned with dancing bananas and oil stains. She slides in on the other side.

She points to the ticking clock above the register. "You're a bit early, ain'tcha darlin'?"

My eyes move from the woman before me and to the clock. Sure enough, I'm early. Twenty minutes early. But in my defense, I had to get away from Wran—so much so that I rushed through a shower and didn't even blow-dry my hair. There had never been a time when I wanted so badly to get away from Wran. Today changed that.

I can't believe he asked me out not even a day home. Sure, I figured it would come up at some point, but I at least thought I had a week to figure out if I wanted him back in my life in that way. I mean, he's all I know. And I know Wran pretty well. If I do indeed agree to go out with him, I know it won't be romance and flowers like it could be with Cade. Not that I'm even entertaining the idea of Cade. Wran won't take me on dates or surprise me with sweet treats even though he very well knows I like that kind of thing. Dating him will be just like it is now with us: Bickering. Disagreeing. Him trying to tell me what to do and how to act. Just like it has been since I met him twelve years ago.

I want more than that.

Especially now.

Aunt May rests her arms on the table and leans in a little closer. "Somethin' goin' on you want to talk about? You know I'm always here."

I shake my head. "I just needed to get away from Wran for a little. That's all. Nothing major." The door to the kitchen opens and Mercedes walks out attempting to balance four trays of food. "I can clock in early if you need me."

"I was hopin' you'd offer, sweetheart. Mercedes is a peach, but the girl could use some help."

Simply smiling at Aunt May, I rise and head over to Mercedes. I grab the two trays that look like they're ready to plummet to the ground. A sigh of relief escapes Mercedes and she shuffles the remaining trays into a more manageable position in her hands. We don't need customers getting antsy. I've only been here a week, but I've seen plenty so far. Besides, poor Mercedes already has enough on her shoulders; frustrated, screaming customers that are hangry aren't going to do her any favors.

Mercedes smiles in relief. "Oh, thank God, girl! It's going to 14."

I turn around to head to that table but stop in my tracks at the sight of Claire's band of loyal followers sitting in that booth. At least Claire is not with them. Then again, I never really see them with Claire outside of school. Maybe Claire's father is still just as strict as he was in middle school. I know back then her father would require her to go straight home. She had after-school studies along with violin lessons, even though she hated violin. I felt bad for her, but her bitchiness over the years has dissolved that entirely.

Taking a much-needed deep breath, I go over to the table and set the trays down. I glance at their empty glasses to keep from looking at them. "Can I get you refills?"

They each ignore my question and grab their trays. I turn to leave but don't make it far.

"Hey, wait!" One of the girls yell for me to stop. "This ain't right. I wanted those crispy fried onions thingies and bacon on this."

I turn back around and glance from the burger to Janet. The veggie burgers here are very distinguishable. You can see specks of black beans in them. Why in the world would anyone want bacon added to a veggie burger?

Grabbing the tray, I force a smile at her. "I'll have this back out to you right away."

"Of course you will. It's not like there are that many customers in this dump."

The forced smile leaves my lips, and I hurry to the kitchen before I do something that will get me fired. I may not need this job, but I want it. I want to be able to care for myself without Wran's paychecks. Slamming a tray full of food in Janet's face will counteract that.

Aunt May's standing at the fryer, eating a French fry when I enter. I hand her the tray and lean against the prep line island that we haven't use since I started here a week ago.

"It needs bacon and fried onion," I tell her.

Aunt May glances at the burger and then at me. "This is a veggie burger."

I shrug my shoulders. "I'm just the messenger. Hey, where's Timothy and Sharon?" They are usually the ones in the kitchen when I arrive. Aunt May does some of the cooking, but when your name is on the sign out front, you don't really have to.

Aunt May waves her hand at me and sets the tray down on the island. She goes over to the fridge and pulls out an onion and two strips of bacon. "Timothy had an accident before you showed, and Sharon had to rush him to the ER."

I watch as the middle-aged woman grabs flour and her special seasoning blend from the pantry and starts making the fried onions. "What kind of accident? What happened?"

Laying the bacon out on the grill, she points to the front. "That girl spilled hot oil on him while changing the fry grease." She shakes her head again.

I glance at the door. I know I shouldn't feel bad for Mercedes, but I do. She was one of them, as Wran likes to refer to the privileged people on the other side of town. Her parents cut her off when she changed her major from pre-law to interior design. I listened to her cry her way through the story when Aunt May interviewed us. But poor Timothy. That's gonna leave real bad burns. My mind wanders back to this morning when I purposefully hurled coffee on Cade, and I cringe. Poor Cade. At least it wasn't hot oil.

"Are you going to fire her?"

Aunt May grabs the tray from the island and removes the top bun, lettuce, and tomato. She slides on the bacon just as the timer for the onions goes off. When the burger is reassembled, she hands me the tray. "As much as I like ya, darlin', you know I can't discuss that with you. Now, please be a doll and take that out for an old lady."

Without another word, I take the tray and head back to the front of the house. Janet and Teri are still sitting in booth 14. I expected them to get up and leave after making me take the burger back, but Janet must be hungry. They're still here. I come to a stop in front of the table and set the tray in front of Janet. She takes the top bun off and inspects the burger. When the sandwich is to her liking, she takes a bite. Her face scrunches up as she spits the mouthful onto the tray.

"What did you do—give me the same burger with added items? That meat isn't even warm anymore!" she shrieks, her angry narrowed eyes pointed directly at me like a dart target.

I don't point out that the burger is not real meat.

I glance around the diner to see a few eyes on us, including Mercedes'. When our eyes lock, she glances away from me and hands the customer she's talking to something before escaping to the kitchen. Great! This is her section and she's just going to leave me with them. How typical. Turning back to Janet, I try to think up a lie. Technically, Aunt May did just add bacon and onions to the previous burger, but I can't admit to that. Mercedes might be klutzy, but she'll be the new favorite if I let that slip.

"I'm not the cook, Janet. Just the server. If you have a problem with the food, I can get Aunt May."

"No, just take it back! We'll go somewhere else."

A laugh bubbles up out of me before I have time to rein it in. We live in a small town. Unless she wants to drive an hour for food, the only place she'll be going is home.

"Is something funny, Roxy?" Teri snaps.

I shake my head. "No, sorry." I shake my head again, voice getting low. For the last couple of days, I've been forgetting that these are the girls in charge. In order to finish high school as peacefully as possible, I need to stay off their radar. That was simpler prior to Cade speaking to me and me deciding to grow a pair of balls. Someone needs to snip them. I don't need any unnecessary conflicts in my life right now.

"This is exactly why you're not one of us. You keep trying to sabotage everyone around you!" Teri says loud enough for the few people in the diner to hear.

I glance back at the kitchen door to see Aunt May and Mercedes watching the exchange.

Turning back to the girls, I let out a sigh. "You're right."

Teri rises from the booth and glares down at me from her Amazonian height. "You better watch your back Monday. After today and now this"—Teri points at the burger—"you're dead."

The girls grab their bags and stomp out of the diner. I let out a breath. That could have gone worse. I could have ended up with more food in my hair. At least that didn't happen. Getting that stuff out of my hair last night was a feat. There are probably still chunks of banana rotting away in there.

Grabbing the trays, I head back toward the kitchen. I do my best not to look any of the remaining customers in the eye as I head back toward Aunt May. It's not the easiest thing in the world, especially since they just witnessed that humiliating confrontation. Aunt May grabs the trays right as I come to a stop in front of her, and immediately shuffles them over to Mercedes. She pulls me into her arms and reluctantly I go. Really, what else can I do? I need the comfort. Actually, what I need is for Claire and her band of bandits not to exist. For them to go back to ignoring me. That's one wish that's not going to happen. Not after today.

Patting me on the back, she whispers in my ear. "You handled that well, darlin', but next time don't be afraid to give them a good ole country whoopin'."

I pull away from the woman and shake my head at her. She thinks everyone needs a whooping.

I squeeze past her and Mercedes and go back into the kitchen. "I should be clocking in now," I tell them.

"You go ahead and do that," Aunt May says as she walks past me and over to the fryer again, plucking another charred fry from a basket.

Just as I enter the back lounge, my phone buzzes. Pulling it from my back pocket, I roll my eyes at Josh's name flashing across my screen. Hesitantly, I press the answer key and bring the phone to my ear.

"What do you want?" I ask him, voice coming out harsh. After learning what I did, he's at the top of my most-loathed list as of now. I can't believe he forced Wran away. How could he watch me go through what I was going through, knowing he was the reason for it in the first place?

"Who pissed you off?" Josh asks, and I can hear the laughter in his mocking voice.

"No one!" I snap.

"Sure, because on any given day little Roxy is snapping at people."

I sign into the phone. "It doesn't matter. What do you want?"

I hear a roaring on the line before he answers. "Headed your way. We need to talk."

"I'm not at the apartment."

"I'm aware of that little job of yours. This is important, Rox. We need to talk."

Yeah, we do. I need to know why he watched me fall apart and soothed me back to sanity after sending my boyfriend to war. "I'll come by the house before going home. Don't come here. I need this job, and I don't want drama here."

He sighs. "How are you gonna get here? I can pick you up."

"I took Wran's car. Expect me around nine."

"Fine. Don't be late. One way or another, we are discussing this."

I roll my eyes. "Whatever, Josh. Bye."

Hanging up the phone, I slump down on the bench. For two years, we haven't needed to discuss this. For two years, I've been able to neglect thinking about telling Wran. And for two years, my life has been sane. Discussing it is going to make what I did even more real than it already is. It's just going to hurt even more. And more than that, it's going to kill Wran. If he finds out, I'm not going to have to decide about the date; he'll just leave again. I don't want him to leave again.

Rising from the bench, I pull my key card out and head over to the machine to swipe it. Everything is going to be fine. Wran is not going to find out. Not until I can handle telling him myself.

CHAPTER 9

ROX

It's nearly ten when my shift ends, and Josh has texted me four times, mainly asking if I'm okay, which is nothing unusual. Whenever I am not on time, he tends to worry. I'm surprised it's not Wran worrying.

When I'm safely tucked away behind the steering wheel, I send Josh a text letting him know I'm on my way. After what I discovered today, I don't know why I'm being so compliant with Josh. He ruined my life. Well, he ruined it if what Wran said is true. I know for a fact that there is more than one side to every story. Sometimes there are multiples. However, something about Wran's confession has me believing it fully. And I honestly don't want to. All the Saturdays I spent with Josh would be tainted. All the consoling would be faux. No matter how he sees me, I at least thought Josh saw me as family. A nuisance family member, but family nevertheless.

Taking in a deep breath, I pull away from the diner. It doesn't take long to reach the house on the other side of the tracks. Lights illuminate the driveway and I pull right up beside his police car. His motorcycle must be in the garage. As I turn the car off, the front door opens and Josh stands there. I bite down on the inside of my cheek to keep me from getting back in the car and driving away from here. Josh and I might loathe one another on a good day, but he has always been truthful with me. I need to know why Wran left. I need to know why I had to give up one of the most important things to me.

I shut the car door and walk up the path to Josh. He steps aside and lets me enter the house. I didn't spend much time on the inside of the place as a child. Josh and Wran were always concerned about their father finding me. What they don't know is that he knew I was here all along; he simply didn't care that his boys were playing house to an orphan. Or maybe he was just too drunk to care. He came down to the cellar one day while the guys were at school. Josh hadn't yet enrolled me in public school. Mr. Belmont came and laid down on the sofa I slept on. He cried into the pillows and clutched a pink furry sweater for dear life. It took him two hours before he noticed my things lying around the cellar. It took him another hour to find me hiding behind one of the huge boxes housing his wife's belongings.

At nine, the only men I was used to were Wran, Josh, and my father. And Mr. Belmont had been drinking. I could smell the pungent odor the entire time he was searching the cellar. The only things I was capable of doing when he discovered me were crying and clutching my rabbit. To me, drinking meant torture; I didn't want to hurt. Mr. Belmont, however, didn't lay a hand on me. He just stared at me as if I was a mirage. When he realized I wasn't going to stop bawling, he backed away and left the cellar. He never came back down there.

I never told the guys about that day.

The sound of the front door locking has me turning to face Josh. My eyes widen at the swelling on his face and the bruises. There's a bandage across his nose. He must have had a tough day at work—although that's shocking considering that crime is a four-letter word in this town. Generally, we have no misconduct.

Josh points toward the family room and I make my way to it. Sitting down on the old, burnt couch, I wait for Josh to say something. When he just sits in his chair and looks at me, I raise a brow at him. He wanted me here; I'm here.

"We really need to discuss what happened and how we're going to proceed. I know this isn't something you want to think about, Roxanna, but you have to. Especially, since he's back," Josh says without taking his eyes off me. One of his eyes has a cut above it, but it never wavers. That steely, unflinching glare is what makes him a great sheriff. It's what made him the youngest sheriff this town has ever had.

"I want to discuss something else first, and I need you to be honest," I tell him. I'm getting my answers before we go down that road. I wish we didn't have to go down that road, but I know he's right. We have to talk about it. I must decide on how to tell Wran. And I really don't need Josh telling Wran before I can come up with some way to keep him from going crazy and burning down this town.

He gets up from the leather chair he's occupying and walks over to the fireplace. He grabs a bottle off the mantel and takes a swig. "Want some?"

I look at the bottle and then at him. Josh doesn't drink. Or at least I've never seen him drink. And he sure as hell doesn't offer it to minors. I shake my head and he recaps the bottle, placing it back on the mantel.

"What's wrong with you? What happened to your face?" I ask him.

He takes his seat again and crosses his legs. He circles his face with a finger. "Your boyfriend did this. Courtesy of me taking your feelings into consideration."

Wran did that? "You know he's not my boyfriend."

"How long is that gonna last, Roxanna?"

I cross my arms over my chest and glare at him. How dare he asks that? "I'm pretty sure if it was up to you it would be permanent."

A grin spreads across Josh's face. He leans forward and rests his elbows on his knees. "Aw, so that's what had little ole Roxy fired up earlier. Wran told you. What exactly did he tell you?"

"That you are the reason he left. You threatened to put him in jail because of me."

Josh shakes his head. "Not because of you. Because he fucked you."

I flinch back at the word fucked. That's not how I see it at all, and quite frankly that word doesn't belong in a sentence about the love I shared with Wran. We made love. It happened once. It was the best and worst night of my life. Wran was so loving and caring during it, but afterwards he was mean and cruel. Back then I was great at reading him, and I knew he only lashed out because he felt guilty. Not because it happened, but because I was so young. I had tried talking to him about it for a while prior to the act, and Wran had made it perfectly clear that it wouldn't happen. He literally threatened the male population if any guy touched me.

That night, though, Wran came home from work upset and covered in grease. He was working at a mechanic shop at the time. He wouldn't talk about what happened; he just kept slamming his fist into the wall. I could feel the rage rolling off him, and I hated it. I had never seen him that livid before. I did the only thing I could think that might calm him down: I kissed him. We had made out plenty of times before. Wran never let it get farther than a make-out session, but he was always calm and relaxed during it. He had just stared at me with wide eyes, frozen in place. The next thing I knew, he was shoving me back on the couch, and I became his new target. It was like I absorbed the rage with each touch. With each kiss. And as he calmed, his touches became more sensual. One thing led to another, and by the next morning I was no longer the innocent little girl he cared deeply for.

"So, you did do it? You sent him away." I'm not sure why I'm asking. He's already admitted it.

Josh nods. "It was for both of you guys' own good. I mean, Jesus Christ, you were only fifteen!"

"You saw what that did to me! How was that for my own good?" I shout at him. "You are the reason—" I can't bring myself to finish that sentence.

"How was I supposed to know you would fall off your damn rocker?"

"Because I had already lost everything else!" I get up from the couch and pace around the room. "You were supposed to know because you were like a brother to me. You were the one that took care of me when Wran wanted to be a teenager and go to parties with his friends." My voice starts coming out in short, weepy gasps. "You were there. You had eyes. You saw."

Josh gets up from the chair and comes over to where I'm standing behind the sofa. He pulls me into a hug, wrapping his arms around my shoulders as if protecting me. Sighing into my hair, he says, "Yes, I saw. But I also saw my little brother turning into someone he shouldn't have been."

I pull back and stare up at Josh. "That should have been his choice."

"You don't get it, Roxanna. I had to watch him grow up before his time. When he was seventeen, he should have been applying to colleges instead of getting a job to stay close to you. He should have been out partying with guys his own age instead of teaching a twelve-year-old about getting her period. Do you not see how fucked up you guys' relationship was? On top of that, people were starting to question it. We live in a small town. Word gets around. He didn't need word getting around that he was a grown-ass man fucking a kid. It would have ruined him."

As hard as it is to hear, I understand it. I wouldn't have when I was younger, but I understand that we weren't conventional. Still, that should have been a choice Wran made on his own without Josh threatening him. Wran has always been clever. Heck, he's the one that got me fake info for school when they decided it was time for me to go to public school. Josh had to sign off as my guardian, but Wran still made it happen. He would have figured something out if word got out about us.

I glance up at Josh. "I understand all of that, but did it ever cross your mind that you would ruin me?"

His eyes dip for a moment, but then they are right back on me. He leans against the couch and lets out a huff. His body relaxes, and I'm not sure I understand the relief gracing his face. "We're not related, Roxanna. And as cold as this might sound, Wran will always be my priority, even if it hurts you."

A loud breath leaves me and I step away from him. That hurt more than knowing he sent Wran away. I search his face for anything telling me he doesn't actually believe his own words, but the relief on his face and in his lean posture tells me otherwise. I'm not his family. He has never seen me as his family. I really am just a nuisance to him.

Silent tears roll down my face and I swipe them away. No, I won't cry over Josh. So what if he doesn't particularly care about me? It's not like I'm a huge fan of his anyways. This only makes it easier to forget I ever cared about him.

I turn on my heel to leave, but a hand lands on my shoulder, halting me. I knock Josh's hand off and walk toward the house door. I have my answers. There's nothing else I need from him.

"We're not done talking," Josh shouts at me. "You walk out that door, Wran will be finding out before you make it to the apartment."

I stop walking and glare at the door.

He wouldn't.

Then again, he did just basically tell me he didn't care about me. Turning around, I rush back down the hall to where Josh hasn't moved. My hand lands against the side of his already swollen cheek, and he doesn't react. Stupid Belmont men think they're so strong.

"You have no right to tell him anything, since you're the cause of it," I scream in his face.

As calm as ever, Josh simply states, "He has a right to know."

"He will know. When I decide it's time for him to know. Just because he's back doesn't mean he gets to be a part of that."

"And what are you going to tell him when you dis-appear every Saturday? What am I supposed to tell my brother when he comes searching for answers?"

"Tell him that it's none of his business."

"Rox, you and I both know it's his business more so than it is mine. Unless you don't want me tagging along anymore. You're eighteen now. You don't need your guardian present anymore."

"What makes you think I would want you to go there with me anymore after you said I didn't matter?"

"You still don't have a car."

Josh grabs my hand, but I pull it away from him. I don't want him touching me ever again. If I'm nothing, then I want him to treat me like nothing. "Don't ever touch me again."

He rolls his eyes. "Fine. When do you plan on telling Wran?"

"I don't know," I whisper. Maybe when I know for sure that I can trust him. When I don't have to see my dad on the news again, reminding me that men can't be trusted.

"Do you still plan on going tomorrow?"

I give him a sharp, pointed stare. He's not stupid. "Of course. I only get to go once a week. Wran being back isn't going to change that. You should know that."

"Should I pick you up at the same time?"

I simply nod. He was right; I don't have a car. Wran would never let me take his car for an entire day without riding along. And it's not like walking to Arlington in February is going to do me any favors. My Saturdays will cease to exist then. They will take them away, and all my progress over the two years won't have even mattered.

"I suppose I'll see you tomorrow." Josh stares down at me for a moment before adding, "I'm really sorry for my part in this, Roxanna."

I nod again and walk to the front of the house. Unfortunately, sorry isn't going to change the last three years of my life. Sorry isn't going to change the fact that I just lost a brother all over again. More tears roll down my face, but this time I don't wipe them again. There's not really a point. I know they won't be stopping anytime soon.

CHAPTER 10

WRAN

I groan from the pecking on my head and reluctantly sit up. My stressed muscles tingle, and I collapse back down. A few more minutes won't hurt anything. Another peck lands on my head, harder this time. I open my eyes, close them, and then abruptly open them again as I realize I fell asleep.

Shit!

Rox!

She never came home last night. Jumping from the sofa, I groan aloud when my back cracks. Damn couch! We need to invest in a new one. Swinging around, I nearly stumble over my own feet when I see Rox standing there in skintight jeans and another one of my old shirts with a mug in her tiny hands. She hands me the mug and rounds the couch. My eyes follow her stride until she sits down. Her face is puffy and red, which only ever happens after she's been crying for hours. I set the coffee mug on the table and sit down beside her. As much as I want to yell at her for not coming home, I'm pretty sure whatever made her cry was punishment enough.

Then again . . .

"Where the hell were you last night?" I'll be damned if I spare her feelings after she had me worrying like a sinner in church.

Her eyes widen for a split second and then they go back to her usually unfazed glaze. "I came home. You were asleep, so I let you sleep."

I shake my head at her, mostly trying to shake off how damn angelic her voice sounds. My little angel. My little angel that didn't fucking come home last night. "Don't lie to me, Rox. Not about this. I waited up for you. I called the diner. Aunt May said you left there around nine thirty. So again, where did you go?"

Rox gets up from the couch. I inhale as she sashays past me in those jeans. It takes everything in me not to grab her and rip those pants off. Or better yet, untuck my shirt from them so she's covered more. She goes over to the kitchen and pours coffee into a pink mug sitting on the counter. Knowing her, she's probably already had three cups. Maybe even more, depending on how long she's been awake. I seize the mug she handed me off the table and gulp down the contents before going over to Rox. The lukewarm liquid does nothing to settle me down.

I walk up behind her just as she takes another sip of her black coffee. I place my hands on both sides of her hips and pull her flush against me. A small gasp leaves her lips, and a small bit of her coffee splashes over the rim of her mug. At least I know I still affect her.

Leaning down, I hiss in her ear. "I asked you a question."

Rox sets the mug down on the small island and turns around in my hold, wiggling her tiny ass as she does so. "I turned eighteen a week ago," she says as if that's a surprise to me. I'm the one that spent nearly a decade planning her parties.

My hands slither up her delicate sides. "Trust me. I know."

"Which means..." She leans forward, snaking her hands under my sweater. Her fingers spread out over my chest, and it's my turn to inhale. She better have no knowledge of what she's doing. I'll murder whoever taught her. "I don't have to answer to you anymore."

Her words are like a cold shower, and for a split second I'm dumbfounded by them. Josh allotted her way too much freedom if she believes this is how this works. My fingers dig into her sides. She winces, and I lean down to her ear. "Try again, sweetheart."

Her nails dig into my stomach and my hands fall from her body. With a sexy little pout gracing her face, she pulls her hands from underneath my sweater and rests her hands on her hips. Her attempting to be mad is honestly the cutest thing I've seen in a while. For someone that wants to be grown up, she still looks like a kid when she does that.

Letting out a breath, I relent. For now. "Fine. You're an adult. But adults, sweetheart, don't play the game you played last night. I was worried."

Her little pout turns downward as she leans her back against the island. "I didn't mean to worry you. Honestly."

I relax against the opposite side and stare at her. "I know, Rox, but I do worry. I worried every day for the last three years because I haven't been here. You have no clue what it's like to come back only to have you disappear."

Her eyes flick up to mine, and I know I've got her. Simple words—that's all it takes, and I know I've got her back where she belongs. Her shoulders slump and she runs a hand through her hair. Rox takes the two steps to my side of the kitchen and wraps her arms around my middle. That's my girl. That's the predictable angel I left behind.

"I'm sorry," she mumbles into my chest.

I rub the back of her head and smirk to myself. "It's okay, Rox. You can always make it up to me."

She pulls back slightly without breaking her hold on me. I look down at her questioning face. "What do you mean by make it up to you?"

I grin down at her. "Well, you could always say yes to that date."

Her hands fall from my waist and she backs away.

Damn! Maybe that was too forward for this version of my girl. I take a step in her direction and she raises her hand to stop me. I stop. Only because she needs to feel like she has some power in this tug-of-war we play so nicely.

"I already have an answer for you about that. I was going to tell you later tonight when I got home."

Blinking, I stand up straighter. She already has an answer? "When did you decide?"

Rox glances away from me and starts fiddling with the beltloops of her jeans. When she does finally look back my way, I can't read her expression. Nervous, maybe? The only way she would be nervous is if she turns down my offer. She'd better not turn down my offer. Granted, the girl has every right to—I did disappear on her for a while—but still. If she turns down my offer for the guy in the truck. . . for one of them, I might hurt her.

"Last night," she responds in a wary voice.

My hands fist at my sides at her tone. Rox never, and I mean never, talks to me the way she's talking now. She has always been one hundred percent confident when it comes to me. She's gonna say no. I know it. That's the only reason she would be so nervous. I take one step across the narrow walkway until we are standing toe to toe. Without thinking, my hands go to the strand of hair hanging in her face. I need her to say yes. "Why do I have to wait until tonight to get your answer?"

Rox pulls her phone from her pocket and looks at it. "Because I have somewhere to be in a couple of hours."

"You can tell me now," I urge her. For some reason, I need to know there's a chance I can win her back.

Biting down on her bottom lip, Rox takes my hand and pulls me over to the sofa. She sits as far away from me as possible, and I don't like it. Frowning, I reach across the sofa and hook a hand around her narrow thigh, pulling her closer to me. She doesn't say anything as I do so. That could be a good sign.

"Rox?" I insist when she starts tearing at her nails. "What's your answer?"

I see her inhale and then she moves in even closer to me. She places a hand on my leg and moves it upward, skimming over a very sensitive area I would rather she not touch until I have an answer. Her hand doesn't stop until she is cradling the side of my face. Her thumb runs lightly across my lips, and I stiffen at her touch.

Someone kill me now.

"I love you," she says so softly.

"I didn't hear that." I beg her to say it again. I haven't heard those words from her innocent voice since the voice-mails she left on my phone three years ago. And even the messages on my phone didn't do her voice any justice.

"I love you," she declares more confidently, dropping her hand from my skin.

My eyes go down to the lip she's biting on, and I desperately want to be the one biting that lip.

"I've loved you since that first day we met, but I'm scared, Wran. You left me once, and I know you had no choice, but I can't handle that again."

My eyes go back to hers as I reassure her. "You can handle anything, Roxy."

And she can.

Rox might not think so, but I know for a fact she can. She escaped an abusive father when she was six. She's managed with me, and I know I've been no picnic to her. I made her early teen years hell. I'll never forget the look on her face when I brought home two girls on her thirteenth birthday. She looked as if her world came crashing down. That was the first time I ever let Rox hear me with someone. As much as hearing her cry the whole night killed me, it also gave me some sick bliss. That bliss vanished the next morning when I saw her bloodshot eyes, puffy face, and the new painting she had hanging on the wall directly across from my bedroom door. A girl lying in a wooden casket with a hole in her chest, eyes wide open as if she could see everything happening around her and a smile on her face. That painting was creepy. That's how I know this girl can handle a hell of a lot more than she gives herself credit for. Any other girl would have cracked under all the bullshit she's had to go through.

She shakes her head. "Don't break my heart again."

I don't need her to say more. Grabbing a handful of her short hair, I gently pull her on my lap and slam my mouth down on hers. Rox freezes under my immediate touch but relaxes as she kisses me back—once, twice, until I can't take another gentle touch. My hands move from her hair and down her slender form, crushing her to me like I did all those years ago when we were first falling in love. Rising without breaking our connection, I ease her back against the couch, feeling the shivers that are making her whole body tremble under my touch. I pull back to look at her flushed face, all rosy and wanting. When she doesn't feel the warmth radiating from me, she lazily opens her eyes.

Any other time I would give her no choice, but I need her to want me just as badly as I want her. "If you want me to stop—"

Rox reaches up and pulls me back down to her, the rest of my words forgotten against her lips. Her kiss is soft and gentle, much like I just kissed her, but unfortunately I don't want that. Not after three years of being away from her. I press myself into her and yank my old shirt she's wearing free of her jeans. I pull away from her supple lips only to pull the shirt over her head.

Before I have time to reclaim her mouth again, a loud knock on the door has her eyes flying open once more. Rox rises on her elbows but I push her back down. Nope. Not happening. I've gone way too long without my girl. Whoever that is will have to take a damn number.

There's another knock on the door.

"Go. The fuck. Away!" I yell at the door.

Leaning back down, I place a kiss on the hollow of Rox's neck. A soft moan leaves her mouth as I trail the kiss down her chest. A loud ping goes off just as whoever is outside persistently knocks on the door. Mood broken\, I reach down to Rox's jeans and pluck her phone from it. A message from my brother graces the screen. Open up, it reads. I turn the phone to her and her once flushed face goes back to pale white. She sits up and reaches for her shirt, sliding it over her head with ease.

Rox reaches for the phone, but I pull it out of range. Like hell. I get up from the couch and go over to the door. Wrenching it open, I glare at my brother. "Do you not understand the meaning of 'go the fuck away'?"

Josh pushes past me and goes inside. "I'm here for her, not you."

I slam the door and turn to see Rox standing and staring at the both of us. Even from over here, she looks tense. Slowly she walks over to me, bypassing my brother. She grabs one of my fisted palms and brings it up to her lips. She mouths I love you, and apparently those are the magic words. Thoughts of slamming my brother's head into the coffee table become extinct.

Josh watches the exchange with drawn brows, hooded eyes, and thinned lips. That only makes me grin. All the trouble he put into keeping us apart, and we're back together less than a week after my arrival. And whatever he had going on with Rox is done. She's mine. We might disagree a lot, but it's me she yearns to wither underneath.

"What do you want, Josh?" I ask him, draping an arm across Rox's shoulders.

"He's here to pick me up." Rox answers for him.

My eyes go down to her at my side.

"I told you I had something to do today."

I nod. Yeah, I vaguely remember her saying she had something to do today before I made her tell me her answer. "I can take—"

"No!" Rox abruptly cuts me off. "Josh is taking me."

"Like hell—"

"Wran," she cuts me off again. "Remember that conversation we had yesterday in the car? You said you'd let me tell you what's going on when I'm ready. This has to do with that. So please let it go."

"Let it go? You're leaving with Josh after we just made out on the damn couch!"

Her eyes dip as she says, "I know, but please trust me."

I shake my head. "Trust is earned, Rox."

"So is forgiveness," she counters, and I have nothing to say to that.

Fuck!

I hate when she does that.

"Fine. Go. When will you be back?"

Relief floods her entire being as she smiles up at me. My brother moves forward and drapes an arm around her shoulders like I did minutes ago. "Don't worry so much, little brother. I'll have our dear Roxanna back home before curfew."

CHAPTER 11

ROX

The tension in the car is heavy all the way to the city. Neither Josh nor I speak. If it wasn't for the fact that I'm not ready to let Wran in on the situation, I would have let him drive me. Unfortunately, I think bringing Wran in on this will derail all the progress I've made. He clearly has problems controlling himself. He was never like that before. Sure, he was controlling, but it was never as bad as it is now. He didn't use to care if I went places with Josh. Then again, that was before Josh threatened to get him arrested.

I glance over at Josh. A childish part of me still doesn't want to believe that he did those things . . . that this man before me is the cold person he admitted to being last night. It makes no sense to me. I can clearly remember him rocking me to sleep when I was seven, whenever it would storm. I remember him taking me to get ice cream when he came home from school during his lunch break if I'd done all the homeschool work. Those memories don't add up to him not caring about me.

"When I was eight, you bought me a blue and white dress with sequins on it because I wanted to be a princess for my birthday," I mutter, eyes still trained on him.

Josh glances at me for a second before focusing back on the road. "What's your point?"

"Last night you said you didn't care about me. That doesn't sound like the actions of a guy that doesn't care," I tell him.

Josh's jaw flexes and his vision remains on the road. "Don't put words into my mouth. I didn't say that last night. I said that Wran was my priority. Besides, you were an innocent kid back then."

"I was a kid when you sent Wran away, too."

"Roxanna, we're not having this conversation. Just sit over there and stay quiet. We'll be at the department soon."

With a groan, I turn back around in my seat. If that's how he wants to play it, then fine. I can't change what he said last night, and he's apparently sticking to that. I know differently. Some part of Josh must care about me, even if it's merely a small piece that thinks of me as a sad orphan girl. I mean come on. He takes time out of his weekend to bring me all the way to Arlington. Yes, he has a reason to, but still . . .

A small part of him has to care.

It takes twenty minutes to get through the traffic to the department. I didn't come last weekend due to my birthday.

My being here on that day wouldn't have benefited anyone involved. Usually I just sit at home and wallow in sorrow. My birthday only reminds me of the one and only time I was with Wran.

"Are you gonna get out or just sit there staring at the building?" Josh asks me, breaking through my train of thought.

"You don't have to rush me." I open the door. "Are you coming in or no?"

"This is the only time I get to spend with her, so yeah," he responds, and slams the door.

I close the car door and walk up the pathway to a set of double glass doors. This building is usually closed on Saturdays unless there are meetings. All my meetings had to be scheduled for Saturdays, since I am in school during the day and Mrs. Adams didn't want to pull me out of school for this. Taking in a deep breath, I open the door and smile at the security guard in the cubicle. He opens the window and gives me a friendly smile.

"Good morning, Roxanna." He glances behind me at Josh, tilting his head in acknowledgment. "Mr. Belmont. I have donuts. Want one, kiddo?"

I shake my head. He offers me one every Saturday, and every Saturday I decline. "No, thanks. I had coffee."

"Alrighty, then. You know the routine."

Nodding again, I take off my shoes and place them in a basket along with my wallet, keys, and phone. I place the basket on the conveyer belt and step through the x-ray machine. When the machine lights up green, I exit the other side and wait for my basket to come through. Josh repeats my actions, and when he's through, we head down the white hall plastered with posters to the check-in.

I tap on the window, and a new girl with blond hair comes over. She opens the window with a big smile that seems all too fake. I know if I were her, I wouldn't want to be here on a Saturday. "May I help you?"

"Um, yes, I'm here to see Lynn Adams."

The girl bends down and types something on the computer. "May I have your name and birthday, please?"

The elderly lady that's regularly here never has to ask me for that information. She would have just opened the door and let me through. I hate having to give people my name. They associate it with my father and then give me a weird look. The identity information Wran got me to get into school became obsolete when it came to this. According to the government, there is no person by the name of Roxanna Belmont. Josh cracked under the scrutiny and had to give the hospital my real name for them to see me.

"Um, it's Roxanna Raine. Born February 12, 2001."

The girl types that into her computer. I see her pause for a second when she puts two and two together. When she glances up at me, I expect to see pity on her face, but it's neutral. Not even the old lady was able to accomplish such an unbiased face. She literally ran out of the office and crushed me to her in a hug, muttered words that should have soothed me but instead had quite the opposite effect. Josh had to pull the lady off me. After that day, though, she never brought up my father or asked me questions.

"They're already waiting for you. You may go in."

I smile at the girl and turn toward the open doors with Josh right on my heels. Turning around, I glance at his relaxed expression. Of all the days and all the meetings, I can't believe he's relaxed on this day. I rub my sweaty palms down my jeans and walk through the double doors. My feet stop moving as soon as Mrs. Adams comes into sight. She's sitting in one of the pink plastic chairs with a toddler on the floor at her feet. When she notices me standing there, Lynn gives me a gentle smile and bends down to retrieve the baby girl. Mrs. Adams walks over toward me, but I can't help but stare at the little girl in her embrace. With big brown eyes and luscious black curls, she gets more and more adorable every time I see her.

The little girl's eyes get big when she notices us standing there, and she starts to struggle in Lynn's arms. When Lynn doesn't let her go, tears well up in her eyes and she starts screaming. Josh and I have gotten used to it over the last two years. She always cries when she sees us. Lynn says it's a good thing.

"Poshy!" she whines, still pronouncing Joshy with a 'p' sound instead of a 'j.'

"Good morning," Lynn says to Josh and hands him the child. "Harley has been very impatient this morning. She only stopped crying when I let her play with the blocks."

Mrs. Adams mutters a happy belated birthday to me, but I don't take my eyes off Harley. For some reason, Harley has always been more drawn to Josh than me. Lynn said that would change when she got older, but it's been two years and she still cries whenever I hold her. Some part of me thinks she remembers what happened and she hates me for it. I've voiced my concerns about that once to Mrs. Adams, and she assured me that babies can't remember anything before a certain age. I don't buy it. That's the only reason I have why Harley doesn't like me.

I turn away from Josh and Harley and face Lynn. "Are we still going to discuss custody today?"

Lynn's eyes flick away from me and at Harley before she nods. "Follow me."

I bite my bottom lip to keep it from trembling. That look didn't mean anything. I've done everything I was supposed to do. I completed the counseling they assigned. I've done the monthly drug tests. Things are good. I will get Harley today.

I shake my head and follow Lynn down another hall.

I will get her. Lynn promised. . .

I glance back at Josh and Harley as a giggle erupts from my daughter. Josh has her held in the air above his head, spinning her around. She always cries when I do that. Nevertheless, the sight of him with her makes me smile. Josh might not like me much, but he has loved that little girl since the moment she was born. As much as it killed me to watch Lynn rip Harley out of my arms not even minutes after the nurse gave her to me, I think it hurt Josh even more.

He hasn't been the same since that day. Harder. . . colder . . . . A lot like his father.

We all come to a stop in front of a wooden door with Mrs. Adams' name on it. She pushes the door open and heads around leather chairs to her desk. She sits, and motions for us to do the same. I take the seat directly in front of her, and Josh sits next to me. He bounces Harley on his blue-jean-clad knee. Josh looks from my daughter to me, frowning, but then hands her to me. Harley shakes her head and clutches onto Josh's arm.

"No!" she cries, and I instantly drop my hands from her, letting Josh keep her. I find it odd that she can say what she doesn't want with clarity but can't say "Joshy."

"You know," Mrs. Adams says, "she'll never stop that until you teach her who's the parent. She needs to be with you in order to get comfortable with you."

I meet Lynn's watchful eyes with a bit more hope than a minute ago. "Does that mean I get to take her home?"

Lynn frowns at my question. "Roxanna, you just turned eighteen."

"I know, but—"

"And you are still in high school." She raises her voice to overtalk me. "My job is to do what's best for that little girl." She points at Harley. "Not you."

"But . . . but you . . . ." My voice trails off as I take in what Mrs. Adams just told me. I won't be getting my daughter today. I shake my head at her, not comprehending what she just told me. I did everything she advised me to do. I'm graduating with honors. I have a job. I have a stable living environment. I have done everything this woman has told me to do. I stand up from my seat and walk over to the door, leaning my head against it to calm my racing heart. This can't be happening. I don't believe this. I'm not getting my daughter.

"I'm not understanding this," Josh says, voice tense. "You told us if all went well that Rox would get her back upon her eighteenth birthday."

"I understand that, Mr. Belmont, but this was not a decision that was made lightly."

I turn back around and go take my seat as she attempts to make us understand.

"The state doesn't care that Roxanna has followed instructions. They care that she is still pretty much a child herself. How is an eighteen-year-old girl still in high school supposed to take care of a toddler?"

"Roxanna has support. She has me, and I wouldn't let anything happen to Harley."

Lynn gives Josh a smile that doesn't reach her eyes and lets out a deep sigh. "I know. You've been here with her the entire time, but you're not Harley's father. Or at least that's what you've been saying for the last two years."

Josh tenses at the accusation in her tone. Social services have been trying to get me to tell them the father since they took Harley from me. I'll never forget the first meeting I had with Lynn, where she literally had investigators come in and question Josh. He was suspended from his job for two weeks while they investigated Lynn's allegations. Not to mention I didn't get to see Harley for the first six months. That all happened when she thought I was lying about Josh. There was no way I was telling her the father after witnessing the treatment Josh went through.

"He's not her father!" I speak up. "Why does that even matter?"

"It matters because you were fifteen when you had her. No one is going to let you take a child into an environment where she could be harmed."

"Please," I beg, my eyes getting watery. "I'll do anything. Name it, and I'll do it. I just want my daughter back."

"Roxanna, you won't be able to take her home today. I think you should consider letting a family adopt her. Give her a chance at a better life."

"No!" Josh yells, and Harley starts to cry. He hands her over to me and gets up.

This time I take her. I run a hand over her head and bounce her on my knee like Josh was doing, but it doesn't stop her sobbing.

"Rox has done everything you people have asked of her. She very well deserves her child. So she made one mistake when she was a kid! That shouldn't be the deciding factor. If I investigate your background, is it going to be spotless?"

With wide eyes, I stare up at Josh. After last night, I'm surprised he would stand up for me. But then again, he has something to lose if I can't get custody of my daughter. I don't want to know how he'll spiral if he can't hold and see

Harley anymore. I place a hand on Josh's forearm to calm him down. I don't need him upsetting Lynn. And I definitely don't need Lynn writing in her reports that my guardian is unfit to handle children.

"Poshy," Harley whines. "Poshy, Poshy, Poshy."

"It's okay, baby," I mutter into Harley's soft curls. "It's okay."

Josh slumps back down in the chair and takes Harley from me as she scrambles to get over to him. "Sorry. I don't understand why after all this time the story has changed. If Roxanna wasn't going to be able to get Harley back, what was the point of all these meetings? Why schedule weekly visits where she gets to hold Harley? Why make her go to AA meetings and see a therapist?"

Lynn folds her arms on the desk. "A decision hasn't actually been made on whether or not Roxanna will get custody. But they are aiming toward letting a stable family adopt her."

"So there's a chance I could get her?" I ask.

"They want to postpone giving you her until her third birthday. It will give them enough time to evaluate how you perform after you graduate. You'll have to have a stable living environment, which I'm aware you already have. They would prefer you live in a house that's childproofed in a safer part of town. You must have a full-time job from the moment you graduate up until they make a decision. And you have to still pass all the drug tests. One small mistake and they're taking her. You won't be able to see Harley again."

"What about college?" Josh asks Lynn. "She can't work full-time and go to college full-time."

Lynn glances from him to me. "You must decide what's more important. Your daughter or. . ."

She doesn't have to say more. If I want to have full and permanent custody of my baby, I have to play by their rules. I can't go to college. Josh reaches over and wipes a tear from my eye. Harley looks between the two of us and then reaches a small hand out my way. I stare at her for a long minute, doing my best not to let more tears roll down my face. People never understand how badly they want something until they are told they can't have it. I never thought about getting pregnant at fifteen and having a family until I watched with blurry vision as Lynn carried Harley away from me. I never thought much about college until now. Yes, I've applied to the community college. And yes, Wran used to drill the importance of a good education into my head, but to me it was simply what you do when you're a senior in high school. It's the natural next step in life.

As I take Harley from Josh, she throws her tiny arms around me and buries her small head against my chest. She mutters something, but it doesn't make much sense to me. I hold her closer. Mrs. Adams is crazy if she thinks I'd choose anything over this little girl.

"I'll do whatever it takes to be able to take her home," I tell Lynn.

She nods and sits back in her chair. "Okay. Make sure you're prepared for anything when the time comes."

I don't respond to that. Lynn knows I won't do less than my best.

Harley pulls out of my embrace and looks up at me. "You 'kay?"

I smile at her innocent question. I haven't been okay since the moment I found out I was having Wran's child and he wouldn't be around to help me through the process. But she doesn't need to know that and neither does my nosy social worker. Leaning forward, I place a peck on my daughter's forehead. I'm going to be okay. Her father's home. In a matter of months, I will have her back. We will be a family. I will have a family.

Those thoughts make me feel okay.

"So," Josh requests, "do we still get to take her for the day?"

"Yes!" Lynn tells him. "I wouldn't think of impeding on the time you do have. You know the routine. Have her back by three."

Josh salutes her, and I roll my eyes. "Will do, Lynn."

Rising from his chair, Josh retrieves Harley from me and walks out of the room. I stand to follow but stop. I need to know if there's truly a chance. While I know what she told me, I need her to spell it out in simpleton language.

"Tell it to me straight, Mrs. Adams. What are the real chances of getting my daughter?"

She rises from her seat and folds her arms across her chest, looking at me straight on. "Honestly, Roxanna, any-thing is possible. But if I had to guess what the judge would rule, it would be against you. You're still a child yourself. And while we don't know for sure who the father is, Judge Jenkins is sure it's one of the Belmonts. Neither of those options leans in your favor."

"Does loving him make a difference?"

"If your judge was a man, then yes. It would. A male judge would see it as consent, but since we are very much trying to make rape culture a nonissue, you're not going to be spared. You're the example. Not to mention your father is walking free in mere days. There's so much that could be used against you regarding Harley's safety."

I nod at her answer. For months, I've been trying not to think about my father getting released. I've tried making it a nonissue when it comes to this aspect of my life, but I knew it would be a problem. He's going to come after me. As much as I want to believe that prison has changed my father, the expression on his face during that news report tells me differently. He's still very much the same man that murdered my nanny. The same man that did horrible things to me. If he finds out about Harley, I'd never forgive myself.

CHAPTER 12

WRAN

I'm losing my mind. Scratch that, I lost my fucking mind years ago when I thought taking in Rox was the decent thing. Her leaving this morning with my brother actually happened. And I let it happen. I let her walk out that door not knowing when she would be back. It's been hours. I've tried everything imaginable to get my mind off the fact that she's with him . . .that she didn't even consider my offer to drive her. Hell, I even baked a cake. A cake!

I look over to the kitchen island where a heaping pile of pink frosting sits on a piece of aluminum foil. I couldn't find the cake stand. I'd like to think of myself as a decent cook—Rox never complained—but hell will freeze over before I can bake. My eyes dip at the sight of the uneven layers that appear to have shifted. That cake was straight when I arranged it earlier. I swear it seemed edible. Oh well. At least the store-bought icing hides the amount of salt I accidentally dumped into it.

Snorting, I grab my phone and check the time for the hundredth time. It's almost four o'clock. Where the hell could they be for this long? I plop down on the couch and reach for the remote as a knock on the door sounds throughout the apartment. Arching a brow, I glance over at it. It's not Rox. She has a key. And my soon-to-be-dead brother is with her. I can't imagine anyone looking for me would show up here. They know this place is off limits. And I can't picture Rox actually having friends that would come. For one, she has always been way too paranoid to make friends—scared they would judge her for her father. She was right to believe that. Kids are cruel. Teenagers are worse.

I get up from the couch and go over to the door, yanking it open. I'm not sure who I expected to see. Someone from the military. That guy that dropped Rox off yesterday, maybe. Although, if he's smart, he'll stay as far away from my girl as possible. I don't know, but I sure wasn't expecting to see Claire Wentworth. She steps inside without being invited and closes the door behind her, smiling up at me as if I'm God himself. Fuck, the last time this girl was in this apartment she was in eighth grade and pretending to be friends with Rox. I couldn't move without her inching closer. I couldn't breathe without her pouncing on me like a cat. She hasn't been back here since she and Rox fell on the outs.

That actually made me happy.

"Rox isn't here," I tell her as I turn my back to her and go back over to the couch. "If you have some project, it'll have to wait until tomorrow."

I know for a fact that is not why this girl is here. One, neither of them would ever partner up with the other. Two, even if they were working on some project, Rox wouldn't have left this morning. She would be in her room preparing to do all the work. And three, I wouldn't have stuck around to see Claire. I don't care how grown-up she appears. Girl is batshit crazy.

Grabbing the remote, I turn the TV on and start flipping channels. Claire comes over and drops down beside me, too close for my liking—leaning sideways so that my right arm rests flush between her breasts. Fucking girls! I scoot over on the couch and flip through one more channel. It lands on the news.

"I saw you were back in town," she says in a raspy voice. "I thought maybe we could hang."

I turn and look at her straight on, tuning out the TV. "There's nothing we could do together that would interest me."

Claire moves in even closer, practically sitting in my lap. "By hang, I mean we could—"

"I know what you meant, and it's never gonna happen." No way in hell would I ruin what I'm regaining with Rox for a piece of ass.

"Why not?" she shouts. "You and Roxy . . ."

"There is no me and Roxy." I know it's a lie, a terrible lie, but I don't need Claire going around town spreading news that I'm into young girls. One young girl, yes. I can admit that. Her being here though—her being seventeen and here—doesn't look right. If she was Rox, I would fight the issue harder than anything, but Claire is no Rox. She will never be my lost girl.

"Then this really shouldn't matter to you."

Claire lunges forward before I have time to process what she's talking about. Her arms weave tightly around my neck as her mouth comes down needy on mine. I shove her away but she crawls right back, hands going underneath my sweater and clawing at my chest. I grip her hands and remove them from my body. She smiles at me, eyes sparkling with lust.

"You can tie me up if you want," she mutters.

I cringe at her suggestion. I wouldn't be opposed to the idea if it wasn't her voicing it, but it is. The thought of her displayed to me in any sexual manner makes me want to binge on that cake and then regurgitate it on her. The thought of being with someone after Rox told me she loved me this morning is sickening. The only woman I want tied up and bent to my every aching whim is her.

I rise from the couch, knocking Claire to the floor in the process, and go over to the door. I jerk it open and glare at Claire on the floor. "Leave now, or I will drag you out."

Claire's face scrunches up in confusion as she gets to her feet. She stomps over to me with her hands on her hips and glares at me. "Are you really turning me down?"

I give her a curt nod.

Her mouth drops open in shock at my dismissal of her. To be fair, any other man probably would have taken her up on her offer. Claire's not a beast to look at, and her short, skin-tight dress has left nothing to the imagination, but she targeted a man in love. A man in love will never let a skimpy dress and a pretty face derail him.

She stomps her feet at my silence. "Your little bitch will pay for all of this!"

Claire's about to turn and leave, but I grab her arm. No one threatens Rox. No one but me. "You lay a hand on her, and I promise you I will deliver ten times worse to you."

Her eyes widen at my promise. I can feel her quivering in my hand, so I let her go. She stumbles back a little and looks out the door I still have wide open. Flipping her hair over her shoulder, she pouts again. She, like everyone else in this town, knows not to mess with me—not when it comes to Rox, at least. In high school, I had to send plenty of my football buddies to the hospital for making accusations that they shouldn't have made. Hell, senior year I somehow ended up getting suspended for a week for choking the principal. He had called me in because Rox had been hiding out in the bathroom for four classes straight. Although I did everything I could to get her a new identity, people knew who she was. This town protected her, but that didn't mean the kids were nice to her. My involvement didn't make it any better.

When Claire doesn't move an inch, I shove her out the door and slam it in her face. I don't have time for petty girls like her. And I certainly don't have time to explain to Rox why her arch enemy is standing in our house when she arrives home.

I go back over to the couch and grab the remote. Just as I'm about to change the channel, an image of a man I haven't seen in twelve years pops up on the screen. His full beard is speckled with gray now, and he has a scar above his right eye. But it's him. My jaw clenches and my hand tightens around the remote as I stare at the man on my tv. I take a step forward as I read the scrolling caption at the bottom of the news report.

After serving twelve years at Fork York Penitentiary, 46-year-old James Raine will be released next Monday at 12pm. He will serve the rest of his sentence under house arrest in Dixie County.

My hands clench onto the remote until I hear a cracking sound. I turn away from the TV. If I have to see that man's face again, I might just crack. How can they let someone like that out? House arrest isn't good enough for what he did. He should have been given the electric chair. I know they have done away with such treatment, calling it inhumane, but what James Raine did to that woman—to all the people that served him loyally for years—needs to be treated with nothing less than cruelty.

I turn to set the remote down before I break it when I catch another glimpse of that man on my TV screen. It's a different photo, from when he was younger. In the photo is a woman with light blond hair and purple eyes, a little girl with pale skin and eyes matching the older woman, and a boy probably a year older than the girl. That image vanishes and one of Rox replaces it. I bite down on my lip when I see her image next to his. As much as I hate him, I hate seeing her next to him more. I hate knowing that she's his daughter. I hate that she put a fucking spell on me, and no matter what I do I will be forever linked to that damn man. Because I can't let her go.

Before I know it, the remote in my hand is flying at the TV. It sparks up, blinks a few times, and then goes black. Damn that man! Damn that entire family. He ruined so many lives, and now they are letting him off with house arrest. Hell, I'm sure his house is the Ritz. What kind of punishment is that? He needs to feel the torment that we all have undergone for twelve years.

I run my hands over my head and let out a deep breath. I need air. I need to get away from here. Turning around, I march down the hall to my room and grab a coat from the closet. A night out, away from Roxanna Raine and every- thing that encompasses, will fix this. At least that's what my anger management coach would tell me. Eliminate the source of my rage. He's been saying that for three fucking years. How do I eradicate the very thing that keeps my heart beating?

I can't.

I have to learn to deal with it through other means. Shaking my head, I head out the apartment and down to the car. I get inside and swerve away from this place.

CHAPTER 13

WRAN

I drive around our small town for a couple of hours with deafening music that could wake the dead before I end up at the small one-bedroom townhome Josh rents for our father. It's in the swanky part of town, so his one-bedroom looks a hell of a lot nicer than the two-bedroom I currently live in with Rox. For some reason my brother still feels the need to take care of our pops. If it was up to me, I would have put him in a group home that could sober him up instead of providing him with luxuries he doesn't deserve. I can feel my teeth breaking as I take in his uneven lawn and the dead plant sitting on his porch. Josh should have left him in that income-based dump. At least he wouldn't be out of coins payin' for this place that our father clearly isn't keeping up.

Turning off the ignition, I hop out of the car and make my way up to my door. I have no clue why this is the place I chose to be, but for some reason, I'm here. I knock on the door once, then twice before it swings open. My pops leans against the door in an old dusty white shirt and a pair of slacks that seem two sizes too big. There's a cigarette hanging out of his mouth, with smoke framing his head like a mane. His beard is untrimmed, like his lawn, and in his hand is a bottle of Jack.

Typical Taylor Belmont.

"Boy," he greets me, and I shove past him into the cloudy house, taking in the piles of dirty laundry in the hall.

The door slams shut behind me, but my eyes continue to take in my pops' living area. I haven't been to this place since Josh moved him in. Nothing has changed since the last apartment. Beer cans still line the floor along with week-old clothes. It still smells as if someone has pissed on everything, and the sight of him still makes me ill. Pathetic. My pops is pathetic. I don't know why I thought that would have changed in my absence.

"I heard ya was back, boy," my father slurs.

I turn around to meet his hooded eyes. He tries to stand taller as he makes his way from the door and over to where I stand, but he can't quite keep his posture upright. My eyes drift over toward the door, and I'm tempted to walk out of it. I don't. I stand my ground. Honestly, watching my train wreck of a father is soothing. I don't know why but seeing him like this calms a part of me that I can't control. Maybe 'cause I know I'll never let myself get this far gone.

My father slams the bottle into my chest, and I reach up to catch it. "You look 'ikeya need it," he says, and saunters on past me.

My hand grips the neck of the bottle, and without contemplating it, I gulp down the whole bottle—not that there was much in it to begin with. I drop the bottle on the already cluttered floor—one more bottle ain't gonna change anything—and follow my pops toward the kitchen.

My nose is assaulted as I make my way to the entry, and I stop shy of it. How the hell can he walk in there when it smells like the sewer backed up into this kitchen? Bringing my hand up to my nose, I take the last few steps in the entry. I stare wide-eyed at the mess. Pitiful. Just fucking pitiful. Boxes upon boxes of half-eaten pizzas lay on the counter, mountains of black trash bags line the floor, and the sink is overfilled with dishes that still have food on them.

Pops opens the refrigerator and pulls out a can of beer, and something in me snaps. I kick the trash bags aside and make my way over to him. Ignoring the smell, I snatch the can from his grubby hands and hurl it to the floor.

"What the hell, Pops?" I yell at him. I point to the garbage lying on the floor. "Do you not see this shit?"

His hand comes up in a fist and slams into my face, and a coppery taste pools in my mouth. "Doncha come in my 'ouse and tell me howta live, boy!"

"Someone needs to!" I yell back at him, spitting blood on the floor. Someone needs to wise up and get him clean.

He's a mess. This place is a mess. He's making everything a mess.

"Notcha!" He grabs another beer and stomps past me.

I glance around the kitchen again before following my pops to the living room. He slumps down in an old rocker. It's made of light brown wicker material and looks oddly familiar. It takes me a minute to remember where I know that chair from, but the moment it comes to me, it just pisses me off even more. It's perfectly fine if he wants to destroy his stuff, but this was Mom's. She used to knit in this chair in my room.

"It's his fault, ya know," my father mumbles as he sips on his beer. "All his fault."

"Who's fault?" I really don't know what he's burbling about, and frankly I don't care. All I know is that I need to get my mom's stuff away from this lowlife mongrel.

"That man on the news. They lettin'im out!" He points to the old square TV sitting on a small table. "Fucker ruined my life, and they lettin'im out!"

I know who and what he's talking about the moment he says that.

James Raine.

The one person I did not want to think about again today. Shaking my head, I try to focus on anything else, but I can't. James Raine is the reason for this. He did ruin my pops. He ruined everything he touched, including my Rox. I can't let my pops know that I agree with him though. He'd never let me live it down—not that he will even remember me showing up here tomorrow.

"No!" It comes out like a roar, and I stomp over behind the rocker. I grab the edge of the back and tip it forward, knocking my pops' lazy ass to the floor with the rest of the trash. "He did nothing. You did this! You let some rich fucker destroy you. You let your kids down. Not him. You. You. You! You are just as worthless as that fucker. You ruined yourself."

Pops stares up at me from his place on the floor, eyes more alert than I've seen in years. He says nothing to my degrading, and I'm glad. There's not really anything he can say. As much as I despise James Raine, Taylor Belmont has his faults too. I grab my mother's wicker rocker and carry it toward the door. That man is not gonna turn my mother's chair into toothpicks. I'll be damned if I let him degrade her memory like that.

I march out of the house into the darkened night. I glance up at the sky. From here, the stars above can be seen as clear as day. They don't seem this in focus from my apartment, but I supposed that's something else that's different on this side. I mumble an apology to the stars and continue to carry the chair to my car. Placing it in the back seat, I hear scampering and turn to see my pops in the doorway with a shotgun aimed at me. He stumbles forward a little and fires, but stumbles backward and lands flat on his ass. My eyes go to where the pellets hit a tree.

Truly pathetic.

Walking back up to the house's door, I bend down and yank the gun from his hold. No man in his state deserves to own a weapon. "Go sober the fuck up."

My pops attempt to spit in my face, but I'm upright before it leaves his lips. I head back to my car and place the gun in the passenger seat. As nice as it was to see him, this didn't help me. I back out of the parking lot and just drive.

CHAPTER 14

Four days.

Two hours.

And forty-five minutes.

That's how long it's been since I last saw Wran Saturday morning. But I'm not counting. I don't care that I basically told him my feelings never changed and then he disappeared. Honestly, I don't, because that's just the thing he would do. He's done it before. This time is no different. I roll my eyes to myself. Nope. None.

I slam my locker a little too hard and let out a deep breath. I'm fine. I'm perfectly fine.

I turn to head to my next class but stop when I notice Cade leaning against the locker directly beside mine with a grin on his face. He grabs my textbook and looks at it. His eyebrows push together and the corners of his lips dip down. That's everyone's expression when they see my textbook for home economics. To the people that are not taking it, it's simply a blow-off class. I thought that too when I chose it as an elective, but nope! I actually have to study and memorize definitions that I will never use once the class is over. I was hoping for an easy cooking class, but apparently there's a lot more to home ec than baking cakes and brownies. If I had known that, I would have chosen a different elective.

I grab my book from Cade and push past him. "I'm late."

He laughs, and I keep on walking. "I think you should take that up with Belmont."

A gasp leaves me and my feet stop moving. Cade walks right into me. "W-what did you say?"

He chuckles again and bends down to retrieve the book that fell from my hold. "Calm down, Roxy. Just cracking a joke."

A joke.

"Oh, right."

He hands me my book and I start walking again. I don't know what I would do if anyone at this school found out about Harley. I've managed to keep it a secret for years, but that didn't stop rumors from flying around like fireflies. People wanted to know why I suddenly decided to be home-schooled after Wran left—especially the teachers. Most of the students didn't care about the why. They just cared that they could use that against me. Claire and her crowd didn't spare my feelings the first couple of months back here.

Worst of all, some of the talk was true, but I couldn't admit to it. It's always the truth that hurts the worst.

"So, you never called, and I waited," Cade says when I make no effort to say anything else. "I was pretty sure I had gotten under your skin enough for you to call."

I glance over at him, trying to hold in my laughter. I didn't think he was the type of guy that would wait on a call. Especially not a call from a girl like me. "I'm sorry. I just didn't think. . . Cade, we have nothing in common. And excuse me if I'm blunt, but I threw coffee on you. It is hard to believe you were serious."

He snorts but keeps walking alongside me. "I have a hard time believing you aren't lying right now."

I stop walking and grab his wrist to stop him as well. I watch as a few students bypass us before giving Cade my full attention. His eyes aren't on my face though; they are trained on my hand at his wrist. I yank my hand away and cradle it against my book, heat rising to my cheeks.

"Sorry," I mutter and start walking toward my class again.

Moments later, Cade is back by my side. My lips curl into a smile at his persistence. It's somewhat refreshing. I never get that type of determination from Wran. Not three years ago and certainly not since he's been home. Sure, he's been insistent on getting me to go out with him, but not with much else. A part of me thinks he's only asking me out because it's something he's comfortable with. And I get that. I've often wondered if the way I feel for him is the same thing. It's always been just us. I never let anyone else into our bubble. I can't figure that out, though, if he's never around. I need to figure that out before Harley's next birthday. I don't want Wran in her life if we're just a convenience to each other.

I come to a halt at my classroom door. So does Cade. He leans against the white concrete wall, grinning down at me. "Have lunch with me. We can go somewhere off campus, so Claire won't see."

His grin is contagious, and while a part of me wants to tell him yes, that I would very much like to have lunch with him, the other part reminds me that we are from different worlds and I don't fit into his. Besides, I have to think about myself. Claire would find out somehow, and then skin me alive. Not to mention I can't be the girl that strings two guys along while she's figuring things out. I can't be the girl that gets to have fun with a guy that doesn't make her want to cry because the other doesn't come home for four days.

"I can't," I finally tell him. "I think you're great, Cade, but I can't go out with you."

"Because of him?" His voice is low so other students entering the class don't hear him.

"Partially." But not entirely.

"I hope Belmont knows what he's getting."

"You don't even know what you would be getting." I'm sure he wouldn't be asking me out if he did. No teenage boy wants the drama that comes with a toddler. I don't even think that's something Wran will want. That scares me more than I would like to admit. Wran saying he's not ready for Harley would crush me, but I suppose that's why he doesn't need to know. No one needs to know. And it will stay like that.

"I know exactly what I would be getting into, Roxanna. And trust me, I can handle it way better than Belmont."

I grin at him as the second bell rings. "Sure, you can, but I have to go now. Mrs. White gets grumpy when students are late."

"I can get you an excuse. Principal loves me."

Smiling, I shake my head and walk into class.

By the time the end of the day rolls around, I'm feeling much more myself. Things have gone good today. I didn't even get any flak from Claire about Cade, which I'm sure got back to her. Her goonies even left me alone. I expected them to make good on their threat from the other night at Aunt May's, but nope—they haven't batted their eyelashes my way. I'm grateful for that. I don't need Lynn or Wran finding out about their harassment the last couple of days.

I maneuver my way down the crowded hall to my locker, ready to go home. If I'm lucky, Wran will be there when I arrive. It will be nice to see him. Plus, I kind of need to talk to him. I need us to move. I know he's not going to like the fact that I want to move over there with them, but I'm sure we can negotiate or something. Besides, it's not like we haven't lived over there before. That side of town was our home up until he turned eighteen. There is not really a good reason we can't make it our home again.

Coming to a stop in front of my locker, I shift my portfolio to my other arm and input my locker combination. A piece of white paper flutters out onto the tiled floor. Shoving my belongings into the locker, I bend down and retrieve the paper. I really hope it's not from Cade. Today has been peaceful, and I would hate for that to be ruined because he doesn't know how to take no as an answer. As I open the note, a whiff of sandalwood and spearmint invades my nostrils. Disregarding the note, I glance around the students fanning out for the day, searching for a pair of amber eyes I know all too well. I've only ever smelled the blend of sandalwood and spearmint as a child. It was an overpowering scent I detested even then. When I don't see those threatening yellow orbs, I glance back down at the piece of paper in my hand.

My heart stops beating and all the air in my lungs suddenly feels like it's been vacuumed out of me. Crisp, orderly handwriting that appears to have been typed on a typewriter taunts me from the page.

```
    I'm watching, and I see everything.
            Love,
            Daddy
```

I ball the paper up and shove it in my pocket, as if that will make the words go away. One day—my father's been out of prison one day, and he's already taunting me. I knew it would happen. I knew when they said he would be staying at our old house in Dixie County that he would try to get in touch with me. Never did I imagine it would be this soon, and at school. I peer around my surroundings, looking for anyone suspicious. This had to be put in my locker last period. It wasn't in there when I picked up my portfolio.

Bringing my bag around to my front, I quickly pull out my cell phone and dial Wran's number. There's no way I'm walking back to the apartment. I don't care if it's just down the street; I'm not taking a chance. When Wran doesn't answer, I immediately press the recall button. The call is forwarded. I bite down on my lip and glance around the hall. I know none of the students in the halls. I open my contacts and go to Josh's number. He might be pissed at me, but he's never let me down—not when I needed him. I press the call button, but it too goes to voicemail.

This cannot be happening.

They cannot strand me at this school!

I lean back against my locker and try to control my breathing. For all I know, whoever put that letter in my locker is long gone. And if some random person was walking the halls for forty-five minutes, I'm sure security would have seen them and escorted them off the campus. I'm probably freaking out over nothing. No one is here. Besides, how would my father know to look for me at this school in this particular town? I ran just like Ms. Wells told me to. She never mentioned a town, and I sure haven't made it a priority to go visit my father to let him know anything about me.

This is just a prank. A horrible, horrible hoax. Someone probably remembered who my father was after seeing the news and decided to wind me up. This is Claire and her friends' doing. They did this. It's just them trying to get me back. They said they would and now they have. I have nothing else to worry about besides sad girls who are going to peak in high school.

A hand comes down on my shoulder and I let out a very piercing scream, dropping down the lockers and onto the floor into the fetal position.

No.

No.

No!

This isn't happening. He isn't here. It's all in my mind. I rock back and forth, cradling my backpack to my chest like I used to cradle my bunny.

"Roxanna!" I hear someone call me in a distant voice. "Can you hear me?"

I nod my head but continue to rock. I'm safe right here. My father can't get to me. No one can get to me. I'll be perfectly safe.

"Help me get her to the nurse's office," I hear, but am unable to react to it. I don't need a nurse. I'm safe right here.

A flash of muscular fingers invades my vision and I shriek again, scooting away from them. My eyes travel up the form to see Cade and two other guys staring at me with wide eyes and creased foreheads as if I'm crazy. Cade slowly bends down next to me and places a hand on mine where I'm clutching the backpack.

"It's just me, Roxy. It's just me," he murmurs in a low, soothing tone. "I'm not going to hurt you."

I stare at him for a long moment, not understanding what he's talking about. Of course he's not going to hurt me. Not unless he's decided to take revenge after all for the coffee, but something tells me that he won't. Taking hold of my arm with ease, Cade helps me up to my feet. He drapes an arm around my shoulder to keep me steady, even though I'm perfectly capable of walking on my own.

"I'm just going to take you to the nurse's office, okay?" He talks to me as if I'm some child that doesn't understand what he is saying.

I shake my head. "I'm fine. I just need to get home."

"Roxy, I think you need a nurse. You were completely out of it."

"No." I shake my head again and pull away from him, still clutching at my backpack. I ease my grip on it to show him I'm fine, but he's not buying it. I'm not even buying it. I glance from him to the other two guys, still looking a bit leery. "Look, I'm okay. Can you just please give me a ride home?"

Cade runs his hands through his blond hair and relents. "Fine. But next time you start screaming in the hallway like a Teletubby with its tail cut off, I'm taking you to the nurse's office."

Hopefully, there won't be a next time. I don't think I can handle anyone else witnessing a breakdown. And I don't think I can handle them finding out why I freaked out. No one can know. My father is my problem and I will deal with it without anyone knowing. Without Lynn knowing.

I nod to him and shift my backpack to my shoulder. Cade immediately takes hold of it and walks toward the exit of the building. I look over to the other football players still watching me warily. I point toward the exit, but they shake their heads.

"Nah, we were just headed to practice," the one with curly ginger locks says. He runs his hands down his thighs and glances awkwardly away from me. I forgot that most of the sport teams here practice year-round. I hated that when Wran was in school.

"Umm. . .yeah. . .Let Cade know to come back when he's done dealing with you."

They rush off down the hall without giving me a chance to respond. Great! Now they think I'm crazy. With a sigh, I walk out the school's exit. Maybe I am crazy. Who freaks out over a piece of paper? It's not like my dad was actually standing there. And it's not like he could have done anything in a hallway full of students. That would have been stupid on his part. Then again, this is the same man that murdered a woman for protecting his daughter and then told a courtroom of people that she should have known her place and stayed in it.

I don't remember the trial, but I've been seeing clips since they announced he would be getting released. Those tiny clips have caused more distress in the past few weeks than Cardi B and her shoe. It's pathetic. I'm pathetic. I shouldn't let these things get to me, but I do.

As I climb inside Cade's truck, he turns the radio to some country station. "I'll Name the Dogs" by Blake Shelton blares through the speakers, and I let out a disgusted groan as I lean my head against the passenger window. The music's volume drops, and I turn to see Cade examining me with his lips parted and brows raised so high he could be browless.

"What?" I ask him.

"How can you not like this song? Every girl I know loves this song," he exclaims.

"Because I'm not the type of girl that's going to be around for a guy's amusement."

Putting the car in reverse, Cade shakes his head at me. "That's not what that song is about."

I roll my eyes and lean my head back against the cool window, a grin gracing my face even though he can't see it. It's nice seeing his passion...to hear the amusement in his voice when he talks about something he loves. It's something I haven't had in three years. I don't think I will ever find another thing that brings me as much joy as art once did.

It's a shame really. Everyone deserves to feel that rush of happiness. Music may not be Cade's true passion, but it's something he loves. The wide grin and sparkle in his eyes attest to that as he continues to tell me why this clearly sexist song is so awesome.

"He's found his lifelong partner in this song. He's showing how much he adores her. Something is wrong with you if you don't want that," Cade continues.

"Mmhmm," I respond as I watch the trees pass.

"Do you like any typical girl music then?"

It doesn't take me long to answer. "Of course. I like Taylor Swift."

I hear Cade gasp, and I turn to him. "You know, I could have guessed that."

Smiling at him, I nod. "What's not to like? She makes awesome music."

"Man-bashing music," he mumbles low, and I laugh.

Of course someone that likes "I'll Name the Dogs" would think that of Taylor's music. That just goes to show that Cade and I would have never worked out. The rest of the short ride to my apartment is spent in silence, which I hate. It only sends my mind to the piece of paper burning a hole in my pocket. By the time we do reach the small parking lot of my building, I'm a fidgeting mess. Cade probably thinks I have issues. I don't understand why I care what he thinks, but I do. And I don't want him believing I'm the psycho that Claire has probably told him I am.

I reach for the handle when the sound of his voice draws me back in. "If you need a ride to and from school, you have my number."

I turn around and face him, confused by his offer. "You would give me rides even after I turned you down? Multiple times."

He nods and I'm baffled. During the time I spent crushing on him, I knew he was a good guy. I knew Cade was someone I wanted to get to know. It was like I was drawn to him for some unknown reason. However, I was also aware that he was one of them. Deep down, I expected the real him to be more like them and less than the persona he puts on for the school. He's not, though. He's the type of person a girl should be drawn to. Not to the Wrans of the world. And in this moment, I hate that I'm not drawn to him like I thought I was for three years.

"When I asked you out," he starts, "I knew it was a long shot. You're Belmont's girl. Everyone knows that. I mean, you do live with him. I figured since no one has seen him in years, I would finally go for it, but the moment he showed up at school, dating you was a lost cause. You love him."

I stare at Cade in complete shock. "Y–you figured all that out by having lunch with me once?"

"No. I figured that out because I see you. I have always seen you, and I'm okay with just being your friend."

A smile I didn't realize was gracing my lips grows wider as I turn away from Cade and get out of the truck. The truck cranks up again and I whirl around, tapping on the glass. Cade puts the car in park and lets down the window.

"Yeah?" he asks.

"Umm . . . W–what time do I need to be ready?"

"7:45?"

It's fifteen minutes later than I usually leave. That doesn't leave me much time to grab coffee from Starbucks, but I can make it work. This may be a bad idea, but I need someone other than Wran. I need friends again. Claire isn't going to like this, I know that for a fact, but it's not like I'm dating the guy. He said he was okay with being friends. He knows I'm with Wran. Nothing can go wrong. Besides, after that letter, I feel a thousand times safer with him driving me back and forth. Who knows? This may be the start of something great.

With a nod, I answer his question and then turn to go inside.

CHAPTER 15

WRAN

It's been thirteen days and four hours since I last saw Rox.

She's gonna be pissed.

Honestly, I don't remember much after ditching my pops' place. Somehow, though, I ended up at a bar and I recall some tatted-up wanker saying something to me before I blacked out. The next day, though, I was in a jail cell—and not the one Josh runs. They just released me an hour ago after someone called in and paid my bail. The dickheads wouldn't tell me who would be stupid enough to bail me out of jail. As I step out the doors, the answer to that question stands before me.

I take the stairs two at a time and make my way over to a guy in front of a red truck. I look him up and down, not quite catching on to the game that's obviously being played. He's one of them. And they're sure as hell not gonna drive an hour to pick up some lowlife from the wrong side of the tracks.

"Who are you?" I ask. I know damn well who this prick is: the guy that brought Rox home that first day. "Why'd you bail me out?

The kid ignores my question and opens my door before walking around to the driver's side. I stare at the interior and scoff. Fucking leather in a truck. Real privilege. I need to get my car back as soon as possible. The officer in there said it was being held at some tow yard. I'll just have this boy drop me off there.

I climb inside the truck and slam the door. The mirror shakes, but I don't care. Not my truck.

He touches the mirror to steady it. "The name's Cade. Cade Jefferson."

Jefferson? "As in Eric Jefferson?"

The kid nods.

Great. Just great. We might only be going to a tow yard, but sitting here with a damn Jefferson is far too long for that short distance. I guess that explains why Rox would ignore years of me telling her that they are bad for us. He's a Jefferson. The Jeffersons owned a third of Rox's father's business. When James Raine went down, though, so did the business. Eric Jefferson ended up opening another firm called Jefferson & Sons.

"Does Rox know who her new little friend truly is?" I ask him, voice sarcastic as hell.

Cade starts up the truck and drives away from the jail before shaking his head. "No. I use my middle name at school. If she knows my surname, she hasn't put it together. She doesn't even seem to remember me." He glances away from the street and over at me. "Please keep it that way."

I sneer at the boy. As if. Why would I lie to her about this? If anything, telling her would assure me that this kid disappears from her life. I don't want her anywhere around that behavior. She doesn't need to be involved in such a toxic environment. It nearly ruined her as a kid. It took me two years to get her to fully trust me and stop clutching that rabbit and Peter Pan book like a shield.

"Why'd you bail me out?" I ask again.

"She's been worried sick for two weeks about you. She doesn't say as much, but the proof is hard to miss. It's been hard not telling her that you've been locked up for two weeks for assault and battery."

I wince at the words in reference to the bar fight. I am grateful Cade didn't mention that to her. As little as I know about her time with her father, I do know he assaulted her. That fucker assaulted a little girl. Rox doesn't talk much about it. I think she must be blocking it out or something. Sometimes it was like she didn't even remember. But I saw the bruises. I've seen the imprint of his fingers that will never leave her delicate skin. Her knowing that I'm capable of such treatment wouldn't be beneficial to me. If anything, it would scare her right into the arms of this boy next to me.

"You like her," is all I'm able to say.

I watch as the boy nods, and my fingers dig into the nice leather of the seat. Of course he likes her. There's nothing not to like about Rox. She sweet and sassy. Smart but not too smart. She cooks, cleans, and she's cultured. She's everything I thought a good woman should be. She's loyal. She's just like my mother. And I'll be damned if I let this boy have her. Cade can bail me out of jail a hundred times, and that still wouldn't buy her. She's mine. I made her mine.

"I've liked her for a long time." He looks over at me, and I can see the fearlessness in his eyes. Then he glances down to where my nails are ruining his perfectly tanned seats. "I know she's yours. She loves you. I know that. Maybe before you came back, I would have had a chance with her, but I know where I fit in her life. I'm just a friend."

"Just a friend doesn't bail boyfriends out of jail."

His eyes flick up to the road, and so do mine. We pull up outside the gate of the tow yard. Cade cuts the ignition and turns to look at me straight on. My eyes remain on the old cardboard cutout that says open in a sans font. I need to be as far away from this kid as possible. I don't believe for one second that he's okay with merely being a friend to Rox. He bailed my ass out of jail for the girl. No guy does that. Hell, I wouldn't do that. Opening the door, I turn back to give the boy a curt wave. I can be tolerable until he leaves.

"The fees have been paid for—"

I cut him off. I don't really want to stand here much longer. "Thanks. I'll send you a check."

"Hey wait!" His voice rises as I turn to leave. Damn, he doesn't take signals well. "I have one question and then you can go play house with her."

I nod. One question isn't too much to ask.

"Roxanna loves you—I've known that since the first time I saw her with you—but do you honestly feel the same way about her?"

I frown at the kid's question. How dare this guy question my feelings? Sure, I haven't always shown them in the proper way. And okay, I've maybe set things into motion that she would hate me for if she knew. That has never stopped the aching I feel every time I see her smile, though.

"I love that girl more than anyone can possibly imagine, but if you mention it to anyone, I will fuckin' end you."

I let out a deep breath as I pull into the parking lot outside the apartments. The streets are pitch black and the stars can be easily seen tonight. On a night like this three years ago, Rox and I would be up on the hilltop stargazing and making plans for a future that would never happen. Now I'm coming home from a jail cell. Glancing up at the place Rox and I have lived for far too long, I frown. The front of the apartment is also as dark as the night sky. For as long as I've known Rox, she hasn't been a fan of the dark, yet the apartment is pitch black. I suppose she could be at work. It is a Friday night. Aunt May does get swamped on Fridays: high school kids' after-game hangout.

Shifting the gears into reverse, I head out of the complex and down the narrow street to the diner. As much as confronting Rox right now feels like heading into a dry wasteland for a week with only one canister of water, it must be done. For all she knows, I left again. I can't have her thinking I abandoned her once more—especially by choice this time around. It would crush her. Once upon a time, I might have reveled in her pain and laughed in her face, but not now. I don't want her to believe I'm that guy.

I park the car across the street from the diner. It's filled to the brim with teens wearing red and white. No one can say this town has no school spirit. I get out of the car and head inside the diner. I glance around for a second before spotting Rox with a tray in her hand on the other side of the diner, in skintight jeans and a cutesy white crop top with a flannel over top. Aunt May must have loosened up a little on her dress code. A few years ago there was no way she would have let the waitresses walk around looking like that.

Rox turns around, and the smile I'm sure she gives to all her customers falls from her pretty pink lips when she sees me. I take a step in her direction when I hear my name. I glance over my shoulder to see a middle-aged woman with big hair and an even bigger grin framed with laugh lines coming my way.

Aunt May.

Man, she hasn't changed since I saw her last.

"If it ain't Wran Belmont, ladies and gentlemen!" she shouts over the roar of the crowd, coming to a stop in front of me. "I was wonderin' when you would grace my li'l ole diner with your presence."

She pulls me into a hug, making me lose sight of Rox.

I pat her on the back, returning her gesture. "It's good to see you too, Aunt May."

"Have a seat, have a seat! Can I getcha anything, darlin'?"

I shake my head at her. As much as I could use one of her burgers, I would much rather talk with Rox. "When does Rox go on break?"

"She wasn't even 'pose to be here today. I gave her the day off. Poor girl been workin' herself to the bone. Go on back. She's probably in the kitchen."

Smiling at her, I lean down and give her a peck on the cheek. I knew there was a reason I liked this old bat. "Thanks."

I walk past her and head to the kitchen. As Aunt May suspected, Rox escaped me to here. Her back is to me and she's leaning her head down against the center island. Slowly, I step up to her and place a hand on her back. She tenses under my touch, and I hate it. I hate it more than anything. When she should have feared me, she didn't. She threw herself at me. She loved me. She gave me a gift I did not deserve. I'm here trying to redeem myself, trying to make up for my absence and past faults, and now she's hesitant.

She straightens but doesn't turn around to see me. Leaning forward, I place a peck on her exposed neck. Her breath catches and it urges me on. I turn her around in my hold only to see tears streaming down her tense face. Her brows dip when her eyes flick to mine. Kisses aren't going to make this better. I take a step back to give her room, but she doesn't move. She doesn't speak. She only glares at me through thick lashes. A chill runs through me and I know for a fact that if Rox possessed the powers of Killer Frost, I would be an ice statue right now. Thank God that's only in TV shows.

"Rox, I'm so—"

My words are cut off when her hand lands hard against my cheek, sending my face back. The smack reverberates throughout the kitchen. I bring my hand up to where hers landed and rub my jaw. Dammit! I knew she'd be pissed. Hell, I'd be pissed if she disappeared for two weeks too, but I didn't expect her to physically assault me in a diner. That's something the old Roxanna would have never even thought about doing.

I take another step away from her, out of her reach. "Okay, I deserved that."

Rox rushes forward and shoves me. When I don't budge, she shoves me again. Tears run down her face in black streaks. Feeling like shit, I stand my ground and let her take out her aggression on my chest. I deserve it. Only an idiot will let a girl being gone all day get to him. I was a fool. If punching me in the chest will make her feel better, I'm not going to object.

When nothing she does affects me, she slaps me again. Somehow, it's harder, and it feels like I've just been knocked in the head with a baseball bat.

"I hate you!" she yells at me as the door to the kitchen opens.

Aunt May and some new waitress stand in the doorway, eyes wide with trays in their hands. The new girl eases her way back out as Aunt May lets the door swing shut. She looks back and forth between us, but then her gaze lands on Rox. She comes over and sets the tray in her hand down on the island. She pulls Rox into her arms, glaring at me over Rox's head. What. The. Hell? I'm the one getting beat on by a five-foot pixie.

A sob leaves Rox's lips, and I roll my eyes. Why are girls so dramatic? She hasn't even let me explain myself. Granted, I know nothing I say will change the fact that to her, I left again right after she told me she loved me. I know my actions were that of a child, but she could have at least heard me out.

Aunt May eases back a little from Rox and wipes at her tears. "What's goin' on here, darlin'?"

"Nothing." I speak before Rox can. As much as I respect Aunt May, I don't need her in my business. Woman is the nicest person you'll ever meet, but woman is also the chattiest person I know. I don't need the whole town knowing I was in jail.

"Wasn't talkin' to you, Belmont." Her eyes narrow on me for a moment before they move back to Rox and soften. "What he do?"

Rox shakes her head. "It was nothing. I overreacted."

Yeah, she did, but then again, I expected it. Rox hasn't been Rox since I came home. But I'm going to get to know her again.

"Can I take her home?" I ask Aunt May.

"No!" Rox responds a little too quickly. "I need the tips."

I roll my eyes at her. "No, you don't. We have plenty of money. We need to talk."

She doesn't react to my statement, and a minute part of me is pissed that she's not reacting. I don't know why she works here. I've always been able to provide her with whatever she needs. Even as a kid, I put her before myself. This job though...I don't like it.

"Aunt May, I can work." Her voice is frantic as she looks to the front of the house. "We have a full house out there, and you only have Mercedes. I can stay. I can work."

I shake my head at this. She would rather work than spend time with me. She's hurt, but damn.

Aunt May smiles at Rox, and for a second I think she's gonna tell Rox to stay. Then her gaze turns to me, and she must see something on my face. She shakes her head at Rox, and Rox lets out a defeated huff.

"You're already over your hours, and I prefer you two hash your problems out within the comforts of your own home and not where my customers can hear. Be back here

Monday evening." Aunt May glares at me over Roxy's head again. "You hurt my girl again, you'll learn just how far a boot can go up a cow's hind."

I raise both my hands up. "I'm doing my best. Besides, she's my girl. I wouldn't hurt her intentionally."

"Mhmm." Aunt May rolls her eyes and walks out of the kitchen, leaving a very pissed off Rox glaring at me with her small arms crossed over her chest. If the look in her eyes didn't scare the hell out of me, I would think she was sexy standing there. Who'm I kiddin'? Girl's still sexy even though she looks like she wants to rip my balls off.

"I'm not going anywhere with you," she says, face tense.

I step to her and pull her arms from her chest. "I'm sorry. I never meant to be gone for that long."

"Where'd you go this time?" I can hear the accusation in her tone. Nothing I say is going to make up for my absence. Not from three years ago and not from two weeks ago. She's not going to forgive me easily for either, even if she does know the truth behind the first time.

"I got arrested," I admit. "You being out with my brother that whole Saturday pissed me the fuck off, and I let my anger get the best of me. I got arrested for starting a bar fight."

Her tense face softens a little, and she reaches out to me but stops. Her hand falls and she shakes her head as if coming to some unspoken conclusion. Her eyes turn to steel again as they meet mine.

"I need someone in my life that I can count on. Not someone that is going to get arrested and act like a child when he loses all control. News flash: life isn't fair or right or just. You taught me that."

Her words assault my ears and I flinch back as if she's hit me again. I hear her words, but I don't understand them. Since I was a kid, I've put her first. Yeah, I've acted like a child on many occasions, but that has never had her saying what she's saying now. I don't even know what she's saying now. She has always been able to count on me. Even when Josh sent me away, I chose something that could keep a roof over her head. I did something I was so against to give her the security she needs. Her words now make no sense. She knows she can count on me. Nothing about that has changed. I haven't changed.

"What do you mean?"

Rox's eyes glisten with unshed tears. My hands immediately go up to her cheeks. She pulls away like she's been stung by a bee and walks to the other side of the island, putting space between us. I round the island and stop in front of her. I hold my tongue to keep from apologizing again. This is never going to work if I keep saying sorry. We're never going to get back to where we were if we can't get past the real issue: she doesn't trust me anymore.

"Whatever it takes," I mutter to her. "I will do whatever it takes to earn your trust again."

She shakes her head. "We will never work again."

"Tell me why and I will fix it."

I will do anything to have her look at me like she used to. Like I hung the very stars she loves. To have her crave my touch instead of fearing it. Rox stares up at me, biting her bottom lip. She opens her mouth to say something but then closes it again and turns away from me. There's something there. There's something she wants to tell me. I know it. I know there is something I can do to get my girl back fully.

"I can't tell you," she whispers. "I want us to be natural. I want us to be us, and if I tell you, it won't be."

I have no idea what she's talking about. Nothing she says can change the way I feel about her. If natural is what she wants, then I'll let this happen as organically as I can. I'll stop trying to force a connection that has clearly changed.

"Okay. We'll start over." I speak to the back of her head. "I don't know how the hell we're supposed to wipe away twelve years, but I will try. You're gonna have to work with me though. Some things I can't pretend never happened."

She turns back around with a small smile on her angelic face. I lean against the island so she can't tell how much that smile affects me. I'd agree to just about anything to see that wonderous expression on her face every day.

"I know," she says to me. "I'm not asking you to erase our past. It all happened."

I nod. I didn't think coming home would mean this. I didn't think I'd have to work so hard to earn her forgiveness. I'm glad that she wants us to start over though. It means that my past is irrelevant. I don't have to admit to things I never want her to know about. I don't have to keep apologizing for all the things I need to be apologizing for. We can just be us.

I hold out a hand to her, and her face scrunches up as she studies my outstretched hand. "Hi. I'm Wran Belmont."

Understanding dawns on her face. She gives me her hand and her smile grows. "Hi, yourself. I'm Roxanna Raine."

"Roxanna Raine. You have such a beautiful name. I'd like to take you somewhere tonight."

She bites down on her lip again, trying to hold in a grin. "Like on a date?"

Her grin is contagious, and I can't help the one that adorns my own face. This all is out of the norm, but if it makes her feel better, I'll be whoever she needs right now. "Just like a date."

"I've never been on a date." Her cheeks flush and a part of me wants to call her out on that. We've been on plenty of dates.

The more I think about her statement though, the more I realize it's true. The outings we had before I left can't really be referred to as dates. It's not like I took her to movies and held her hand and kissed her in public. We couldn't do those things. And to be honest, I was a dick most of the time. For all intents and purposes, I was still very much the child whose life had been ruined by this girl's father. I'm still very much that guy, but three years away from her changed my perspective a hell of a lot. Yeah, seeing her squirm is still enticing, but I'd much rather have her in my life than not.

This girl has rooted herself so deep into me that without her I can't breathe.

I bring her hand to my lips and place a peck on it. "In that case, I'm gonna make this the best damn date you'll ever have."

CHAPTER 16

WRAN

We come to a stop in front of the apartment and Rox gives me a skeptical look. I know this is supposed to be the best date ever, but I wasn't really planning on going out when I came home. So I'm winging this. Sue me. As promised, though, I'm gonna give her the best date of her life. I just need to pick up a few things first.

I open the car door and hop out. Rox starts to open her door, but I bend down to stop her. Although I'm winging this, I kinda don't want her to know my makeshift plans.

"Stay here and close your eyes," I tell her, a little too much excitement in my voice. I don't even try to hide it. I am excited. I'm going on a date with Rox. A real date. Not an outing where I'm pretending that we're friends or family or all the other excuses I used to tell people. A real, honest-to-God date with the girl I've been in love with since I was eleven.

And there's nothing stopping us now.

She nods and removes her hand from the door, placing it in her lap. When I'm certain she's not gonna get out, I race up the stairs that lead to our home and rush inside. My feet immediately move me to the bookshelf by a replacement TV. I spot the Peter Pan book right away and grab it. I head to my bedroom and go to my closet. The telescope we built together when she still believed in Neverland is sitting in the corner. It's probably not the best telescope, but it will do for tonight.

I glance around my room trying to think of something else. She's probably been at work since school let out, so she'll be hungry. I go back to the living room and set the telescope and book down on the couch before heading to the kitchen. Opening the cupboards, I growl at the lack of options. I know Rox doesn't require much, but we literally have nothing that can even be remotely perceived as fancy.

I'm gonna need help.

Pulling out my phone and opening my contacts, I scroll down to the one person I know for a fact can help with this. I press the call button on Janice and wait for her to answer. She picks up on the second ring.

"A little late for Wran Belmont to be calling me, ain't it?" she says into the phone. "Are you taking me up on that offer, handsome?"

I let out a half laugh, half groan. Not gonna lie, most days I love the attention from the opposite sex, but not right now. "Nah. I need your help."

"Help? What kinda help could you need from me?" she asks, and I can tell she's all serious now. "You in some kinda trouble?"

"No. I'm going on a date. With Rox. I need help," I exclaim. I have no clue what I'm actually doing. The girls I've taken out before weren't Rox, so I didn't have to try with them. I knew what they wanted. And they knew what I wanted. It was easy with them, and in the morning I could send them away. It's not like that with Rox. And I can't mess this up. I want her to know I'm serious about this. About us. I want her. I want her more than anything I've ever wanted before.

"I need food. Fancy food," I say when Janice doesn't say anything. "And maybe some wine. That fruity shit that girls like."

"Okay," she finally says after a minute of silence. "I can do that. Should I bring it to the apartment?"

"No. Take it to the clearing on the hill. Oh, and if you have candles, bring those too."

"The clearing on the hill? You do know there's slush all over da grounds, right?"

Shit! It's the beginning of March and our snow is just now melting. I forgot about that. "Umm, do you have a tent?"

"Yeah, I'll take it."

"Thank you."

"You know I'll do anythin' for ya, handsome."

I end the call and go grab the book and telescope. I take the throw blanket on the back of the couch as well. Locking up the apartment, I rush down the stairs and peer through the driver's window at Rox. Her eyes are closed and she seems at peace. I smile before going to the trunk and tucking the book and telescope in it.

Getting back inside the car, I throw the blanket in the back seat.

Rox's eyes flutter open and she gives me an inquisitive glare. "What took so long?"

"It's a surprise." I check the clock on the dashboard. It's not even eight yet. We have time to catch a movie at the drive-in. That'll give Janice time to prepare some food and set up. "How do you feel about going to the drive-in?"

Her eyes widen, but then she shrugs her shoulders as if it's no big deal. We've never gone to the drive-in together. It was always a couple's trap, and well...we couldn't really be a couple. To some degree we were, I guess, but only behind closed doors. I know Rox wanted to go though. She made a comment a while ago about it. She must have been in seventh grade. Back when she and Claire were still friends, I overheard them talking about it. Yes, I eavesdropped on her. Sue me. I didn't like Claire even as a twelve-year-old. She was using Rox just to get close to me, and that was not okay by any means.

Claire had told Rox that all the high school students went to the drive-in to make out. It was true, but Rox was so innocent. I didn't want Claire to taint that about her. And I most certainly didn't want Rox thinking about making out with some pimply-faced boy. But Claire, being Claire, made going to the drive-in sound like something they needed to do before they reached high school. Rox, being Rox, told her there was no boy she wanted to make out with.

Later that night, Rox asked me if we could go to the drive-in. She had this wistful look in her eyes, like it was the only thing that mattered to her. She practically begged me with those big purple orbs, and I almost gave in to her right then and there. Instead, I told her no and that I was going with someone else. Actually, I told her I was going with someone that knew what to do at a drive-in.

My words were much more descriptive back then—probably too graphic for the ears of a thirteen-year-old. I didn't care though. I would have told her anything to get the thoughts of me with her at the drive-in out of my mind.

"What are you thinking about?" Rox asks, breaking through my thoughts.

I shake my head at her. "Nothing worth bringing up. A new start, right?"

Her lips turn down at the corners, but she nods. I put the car in reverse and back out of the parking lot. The entire ride to the drive-in, Rox has a frown on her face. She doesn't say a word to me, and I'm worried that telling her nothing was the wrong way to go. I don't know how to do this with her, and I'm already ruining this date. It wouldn't have been hard to tell her I was thinking about the first time she asked me to go the drive-in. It just wouldn't have been the fresh start she wants.

The field is mostly empty of cars when we pull up. I figured it would be. Most everyone is at the diner, and it's too early to be here. The high schoolers will most likely be catching the ten o'clock showing. There's no security guard scheduled at that time—or at least it used to be like that. Ten to twelve at the drive-in was like happy hour at Joe's Bar for us back in the day.

Did I really just think that?

Damn, I'm getting old.

I cut off the engine and stare at the movie playing on the screen. Some black-and-white film with captions is showing. The one night I want one of those girly comedies to be on, and they are playing some film we have to read. I pull my eyes from the movie and turn to Rox. She's already watching me. I point to the back seat. There's more space back there and well, it's cozier. A nice pink creeps to Rox's cheeks as she bites down on her lip. She glances at the back seat and then at me. Unbuckling her seat belt, she crawls back there. The light from the screen illuminates her pale skin, and I audibly gulp at the sight of her in my back seat, all flushed and innocent and perfect.

This night has to go right.

Knowing there's no way my tall ass is going to be able to crawl back there without knocking my head against the roof of the car, I open my door and hop in the back. Rox moves over a little, but not much. She grabs the throw blanket and clutches it to her chest as I close the door. Without saying a word, she turns to the movie, leaving a small distance between us.

I stare down at the foot of space separating us, not sure what to do. If Rox wanted me to touch her, there wouldn't be space. Then again, she didn't move much when I got back here. My eyes flick from the screen to the side of her face and back down at the space. I don't want there to be anything between us, but she obviously does if she didn't bother to close the distance.

Fuck...

I lean back against the seat and try to focus on the movie playing in front of me. If Rox wants to come over here, she will. I'm not going to do anything that will jeopardize her and me. I'm certainly not going to do anything that will make her say she hates me again. Those words on her lips hurt more than the slap. I never thought I'd hear her say anything remotely close to she hates me.

After what feels like a fucking lifetime, I turn back to her only to find her watching me instead of the movie. Her eyes dip to the space between us and then back up to me. Okay, so she doesn't want the space? Girls are so complicated.

Fuck this.

I grab the blanket she's been clutching for dear life and unfold it. Arranging it so that it covers both of us, I then drape my arm across her shoulder and pull her to me. Rox gives me one of those half smiles that she's usually on the receiving end of before lowering her head to my chest and throwing her arms around my middle.

Chicks. She could have done that instead of making me anticipate what the hell she wants.

We stay cuddled together in the back of my car, reading words on a screen, until my phone chimes with an incoming text. I quickly glance away from the movie to read the message.

JJ: It's done. Don't ask for anything else, loverboy.

ME: Thx

Finally.

If I'm honest, reading words on a screen isn't my idea of fun. Holding Rox without touching her is also pretty unbearable. I swear by the time she finally forgives me I'll be in a coma induced by permanent blue balls. An unpleasant groan burrows out of me at the thought of waiting that much longer before Rox will let me love her again. I've already had to go three years without. Three. Fucking. Long. Years. It wasn't from a lack of trying. It's just that whenever I tried to let loose, those damn messages Rox left on my voicemail would creep back into my mind and I couldn't bring myself to follow through with the deed.

Yeah, call me a pussy-whipped piece of trash.

I don't care.

"Everything okay?" Rox asks with her eyes on my phone. "Who's JJ?"

To keep her from seeing her surprise, I press the power button. As the phone goes black, I nod at her. "Yeah, things are great and that's no one. Do you want to leave?"

Rox bites down on her lip and looks at me through hooded lids. My eyes drop down to the lip she's biting, and I feel myself harden. Fuck, I wish I was the one biting that lip. Without much thought, I dip down and pull her lip free with my teeth. A soft purr leaves her mouth, a spark flashing in her lust–filled eyes.

I pull my eyes away from her rosy lips and back to the movie playing. Get. A. Fucking. Grip. "We should get out of here. There's somewhere else I want to take you."

"Where are we going?" Rox whispers, pulling out of my arms.

My head drops in her direction only to see a frown on her face. "It's a surprise, but you'll like it."

I hope.

Rox pulls her phone out of her pocket and looks at the time before giving me her full attention. "Okay, but I need to be back home before midnight. I have something to do tomorrow, and I need to be well rested."

My mouth turns down at her words. She had something to do two Saturdays ago as well. I kinda wanted to spend the night under the stars like we used to do. Running a hand over my head, I give her a simple nod. It's not like I can tell her no or make her stay the night with me. I mean

I could, but then I would be going back on my word to give her the best date ever. Surely, kidnapping and forcing her to stay out with me would lead this in the opposite direction.

"What do you have planned tomorrow? Mind if I tag along?" I don't mean to ask that; I already know the answer. She's not gonna want me to come.

Rox bites down on her lip again, which I'm learning is a nervous habit of hers now. She never did it before. "Actually, Josh is taking me."

My jaw locks in place as she looks away from me and turns straight in her seat. Following her example, I turn away from her too. Damn Josh. I don't know why the hell she's spending her weekends with my brother, but it's really starting to piss me the fuck off. If she's gonna give her time to anyone, it should be me. Maybe kidnapping her isn't a bad idea anymore. Besides, it's not kidnapping when she lives in my apartment, right?

Shaking my head, I open the car door and head to the front. Rox doesn't move a muscle. I take the front seat, starting the car up and leaving. Fuck this damn date. She can have Josh take her out. Seems as if that's what he's doing anyway. No one spends that much time with a girl unless he's gettin' some. I don't care what they tell me. I know what my head is telling me, and it's saying this shit is fishy.

I pull back into our apartment complex five minutes later and get out of the car without saying a word to Rox. There's no way in hell I can handle this. She's supposed to be mine. I'm supposed to be the one taking her places and spending Saturdays doing whatever. Not Josh. Not some fucking rich kid from the other side of town. Me. I march up the stairs to my apartment and enter before Rox has a chance to get out of the car. Marching over to the kitchen, I yank the fridge open and peer inside. Water. Water. Water. Nothing that will take the edge off tonight.

I slam the fridge door and sigh.

What the hell am I doing?

I don't drink. Not like this.

I don't let chicks get to me.

And I most certainly don't let the daughter of a murderer make me act like an insipid loser.

No. I need to remember who Rox is. I need to remember who I am. I will not let my feelings for this girl turn me into such a pussy-whipped mess. I need to compartmentalize like I did before she grew a pair of boobs and looked at me as if I was the answer to all her problems. She is the enemy. I am her torturer. It's time to get back to that. Especially since she seems to have moved on. I need to move on.

The door to the place opens and closes with a soft thump, the opposite of the thunder that erupted when I slammed it. I hear the soft steps of her feet before I see her. She strolls into the kitchen with her head down, not meeting my hard gaze. She used to look at the floor all the time as a kid, too afraid to meet anyone's eyes. I smile at the top of her head for a second before realizing what that means. She's terrified she's done something wrong. She hasn't, but she doesn't need to know that. All she needs to be aware of is how pissed I am right now.

After what seems like an eternity of her standing in front of me, not saying a word, she finally raises her head and looks me in the eyes.

She bites the corner of her lips before words finally make their way out of her pink mouth. "I–I thought we were going somewhere else."

I glare down at her.

Rox takes a step back and angles her head up.

"And I thought I made it perfectly clear that I didn't want you around my goddamn brother. Or did him threatening me not register in that pea brain of yours?"

Her eyebrows shoot up at the same time her eyes get saucer-wide. She goes to move away from me, which is probably the smart thing to do now, but I grip the front of her frilly shirt and haul her toward me. She's not leaving without knowing my intent.

Both her hands go to my one holding her against me. "Let. Me. Go."

She doesn't stutter once, and those beautiful purple irises have hardened into narrow slits.

My hand slowly unwinds from her shirt only to skim down her side. She doesn't budge as my arm snakes around her tiny waist. I yank her against me and a low gasp leaves her. Her eyes drop from mine. With my free hand, I grab her chin and force her eyes back up to me. Water pools in her eyes, and a sick part of me basks in seeing her unshed tears. I did that. I still have all the power in the world to make this little flower wither. She should have known she wouldn't get away with rejecting me. For him. Him, of all the people. Him, who tore us apart to begin with.

"Don't," she whispers and jerks her face from me.

My grin widens. "I haven't done anything yet."

"I haven't done anything wrong," she whimpers.

A low growl leaves me as I shove her away from me. Is she really so naïve to think that? Rox knows me, probably better than I know myself, yet she honestly believes she did nothing. I shake my head at her. This is ridiculous. This whole fucking night was a fucking fantasy—for her or me, I'm not sure. But the one thing I know is that fantasies don't exist in this life. Why I thought I could make us both happy is beyond me. Neither of us deserves that peace. Certainly not her, with all her lies and secrets.

"Tell me once and for all what's going on with Josh. Why must you go off with him every Saturday?" I ask her. That's all I want to know. If she would just give me a damn answer instead of evading the fucking question, we could be watching the fucking stars right now and basking in the night sky.

Her hands are balled into fists. Her tears are no more. Her pretty mouth is pursed and pouty, instantly making my dick forget the situation. "None of your damn business! You would damn well know if you would have answered your fucking phone three years ago. You didn't! You gave up your right to know anything about me and my Saturdays.

Your brother has been my support system for these past years. And while yes, I'm pissed at him for his part in this nightmare, you made your choice. I called you for months! Months, Wran! You will not come back into my life and ruin what I worked for."

Rox turns to walk away, but I grab her forearm. She jerks against the hold, but I'm not letting her go.

"I can be your support system now."

She shakes her head. "No. I don't need you and your bullshit now. You would only ruin the progress I've made, and I won't let that happen for anyone. Not even you."

I drop her arm, trying to figure out what the hell that means. I wouldn't ruin anything for her. I know I've done things, but I wouldn't ruin anything that actually meant something to my girl.

Rox stares me straight in the eyes, which doesn't happen a whole lot. She's being serious right now. She doesn't need me.

Running my hand over my head, I take a step back, giving her space. Something tells me she's not going to play the game now. She's not going to run, even if I chase her.

"We're done," she says in a barely audible voice. "You need to leave."

My brows scrunch up at her statement. "Excuse me?"

Rox looks away from me then. "I think you need to leave."

"This is my damn apartment!" I shout at her. No way am I leaving. She can forget that.

Her head shoots back to me, nostrils flaring and eyes wild. "Then I will leave!"

"Cool your fucking rockets, Rox! What are you, PSMing? Calm the fuck down. No one is leaving!"

Turning around, Rox storms away and down the hall to her bedroom. She slams the door, and I swear the walls shake. Times like this remind me that she's still a fucking teenager, and I need to learn how to handle her better. I start to head down the hall but think better of it. She needs time. That's all. Let her calm down and then we'll talk. No one is leaving. Hell, I can't wrap my mind around the fact that she let those words leave her lips. She knew before she suggested it that I wasn't going to leave my own place, let alone let her leave.

With a heavy sigh, I turn away from the narrow hall leading to our rooms and head over to the sofa, slumping down and running my hands over my face. Today has been long. Leaning my head against the plush backing of the couch, I let my eyes drift closed on the events of today. Tomorrow is a different day. Tomorrow I will wake up and make things right once again, if only to fuck them up.

Tomorrow I will make this place her home once more, and she will forget the silly statement she made.

Tomorrow she will heal my scars.

Tomorrow we will be whole again.

If only for a fucking day.

CHAPTER 17

ROX

The smell of bacon and fresh-ground coffee assault my nose as I sit up in bed, throwing the sheets off and yawning. He isn't playing fair. He knows I can't resist caffeine. Getting up, I slip on my fluffy pink bunny slippers and pad my way down the hall where I find Wran standing shirtless and pantsless in the kitchen, only in a pair of boxer briefs I bought him for Christmas years ago. And they're too small now.

He is so not playing fair.

Wran turns around and smirks at me as he places a plate on the island, followed by my favorite mug. I stretch my neck to see what's on the plate and my mouth instantly waters at the sight of bacon and chocolate chip pancakes topped with whipped cream and chocolate sauce. How am I supposed to stay mad at him when he's cooking all my favorite breakfast items and walking around in teeny tiny boxers?

Hesitantly, I go over to the island and stare down at the food. My stupid stomach chooses this moment to growl and let him know that I'm hungry. But seeing as I didn't eat last night after my shift at the diner, I suppose my stomach has the right to be growling at me and begging me to succumb to this setting. Glancing up, I meet Wran's eyes as he watches me, the corner of his mouth tilts up as if he knows this will win me over. It won't. I won't eat this no matter how good it looks. Eating this is basically saying that I'm okay with his treatment of me. It would be like letting the bull trample me. I won't eat this. I won't let him win. Not this time.

Rolling my eyes, I turn away from his apology and head right back to my room, plucking my phone from the charger as I do. I plop down on the bed and check the time. It's early—far earlier than my normal Saturday wakeup time. I place it back on my bedside table as the door to my room opens, Wran stepping through with the breakfast plate in one hand and the sparkly pink mug in the other. He walks over to me and sets the plate on the table next to me. We stare at each other for a long second before he sighs and sits on the edge of my bed, making sure to keep some distance between us.

"Roxanna, I'm sorry," he says, head held low.

The only thing I can do is scoff. He isn't sorry. If he was, he wouldn't have let last night happen. We would have gone wherever he had planned, and we would have talked and laughed, and things would have gone back to normal. It would have been the perfect first date, but he just had to shove. I don't even know why I went ballistic. It's not like I don't know Wran. He likes control. He likes knowing that people will bend to his will. And when they don't, he doesn't know how to handle them. I just wish he would stop trying to handle me. If I thought for one second that telling him about Harley would do either of us any good, I would. Like I said, though, I know Wran. He finds out about her right now, he'll be the new king of hell.

I don't need that.

Harley doesn't need that.

"I accept your apology," I tell him, taking the mug from the side table and sipping.

His smile grows wide as he slides in closer to me. I raise my hand to stop him, shaking my head at this sudden movement.

"No. Just because I accept your apology doesn't mean what I said last night doesn't apply."

The grin splattered across his sharp features turns down the moment he realizes I'm not backing down, and I can see the stone-cold expression move into place, just like it used to do when we were kids and he didn't get his way.

"What do you mean?" he asks, crossing his arms.

I peer at him over the rim of my mug, but look away when I see the anger rolling across his face. I've only ever been at the receiving end of that hateful leer once. And that was the last week of eighth grade when he caught me pleasuring myself and then gave me the birds and the bees talk. I didn't understand why he gave me that look then, but I suppose it's pretty obvious now.

"I mean, I still think we need separate living arrangements."

"No." He doesn't even think it over.

"No? It wasn't really a suggestion."

"Neither was my no. Roxy, what's the real problem?" he asks me. "We've never had a problem living together."

"Yeah, well, things have changed. I have changed. And I want different things now. Like more privacy. And space."

"Privacy and space?" he hisses at me. "You've had that for three years! Was that not enough space for you? What the hell do you need space for anyways? You're a barely eighteen-year-old girl!"

I glance away from his seething leer, knowing for a fact that I don't really need the space I just claimed I did. No, I just want to be as far away from Wran as possible right now. I do stupid things around him. I fall for him when I'm around him, and I can't fall right now. Not until after I get my daughter back.

Wran reaches out and lifts my chin, bringing my gaze back to his. "Space and privacy, huh? I can do that. Just don't leave. I'll stay in my room. It'll be like I didn't even come home."

I don't want that.

But I need that.

Ugh! I hate this!

My phone buzzes from the side table and I glance over at it. Wran does the same. I pluck it up and silence my alarm. I set it back down and retrieve the plate Wran made. I know I shouldn't eat this, but I'm hungry. I look at Wran to see his eyes still glued to my phone. A sigh leaves me and I set my breakfast to the side. I know how unfair this is to him. I can see it all over his face. He's dying to ask me about it again. I know eventually he will find out about Harley and my Saturdays, but right now. . . I don't want to see him hurt any further.

"I'm going to the mall today. Prom is in a few months, and I need a dress." It's not a lie. I am going to the mall and I do need said dress, but I'm mostly going because I want to spend the tips I made doing something nice for Harley. The last time I took her to the mall, I didn't have a job and she wanted a Build-a-Bear. I had to tell her no because I didn't want Josh buying it and I didn't want to cash any of the checks Wran sent home. I actually made enough this week to get her a bear.

Wran sits up straighter, brows knitted together. "Prom?"

He asks that as if it's a foreign concept. I nod. "Yeah. You know, that thing most seniors attend in big formal dresses and tuxes and stuff."

"I know what a prom is!" he snaps. "Do you plan on going with anyone in particular?"

I shake my head and give him the truth. "People generally don't talk to me, and I tend to stay to myself. No one is going to ask me."

"Do you want someone to ask you?"

I smile at his question and nod, giving him as much of the truth as I possibly can. "No girl wants to go to prom alone."

Wran's jaw clenches and he does his best to look and seem composed. His eyes dart to my phone, to the door of my room, and then back to me, making it very clear that he doesn't like the idea of me going to prom with someone. If only he knew I wanted to go with him. I can't, but I can hope. My situation wouldn't allow me that sliver of happiness. Not even for a few hours.

As my phone dings again, Wran rises from my bed and scratches the back of his neck. "I guess I'll see you whenever you get home. Or not. Privacy and space, right?"

I frown at the way he says that. Yes, I need a little bit of space, but not for the reason he's assuming. My case worker already believes one of the Belmonts fathered Harley. Even though she's right, I don't want her going after Wran. Us becoming what we used to be can't happen. Not until it's safe. Not until I have Harley back in my custody. Besides, I'm not going to be the reason he must go away again.

"Yeah, privacy and space," I confirm. My heart breaks at the thought of even needing that. Last night I blurted that out of anger. I was pissed. He promised me a perfect date, and while the drive-in was great, I know he had something else in mind. I didn't honestly mean we should get different apartments. As I lay here and cried myself to sleep, I realized space from each other is the only way for me to get Harley back. I can follow their orders and do whatever they want, but if I'm caught with Wran in any way other than what we should be, their suspicions will be corroborated and both Wran and I will be screwed. I don't know much about the law pertaining to our situation, but I do know we shouldn't have happened back then. I hadn't yet reached the age of consent and he was over eighteen. I consented. I can tell a judge that a million times, but as Lynn said before, I'm the example, and they will roast Wran.

I won't let that happen.

Grabbing my phone, I open it up to see a message from Josh, letting me know he'll be here in a few hours. I glance up to see Wran's retreating back as he stomps out my room, closing the door behind him.

Ugh! Why does life have to be so complicated?

CHAPTER 18

ROX

The drive to get Harley is filled with even more silence be–tween Josh and me, but I'm used to that, for the most part. Things have been rocky between us since Harley came into the world. It's only worse now since I know how he truly feels about me.

The moment Harley came racing out of the building, though, with Lynn right behind her, Josh's emotionless face turned into one of joy. A huge grin covered his face as Harley leaped into his arms.

That was an hour ago.

Now he's back to staring at me as if I peed in his coffee. I've tried to ignore his glares, but today they seem to be magnified. I have no clue why, but whatever is making him act like a major douche is pissing me off. Josh isn't even trying to hide the fact that something is wrong. Don't get me wrong, he doesn't normally hide anything. He doesn't let it show, though, when he's with Harley. Those snide stares are only for my eyes.

With a sigh, I reach down to get Harley. She lets the waterworks loose, but I don't really care right now. I need something to distract me from Josh, and while I know using my baby isn't the right thing to do, Josh won't keep sending me those glances with her in my arms. He wouldn't want her to see that side of him.

Josh reaches over and takes the screaming child from my hold, silencing her with one pat on the back. I shake my head because I honestly don't know what to do. Taking her back would just make her cry again, and that would cause people to stare at us. I don't need a reason for Lynn to think I'm even more incapable of taking care of Harley.

"I'm gonna take her to the bouncing ball pit," Josh says and marches forward.

"Wait!" I shout after him, only for him to ignore me. When my stride finally catches his, I pull him to a halt outside of GAP. "Don't you think she's a little young to be in the ball pen? What if she gets hurt or can't get through the balls?"

"Really, Rox? She's almost three." Josh scoffs at me.

"I know, but—"

"Josh Belmont?"

My protest is cut off when I hear a familiar voice. I turn to the entrance of the store, only to see Ms. Flannigan, my school counselor, walking right toward us. The last time I talked to Ms. Flannigan was a few weeks ago when she was asking me about my future and questioning my decision to not go into art. I never gave her an answer to her questions, and I know for a fact she's been keeping an eye on me. Although right now she seems to only have eyes for Josh. She comes to a stop in front of him and beams up at him. Her eyes briefly move to Harley but go right back to Josh.

"Tasha?" Josh asks as he shifts Harley in his arms.

She nods and finally acknowledges my presence beside Josh. "Good to see you, Roxanna. I was afraid you only worked and went home after school. It's nice to see you out."

I give her a gentle smile and shrink behind Josh a little. One reason we stay in the city on Saturdays is that not many people care to venture outside of Kingston if they don't have to—meaning there is only a slight chance we run into people that know me. "Thanks, Ms. Flannigan."

Josh hands Harley over to me, his eyes never leaving Ms. Flannigan. I take her in my arms and she shakes her head in protest. Josh doesn't seem to notice, which is really strange. Nothing takes his attention away from Harley on the one day a week we get to spend with her. Well, nothing before Tasha.

I look my counselor up and down, trying to find the appeal. She's nothing special. Small frame with glasses too big for her face. Although she does have amazing strawberry blonde locks, I don't see why Josh would just hand Harley over for her.

"Poshy!" Harley screams. "Poshy, Poshy, Poshy!"

The sound of Harley's struggle pulls his eyes from Tasha. He takes her from me, and the confusion on my counselor's face has me immediately regretting coming to the mall today. Someone finding out about Harley is not worth a stuffed bear. Tasha's eyes move from Josh to Harley and then over to me. She does that a few times before planting another grin on her face. It's fake—oh, so fake, and I can already see the questions forming in her brain. It wouldn't be the first time people have wondered. And it's most certainly not the first time people have thought Josh, Harley, and I are some happy little family. Besides Lynn and the rest of family services, mostly strangers comment on the outings we all share; it has never been someone that we both know. Someone that can look at Harley and compare her to us. Yeah, she has my pale complexion, but for the most part she looks exactly like Wran. And well, Josh is Wran's brother. They share features. We've never had to actually correct someone before.

"I didn't know you had a daughter," Tasha says to Josh. "She's so cute."

"I don't," Josh says without thinking, and my eyes widen.

Tasha's eyes roam down to Harley and then to me. The moment she makes the connection, I want to throw something at Josh for his slip. It's best if they believe she's his.

"Ohmygod!" my counselor says. Her head whips back and forth between us all and she steps back.

I shake my head at her, trying to think up some lie to get us out of this. I don't need my counselor thinking what she is thinking. I'm in enough trouble with family services; I don't need even more crap on my plate.

"That's not what I meant." Josh intervenes. "She's not mine, but she's a relative. A cousin on my mother's side of the family. I'm babysitting for the day."

Tasha shakes her head, not believing a word leaving his lips. "Roxanna, is she. . . ?"

I stare down at the tan tile of the mall floor. What do I do? Do I really reject my own daughter so openly? What type of mother would that make me? But I can't let my counselor find out about her either. Not when she's thinking the worst.

Before I have a chance to come up with anything, Tasha is asking even more questions. "How old is she? Did someone take advantage of you? Ohmygod, are you okay?"

I shake my head at the school counselor. "Ms. Flannigan, please stop. It's not what you think."

"Poshy?" Harley asks again. I look over to my daughter, and she points at me.

When neither Josh nor I respond to Harley, she starts screaming. I glance around to see a few people staring at us, and all I want to do is shrink into myself. This is bad. So, so bad. We should have just gone to the park or zoo like we always do. Heck, we could have even gone to that little indoor toy world that Josh suggested that just opened. I just had to come to the mall, a place I know that people my age like to hang out at, all for a stupid bear. And now I'm going to lose my baby forever. All for a stupid bear.

Josh turns from Tasha and places a hand on my shoulder. "Breathe, Roxy. In. Out. In. Out," he utters, and I force myself to obey. He shifts Harley into my arms, and I take her too eagerly. "Take her to get the bear. I'll handle things here. Meet me in the food court in an hour."

I walk, almost run, away from the situation, coming to a stop only when I see the stuffed animals with frilly clothes on display in the window. Harley points to a white bear in a Wonder Woman costume and fights to get to the floor. I set her down only to take hold of her hand and guide her inside the store. She pulls her way over to the window and reaches her short arm up to the bear.

I bend down and shake my head at her. "You can't take that one. Let's make you one."

She frowns, bottom lip trembling, and stomps her feet. "That one."

"We can make you one just like that. Besides, don't you want to make Poshy one too?"

She nods her head, and her curls bounce back and forth. "He wants boy one."

I smile at her. "Yes, he does. Now, let's make him one."

For the next half hour, we spend our time building multiple bears, dressing them in whatever Harley picks out, and overstuffing them. A few of the seams burst, but Harley seems to like when white fluff rains down on us. She wants in the machine. But as much fun as building bears is with my daughter, my mind keeps going back to the counselor and Josh. There's not much he can do to get her to unsee Harley or for her to unvoice her concerns. Something in the pit of my stomach tells me Tasha isn't going to let this go so easily. I wouldn't if I was concerned about a student. Josh has always been able to handle things though. I'm counting on him. I can't lose Harley. These Saturday visitations are already limiting. I might go crazy if this gets back to Lynn and she takes these away from me too.

Picking Harley up, I go pay for the five bears we end up with. I don't know how I let a two-year-old talk me into getting five bears, but I did. Good thing I haven't really touched my account. Build-a-Bear is not cheap.

"Let's go find Poshy and get some lunch," I tell Harley.

"I want two Happy Meals," she boasts, and I arch a brow at her. She's never even eaten a full Happy Meal and now she wants two.

"Why do you need two?"

"Princess Cee hungry too."

I smile at her and the bear in her arms dressed like a troll doll. "I don't think Princess Cee can eat."

"Yes she can!" Harley's little face scrunches up and her mouth pokes out in a pout. I would be lying if I said it wasn't the cutest thing she's ever done—at least in my presence.

"Okay, okay, okay. We'll get her a Happy Meal too."

Harley's face immediately brightens, and she throws herself into me. Awkwardly, I pull her closer while trying not to drop the bag in my other hand. A grin spreads across my face as I hold her close. I don't get many of these moments with her; hugs and stuff are usually reserved for Josh. I'm jealous about that. I can say that. It's hard watching my own daughter choose him over me, but moments like this remind me that I'm still her mother. Even if I only see her on Saturdays.

Josh is sitting in the center of the food court when I make it down the elevator to the bottom floor. He has two Starbucks cups in his hand. As I come to a stop in front of him, he hands me one cup and takes Harley in exchange, placing a peck on her forehead. I glance around the food area just to make sure no one saw that—well, no one that we may know saw that. After my counselor, I don't need more eyes on us.

I take a sip of the coffee and let out a throaty moan. God, I needed that.

"Keep doing that, and Wran might have all coffee cafes removed from your reach," Josh says with a chuckle.

I stare at him with wide eyes, shocked to see him laughing after literally glaring at me all morning. I don't know, but I was expecting his douchery to go up ten notches after having to "handle" Ms. Flannigan.

Ignoring his Wran remark, I ask him, "What happened with Ms. Flannigan?"

He glances down at Harley in his hands before returning his eyes to me. "I handled it. For all intents and purposes, Harley is your sister."

"What?"

"Your father raped a woman in prison. She got pregnant. Child services have Harley, and you get visitation."

I set my coffee down on the table and glare at him. "What?"

"It's not all that unbelievable. Your father did murder a woman and some cops."

"Ms. Flannigan bought that?"

Josh's eyes move back to Harley, and he watches her play with the bear. "What's not to buy, Roxy? She looks like you."

"She also looks identical to Wran."

"I guess it was a good thing he wasn't here."

I sit down in the cold metal chair across from Josh. "I don't like this."

"Well I don't like the fact that you still haven't told Wran about Harley. It's been almost a month since he's been home."

"You can't think that's a good idea, Josh," I hiss at him. We've had this conversation before. And I don't want to have it again. Not in front of Harley, and most certainly not in a food court where anyone could hear us talking.

"I think my brother has the right to know that he's a father. It might not be the right time, but it's never going to be the right time to drop a bomb like this."

Dropping the subject, I rise from my seat. "I'm going to get her a Happy Meal and then we can leave."

"We still have three hours left with her," Josh protests.

"Then we'll go to the zoo."

As I walk off, I hear Harley saying something about cats but ignore it. As awful as it sounds, I'm ready to drop Harley off and go home. Today has been a pain in my butt. Maybe Lynn was right—maybe Harley does deserve to be with a family that could provide her with everything. A family that wouldn't have to lie about who she is to them. I peek over my shoulder to see Josh bouncing Harley on his knees, a real grin on his face for the first time all day.

I quickly place my order for two Happy Meals and go back to our table. As soon as I sit, Harley points at the bag in the vacant chair and I instantly know what she's after: the blue bunny in a cop uniform she put together for Josh. I highly doubt she understands how fitting the toy she created for him is. Opening the bag, I pull the bunny out and hand it over to her. She thrusts it in Josh's face, and he must lean back to get a little space to take in the toy. He takes it from her and looks it over before turning to me with a questioning gleam in his eyes.

"It's for you, Poshy," Harley says, as chipper as ever. "I made it."

Josh smiles at the bear before kissing the top of Harley's head. "I love it."

Just then, the guy who took my order comes over carrying a tray. He sets it on the table. I frown at the tray and then look up at him. This isn't my order. "Umm. . . I just ordered the Happy Meals."

The guy looks a little taken aback. "I know. There was a man behind you that added the coffee and cookies to your order."

"Oh." That's weird. "Well, umm, okay. Thank you."

"No problem. If you need anything else, let me know."

I nod to the guy and he walks away. Josh takes the bag from the chair so Harley can sit. He takes the Happy Meal from the tray and starts arranging the chicken pieces and fries in front of her. She shakes her head and points to the cookies. Of course she would want the cookies now instead of the Happy Meal. Child has a serious sweet tooth, but I can't blame her. Wran does as well. I take the pack of cookies and pull one out, only to see something small and folded in between the cookies. I pull out the paper and unfold it, sucking in a breath as soon as I realize what it is.

"Cookie!" Harley harps out, and I drop it back on the tray.

"What's that?" Josh asks, but I'm too busy reading over the words again.

```
Once there was a lost girl who played with Peter
                      Pan.
 She gave him an heir and that made daddy mad.
 Such an innocent little thing, all pretty and
                     sweet.
 She looks like mommy and you know what that
                     means.
                     Love,
                     Daddy
```

Jumping up from my seat, letter in hand, I rush back over to the guy. His eyes widen as he sees my panicked face and takes a few steps back. From behind me, I can hear Josh calling my name, but I make a beeline for the guy. I've been receiving letters every other day since that first one. I chalked it up to someone playing a mean joke, but this isn't one of my tormentors. This is real. He's really sending them.

"Who gave you this?" I ask the guy at the counter.

He looks over my shoulder as if trying to find the person, but I know he won't. Whoever gave him this letter is long gone. The guy shakes his head and backs up some more.

"I–I don't know. He just said to add the coffee and peanut butter cookies to your tray with the letter. I didn't read it. I figured it was just an old guy trying to hit on you."

Peanut butter?

Ohmygod!

I take a step from the guy at the realization of what he just admitted. Peanut butter. He wanted to hurt me that badly. And Harley . . . I don't know if she has the allergy, but that stuff runs in families. I was about to give my baby peanut butter.

"What's going on?" I hear from behind me.

Ignoring Josh, I push the rising panic down and ask the cashier, "What did he look like?"

"I don't know. F-familiar. I've seen him somewhere. I-I'm sorry."

A woman from the back comes out and glances between me and her wide-eyed, trembling worker. She crosses her arms and gives me a pointed look. "Do we have a problem here? I can call mall security."

I shake my head and ball the letter up, shoving it in my pocket. Turning back around to Josh, I can clearly see the question on his face. I shake my head at him as well and grab Harley from his arms.

"We're leaving," I tell him. "Now."

Josh points back at the table where the Happy Meals lie. The sight of them makes me want to hurl. "She hasn't even finished eating, Rox."

"I don't care," I yell at him, panic lining every word I speak. "I'm leaving and I'm taking Harley, with or without you, Josh."

Without waiting on Josh, I stomp off toward the mall exit we entered. I need to get out of here. I need to get Harley out of here. Back to Lynn. Lynn can keep her safe.

Ohmygod, I can't believe this is happening.

He knows.

He knows about her.

How am I supposed to keep her safe from this? I shake my head as a tear rolls down my cheek. I don't make a move to wipe it away.

"Roxy?" Harley asks.

I look at the little girl in my arms and more tears fall.

Harley reaches up and wipes my eyes.

"It's going to be okay, baby. Mommy promise."

"Mommy," leaves her lips for the first time ever, and it breaks me. The first time she's calling me that, and I can't enjoy it.

CHAPTER 19

WRAN

Rox bolted from the apartment this morning like the cops were after her. She didn't even stop to get coffee. Ever since she came back home Saturday, she's been on guard. I know for a fact that she hasn't eaten or slept. The one time she did try to sleep, yesterday evening, she woke up screaming and mumbling something about her baby. She made no sense whatsoever. I tried talking to her, but the girl is fucking stubborn. I called Josh because, well, he was with her Saturday. He's been ignoring all my calls though. The only people I can possibly think would know what is going on with her are Cade and Aunt May. There's no way in hell I'm talking to one of them again. And I might just lose my shit if she confided in Cade instead of me.

I push through the doors of the diner and glance around. The place is a ghost town, but that's nothing new for the diner this time of day. None of the employees being out front is strange though. Aunt May is lucky she decided to set up shop in Kingston. Any other town and this place would be robbed cold by now. I go over to the bar and ring the bell at the register. Aunt May comes prancing out with an oil-stained apron on, the other new girl on her heels. I think her name was Macy, Mercedes, or something. The old lady comes over and leans her weight against the counter.

"If Rox ain't at school, I don't know where she at," Aunt Mays says.

The new girl—Mercedes, her nametag says—comes around the counter and plops down on the stool next to me. I look her up and down and scowl at her. The straightness of her posture, the way she has her ankles crossed and her hands laid in her lap like she's the fucking queen of England screams them. I don't know why this chick is working at this diner on this side of town when she's so obviously one of them, but I know I don't like her. She needs to go back where she belongs. Pretty sure she can only cause trouble for Aunt May.

"Rox's at school. Not what I'm here for," I tell Aunt May, dismissing the chick to my side.

Aunt May bends and retrieves a menu from below the greasy counter and hands it over. "Then what can I getcha, Belmont?"

I shake my hand and move the menu over. "Not here for that either. I need to talk to you about Roxy. Something's goin' on."

A sigh leaves May's lips as she slumps forward on her elbows, like the mere mention of Roxy being off balance has caused her to be as well. She unties her apron, removing it from her petite figure, and saunters around to me with one hand placed on her hip. She shakes her graying strands before perching herself up on a stool and searching her diner. When even she notices that the place is a ghost town, she shakes her head one more time.

"I thought the old lady in me was seein' things. Girl looks like she ain't slept in weeks," Aunt May says, like the words literally pain her to say. "All she been doin' is workin', and when I try to send her home, she protests."

I nod and look at Mercedes. "Have you noticed the same thing?"

The girl shrugs and goes back to biting her nails. "First day back since last week."

I roll my eyes at the ditz and turn back to Aunt May. "Josh dropped her off Saturday and it's been like she's terrified of something. I was hoping she maybe said something to you. I'm at my wits' end."

May shakes her head. "You know her better than anyone, Wran. Girl don't talk much. The last time I saw her this on edge, not sleeping, was right after you left."

Right. 'Cause everything comes back to me leaving.

"What was she like when I left?"

I've heard the rumors—drugs...partying—but none of that sounds like the Roxy I know. She wouldn't do that. Not after the childhood she had with that dickwad of a father. She doesn't talk about it, but I can picture what her life was like. The bruising on her arms and legs—old and fresh, yellowing and purple when I first found her—haunted me. After seeing those, I didn't touch her for months. Hell, she still has scars now. Neither one of us give them much attention, but they are still there. Underneath the clothes and bravery and shyness, they are still very much there.

I clench my teeth at the thought of that man laying his hands on my Roxy. He was lucky I wasn't around then. He would have been the one rotting ten feet under instead of living in a prison cell receiving daily meals and rewards and whatever else privileged fuckers like him get. The fact that they freed him is enough to make me want to hunt him down and attempt the job. Roxy is the only reason I'm not. She needs me, whether she knows it or not, and I doubt she wants to visit me in a prison cell.

"She didn't come in here much after you left, Wran, so I only know what I heard. And the few times she did come, she was always out of it. I don't think it was drugs or anything, but it was like she was in a state of denial. She seemed void of any emotions and Josh had to feed her in order to get her to eat."

I straighten on the stool, struggling to comprehend what May is telling me. It makes no fucking sense. Some people say she became a huge partier, drunk and high all the time, but Aunt May is saying that's not the case. I don't know what to believe anymore. If I broke her that badly, I see why she's been hesitant to let me back into her life. The Rox

I know, though, was strong; I made sure of that. Yeah, she was quiet and reserved, only truly showing how she felt in artwork and paintings, but I never thought she was weak. I never thought she couldn't handle being on her own.

"Umm, I don't know if this makes a difference, but, umm, there was a rumor going around that she might have been preggers," Mercedes says as she moves around on the stool, still biting her nails like a damn five-year-old.

I put a hand out to stop her from spinning back and forth, narrowing my eyes at the girl. How the hell would she have heard that? She's from the other side of town. Pretty damn sure Rox had no reason to socialize with them before Cade came along. Not to mention that this chick looks older than Rox. She must be around my age.

Mercedes shrugs her shoulders. "It was just something I heard one time at a party. Kingston High seniors know how to throw really awesome parties. Better than some of the sorority parties on campus."

"Unfortunately," May begins, "I heard that too, but figured it was just a rumor. Nobody's seen her with a kid. I figured Josh pulled her outta school 'cause she was depressed 'bout you."

Pulled her out of school?

What the fuck?

Why is this the first time I'm hearing about this?

Running my hands over my head, I get up from the stool and bend over to squeeze May. She gives me a gentle hug back.

"Thanks. I think I need to go talk to Josh."

Aunt May nods. "I'll see what I can get out of Rox when she comes in tonight and relay it to ya."

I give her one last smile before heading outside and leaving. It takes no time at all to get to the house, but when I don't see his motorcycle I head to the jail. Sure enough he's here, sitting and doing some paperwork right underneath that stupid buck that's missing one eye.

Dropping down in the shit-green chair in front of his desk, I put my feet up on the desk, deliberately shoving them on his paperwork. I need his attention. My gut's telling me he knows what the hell is going on with my girl. He was with her Saturday. He's been with her for the three years I have not been. He has answers.

"We need to talk," I state when his head pops up.

Josh shoves my feet off his desk and brushes the dirt from his papers. "I'm busy."

My palms slam down on this desk, sending a jarring echo throughout the jail. "Then get unbusy!"

"Do that again and you'll be spending a night in a cell," Josh says, giving me a pointed look.

I laugh at his pathetic threat. He's threatened me with worse. I'd happily spend a damn night behind rusty bars if it means knowing what's up with Roxy.

"What the hell is wrong with Roxanna? You were with her Saturday, and she's been off since then."

My brother stares me in the eyes for a long minute, lips thinned, not saying a word. Then his eyes drop. "I don't know. She freaked out at McDonald's and rushed out of the mall."

The mall?

They were at the fucking mall?

Together?

"We cut our day short," Josh finishes.

My eyes widen at that and my vision tints red. They were on a fucking date! I grab my brother by the collar of his brown shirt and pull him up, his paper scattering to the floor. Josh pulls his gun from his holster and points it at me. My lips turn up. He wouldn't think of pulling that trigger, but I release him nevertheless. He bends down and retrieves his papers before giving me a cold scowl.

"I should lock your punk ass up," he declares.

"Then why aren't you?"

"Because I am just as worried about her as you. She's never cut a Saturday short."

Curious, I ask, "How many Saturdays have you spent with her?"

Josh's jaw tics and I see a smirk forming on his face before he wipes it away. "Almost three years' worth."

My hands ball into fists at his admission. I knew it. I fucking knew something was going on with them. All the damn signs pointed at it. I shake my head at him and turn away from him. He sent me the fuck away to stay away from her, and yet the moment I leave, he's trying to get in her fucking panties.

"How the fuck could you?" I whirl around on him. "You sent me away for the same damn thing you're doing! I hope you're happy with my fucking sloppy seconds."

"Now, you're making accusations," Josh utters as he gets up from his chair and walks around the desk, leaning on it. "I never said I was fucking her. Like I've told you before, she's not my type. I like them legal."

"Then what are you doing with her every Saturday?"

"It's not what you think."

"Then tell me! I can't soothe her if I have no clue what the hell is goin' on, Josh."

"I can't tell you. She doesn't want you to know."

"Why?" I know I sound like a punk-ass kid right now, with my millions of questions, but I don't care. I need answers. This helpless feeling is not something I'm used to, and I don't like it. Not at all. Rox is supposed to be my girl. I'm supposed to take care of her, and I feel like I'm failing her. I might as well still be away.

Josh snorts at me and crosses his arms. "You ruined her, bro. I sent you away because you were ruining yourself as well. And all I could do was watch."

I shake my head at his statement and drop back down to the chair in front of him. "She was making me better."

"Better? You paid kids in her class to tease her. You brought women home and fucked them in front of her. She was literally a kid, Wran, and she listened to you banging women right next door. What do you think that did to her?"

"I was stopping. I was forgiving." I looked up at him. "I love her. You know that. I would do anything for her."

He nods, acknowledging my words but saying nothing.

I run my hands over my face, and I exhale before looking up at my brother. There have been so many rumors regarding Rox after I left. I need to know if they are true. "What happened when I left? Some people told me that you took her out of school. Others say that she was, well, that she was fucking pregnant."

Josh's face pales at the last statement and his eyes widen a bit. As swift as the expression came, though, it's gone. But I don't need any other answer. Him going pale tells all: Rox was pregnant . . . with my child. I gave her a child. My head drops into my hands. It all makes sense now. The voicemails. Her being scared. The voicemails ending.

Wran, I know you don't want to talk to me, but I need you. S–something happened. I did something bad. I–I don't know what to do. I'm scared. Please, please call me. Text me. Anything, please. I just need to hear you.

I get up from the chair and pace around the room. All I had to do was answer the damn phone or send her a letter or something. Anything. I walk over to the wall and lean my head against it. I fathered a damn child. My fist slams into the concrete wall and I hear the pops before I feel the pain.

"Jesus, Wran. Stop acting like a damn boy!" Josh yells over to me.

Shaking my hand out, I march back over to Josh and grab him again. "Why didn't you tell me?"

He takes my hands and shoves them away from his shirt. "Because she doesn't want you to know. That was a difficult time for her."

"Difficult time?" I mutter to him. Does that mean...?

"You just punched a fucking wall, Wran. She has every right not to tell you anything about the last three years."

"Did she lose it?" I need to know.

"Yes."

I suck in a breath and ease back down to the chair. Shaking my head, I bite down on the inside of my lip and let a tear fall. I lost a child. Rox lost a child. And I wasn't here for her. I didn't get to soothe her. I didn't get to grieve with her. She was alone. All because I didn't answer her messages. A hand goes to my mouth. I got a fifteen-year-old pregnant.

Fuck!

My eyes shoot up to my brother. He was here. He comforted my girl. This is all his fault. She would have the baby if it wasn't for him. She was probably stressed. Upset. All because he made me go away. I rise from the seat and scowl at Josh. Before I know it, my fist lands against his cheek and I hear a snap. Blood trickles from Josh's nose. He wipes it away with the back of his hand and shakes his head at me as if he's disappointed in me.

"And you wonder why she doesn't talk to you anymore. You have issues, brother."

"You didn't tell me about my child, so we have issues."

"Neither one of you are ready for a kid. Hell, she's still a kid. And you"—Josh scoffs and spits a mouthful of blood on the floor, wiping a hand across his mouth—"have more issues than getting a kid pregnant. What do you think would have happened? No one could have known it was yours."

"I would have figured something out!" I shouted at him. "You didn't give me a damn chance to do the right thing!"

Josh stares at me with unrelenting eyes, as if he didn't just tell me that the love of my life gave me something precious and then lost it. He can try to justify his actions, but as of this moment, we are done. I have nothing else to say to this prick. Nothing in this damn world would have made me keep something like this from him if the roles were reversed.

Turning from him, I stomp out of the precinct and just drive.

I wait for the lunch bell to ring before grabbing the coffees and getting out of the car. Coming to the school wasn't my plan when I left the precinct, but I needed to see Rox. It's weird. After finding out about the baby, all I want is to be around her. To make sure she's okay. It happened three years ago, but something is making her act standoffish and scared now. And if I can ease that just a little, then maybe she will open up to me about the baby.

Josh says that she doesn't want me to know, and normally I would just bulldoze the information out of her, but I can't with this. It is too sensitive a topic, and apparently losing the baby had a monumental effect on her. She's different, and that's my fault—more than I originally thought. I'm not going to pressure her to tell me about it.

As I walk down the checkered hall, a few students meet my eyes. I tilt my head in acknowledgment but don't stop until I get to the cafeteria. I search the round tables that haven't changed since my days in this school, and look for Rox, but don't see her anywhere. Claire spots me, though, and waves. I frown at her and exit the way I came.

I pop my head in a few classes to see if she maybe stayed behind in one, but nope. Maybe I should have waited at her locker like before. Kingston High isn't a big school, but it's big enough that if you can't immediately find someone, you're more than likely not gonna find them. I start to head back to my car when I pass by the glass doors that lead to the common area. Sitting there at one of the outdoor tables is Rox. With Cade. My hand tightens around the coffee cups as I watch him drape an arm around her shoulders. She doesn't make a move to shove him away. Instead, Rox looks up at him and gives him one of those shy smiles. He says something else and she shakes her head.

Stepping up to the doors, I nudge one open a little to hear what he's saying to her.

He covers his heart with one hand and tosses his head back. "Come on, Rox. You're breaking my heart here."

My lips quirk up at that.

"Sorry, but I can't," she mutters with his other arm still firmly around her shoulders. He might want to move that before I march over there and remove it for him.

"It's just a party. All you do is work and go to school. You have to have fun sometimes."

"I wouldn't fit in with them."

"You'd be with me. That alone means you fit in."

She looks up at him, biting the corner of her bottom lip. I know that damn look. She's actually thinking about going to a fucking party with this prick. She shakes her head again.

"I can't. I have work."

"Okay, but are we at least still on for tomorrow? I need a tux for prom, and you need a dress."

Rox nods, and I narrow my eyes on Cade. I thought I made myself clear when he bailed me out of jail.

She's.

Fucking.

Mine.

I turn away from the scene in front of me and march outside to my car, dropping the coffees in the nearest can. Fuck this shit. If she wants to hang with one of them, then fine. She doesn't want to tell me about my child, not fine. Not fucking fine at all. She can't pretend like it didn't happen. I don't care what Josh has to say about the situation. I have a right to know. I had a right to know then, and I have a right to know now. I'll be damned if Cade is going to weasel his way in and claim what's mine.

CHAPTER 20

ROX

I run my hands over the pretty pink sequins and beads as I wait for Cade to come from the dressing room. Why he needed me with him to try on tuxedos is beyond me; they are all the same—well, mostly the same. It's not like he can choose one that is not pants and a jacket with lapels. The only difference is color and material and fit. As long as his suit complements his date, he'll be fine.

Making my way back over to the fitting room, I sit down on the bench, all thoughts of pink dresses and limos and corsages leaving my mind. I can't go, and even if I did, it would be miserable. I would be with someone I don't want to be with and wearing a dress that is probably from the bargain bin. Cade asked me to be his date a few times before giving up and asking Claire. That's the only reason I've been able to hang out with him today without getting pig's blood dumped over my head and looking like a scene from Carrie.

Don't get me wrong, Claire made her claim on him very clear on Tuesday after he asked her out. I'm still finding pieces of rice in my hair after she cornered me in the bathroom and flaunted her new date status.

The curtain to the fitting room swings open and Cade steps out plucking his lapels and spinning on his soles like you see in 1920s movies. Suave, really suave.

"I think this one might be it," he says, moving to the mirror and checking himself out.

I stand and peek over his shoulder to see him running a hand up and down his chest and across the lapels of the suit jacket. "You look good."

"You said that about the last ones too."

"I think they all looked good," I say as I retake my seat. There's not really more to say about a guy trying on suits. If he was trying on prom dresses, then I might have an opinion. "Besides, you're going to prom with Claire. Does it really matter?"

"Guys like to look good too, you know. And I'm only going with her because you turned me down. Five times."

I roll my eyes at him and then take in the tuxedo again. This one is navy with black satin lapels and a matching tuxedo stripe going down the side of each leg. The fabric seems luxe even though it doesn't give off that shiny gleam you would expect formalwear to have. The only sheen is on the lapels and stripes. This one is nice. It fits him really well. It'll go great with whatever the she–devil picks. The only thing she told Cade was that her dress was blue.

"I think I'm going to get the matching top hat," Cade states as he turns from his reflection in the mirror and gives me his signature panty–dropping smile. "What do you think?"

"I think you should be asking Claire."

"Come on, Rox. Participate and I'll buy you a coffee."

I roll my eyes at him and hop up, planting a grin on my face. "You already have. This morning."

"I'll buy you another one."

Shaking my head, I give him another once–over. He really does look good in this suit. "You look great, Cade."

He steps forward and I have to crane my neck to see him. He drops his arms over my shoulders and smiles down at me. A real smile, not one of those smiles that he gives all the cheerleaders and Claire and even some of the teachers at Kingston High.

"Good enough that I can ditch Claire and take you?" he asks with all seriousness.

I shake my head and his arms fall from my shoulders.

"Just thought I'd try again."

He heads back to the dressing room. Another ten minutes of waiting and he reemerges in the black jeans and pastel polo and his letterman jacket. The playfulness from a moment ago is gone and he holds the tux by the hanger and walks right past me. I jump up from the bench and follow him. I frown at his back as he hands the suit to the guy over the counter. Once his tuxedo is packaged in a garment bag, we leave the store.

I hop in the passenger side of Cade's truck just as he gets in the driver's seat. He puts the truck in drive, revving up to leave, but I put a hand on his arm to stop him for a minute. I don't know why, but I feel like I owe him an explanation. He's befriended me, even though that's something he didn't have to do. He's kept Claire at bay, and beyond that, he's been super understanding about everything. I know I'm not the easiest person to befriend. But he did, and he's been the one here for me and listening to all the drama about Wran.

"I'm sorry," I mutter to him. "I really do think you're a great guy. And maybe in another life, I would say yes to you. Another life where I never met Wran and I never came to Kingston. I don't want you to be mad at me."

Cade turns in his seat to look at me full on. "I'm not mad at you. I could never be mad at you, Roxy. I just don't think Wran Belmont deserves your loyalty or you."

I nod. "But he has it."

Cade looks past me and out my window before giving me his full attention. "May I ask you a question?"

I nod again.

"Does he have it because you love him or because of Harley?"

My eyes widen as he speaks my daughter's name, and I shake my head. No, he doesn't know about her. No one in Kingston knows about her. "I–I don't k–know what you're talking about."

My gaze falls from him and toward the leather seat cushion. If he knows about her, that means others could know about her. The rumors. . . Rumors come from somewhere. Wran has always told me that. That means someone knew or suspected. Ohmygod, they know. The students at my school know. Claire knows.

"Hey, hey." Cade grabs hold of my chin and raises my face back to his. "It's okay. Stop freaking out. No one at school knows about her."

"You're mistaken," I lie. "I don't know a Harley."

Ghh! Saying that out loud makes me feel like a thousand-pound ball has been set on my chest. Why am I lying? He obviously knows about her.

"I'm not gonna tell anyone, but you do have to stop lying to me. You come to Arlington every Saturday to see her. I've seen you and the other Belmont with her. It's nothing to be ashamed of."

I shake my head at him, giving up on the lie. He knows. "I'm not ashamed of her. I'm ashamed that I made one mistake—one stupid mistake that I don't even remember making—and I lost her."

Cade takes my hand and squeezes it as I wipe at the tears. "Do you want to talk about it? I doubt you've had many people you could talk to."

"No. It's hard to talk about something you don't really remember happening."

"Does Wran know about her?"

I roll my eyes at his question. "Of course not. We wouldn't be sitting here in your truck if he did."

"He sounds like a controlling dick."

"You sound like a jealous friend."

"I am a jealous friend," he says, not looking away from me.

I let my gaze fall from his. That is too much of a confession. Sure, I know he's been trying to get me to go on a date, but damn. . . I didn't know he felt that way. Sitting back in the seat, I fasten myself in as Cade pulls away from the curb. I can't believe he knows about Harley and isn't judging me. If anything, I expected him to look at me in disgust. Call me a slut or something. That's what Claire would have done. That's what any other person at my high school would have done.

Shamed me.

Shunned me.

Crumbled me up and destroyed me.

But not Cade.

He accepts that part of me.

He likes me.

With my head down, I observe him from beneath long lashes and grin. He really, really likes me. At least now I know he's not pretending. While this whole friendship has felt genuine, I was waiting for him to retaliate anyways. Most people would have. Or at least the people I know would have reacted to coffee getting thrown on them.

The moment my eyes move from him, I can feel his gaze on me, and it makes me smile even more. This feels great. I haven't had a true friend in such a long time. It's nice to have one again.

"I want to take you somewhere," Cade says out of nowhere.

I pull my phone for my skirt pocket and read the time. "As long as you get me home before five, I'm good."

"You're working tonight?"

"Yeah."

"Then we'll make this fast," he says and starts weaving in and out of traffic.

We don't come to a stop until we are at a concrete building with a rounded top on the outer edge of Arlington, far from any city life. Cade jumps out of the truck and comes around to my door, opening it. He holds out a hand to me. I arch a brow before looking over at the building again. This building seems familiar somehow. I know I've never been here. This doesn't look like a place Wran would have brought me.

When I don't give Cade my hand, he grabs it and pulls me from the truck. He shuts the door and locks it, all while dragging me to the entrance of the building. He pulls out a key, causing me to arch a brow at him again. Why does he have a key to this building? Cade just grins at me like it's freaking Christmas and whatever is in this building holds all the presents he could want. I roll my eyes as he opens the door and goes inside.

I follow him and come to a stop immediately once inside. My eyes widen and I let out a gasp as I stare up at the dome-shaped ceiling, blacked out except for the tiny little lights arranged in the shapes of the constellations. A telescope stands dead center. Pulling my eyes away from the stars, I let them explore the room. There are a few movie-theatre-like chairs and a door on the other side. There's also a big red button on the wall that screams "push me, push me." Tilting my head to the side, I narrow my eyes and bite down on my lip. This place is more than familiar. I've been here. I know I have. I just don't remember when.

"Something about this place is familiar," I mutter out.

"It does? How so?" Cade walks over to me and takes my hand, pulling me to one of the chairs.

I search my memory for anything, but nothing comes. "I don't know."

Cade crosses his legs and rests them on the back of the chair in front of him. "I used to come here all the time. My father would bring me with a family friend." He pauses for a minute as if remembering. "But that stopped when her mother died. I bought this place a few years ago."

"You own this?"

He nods. "When you told me you like stargazing, I thought you'd enjoy this place."

I turn around in my chair. "You remember me telling you that?"

He nods again. "The ceiling opens up and you can see the stars at night. It's a wonder. You'll have to come back one night when you are not working."

"I'd really like that."

Cade takes my hand again, and I feel something cool fall into my palm. I look down to see the key he used to get us inside. My eyes snap to him, the questions clear in my gaze.

"I'm giving this place to you. You'll get more use out of it than me."

I shake my head back and forth. "W–what?"

"You can have it."

The key drops from my hand as if it burned me, and I shake my head again. "No. I don't want it." No one gives people buildings. "I can't accept this. Thanks, but no thanks. I think we should probably go."

"Why?" he questions me.

I blink a few times, not understanding his question. That's obvious. He just tried to give me an observatory. No one gives a random person they've known for a month something like this. I don't know what it means, and I don't want to owe anyone anything.

"Roxanna, I'm giving this to you because it doesn't mean anything to me anymore. It only held memories for me, but I don't need those memories anymore."

"Why not?"

He looks away from me without answering the question. When I realize he's not going to answer, I turn back to the stars illuminating the ceiling like the night sky.

We must stay there stargazing for at least an hour before my stomach growls and Cade decides it's time to leave. He stops by a Mexican restaurant and orders us burritos to go. I sit in the silent car, the only noise coming from the paper wrapper around my burrito and my chewing as he drives back to Kingston.

He pulls up outside my apartment and puts his truck in park. Neither one of us says anything for a while, and the silence is a little awkward. I really wish he hadn't offered to give me an observatory. That changes things.

Breaking the silence, I tell him, "Thank you for convincing me to skip classes today. I had fun."

He shakes his head. "Don't thank me for that. You needed to get out of your head. Even if for a few hours."

I don't know what to say to that, so instead I grab the door handle, readying myself to hop out of the truck. There's no getting out of my head. Today was nice, but it is not going to keep the nightmares at bay. It's not going to keep the letters from coming. If Cade only knew half the things I had to worry about, he would not have even said it. He grabs my wrist to keep me from moving though.

"Thank you for the date," he says.

I spin back to him, shaking my head. No. This was not a date. It was two friends hanging out and picking out prom clothes. A cocky grin spreads across Cade's face at my reaction. I punch him playfully in the shoulder and grin back.

"This was not a date."

Releasing my wrist, he leans back against his door and crosses his arms. A grin matching my own replaces the cocky smirk he had on his face. "I don't know. We went shopping, had lunch, and watched the stars. Not to mention you agreed to go on spring break with me this coming up week. Sounds like a date to me. A really good date."

"I did not agree to go on spring break with you."

"No, but you will. I'm picking you up Sunday, and we'll be back before next Saturday. You can even bring Belmont."

The smile falls from my face. "Cade, this was not a date."

His smile doesn't fall as he nods his head, his blond hair not falling out of its gelled state. "I know that, Rox. I'm just messing with you. Well, about the date. Not spring break. Trust me, if we were on a date, I wouldn't be returning you to Belmont."

CHAPTER 21

ROX

I stand outside long enough to watch the taillights of Cade's Ford disappear down the street. Once I can no longer see them, a breath I don't realize is bottled up comes whooshing out. He doesn't just like me and that's not a good thing. I turn away from the street and head up the stairs to the apartment. I don't make it a foot inside before the pungent smell of booze slams into me. I search the living room only to find Wran passed out on the couch. Beer cans litter the floor and the sofa.

Rushing over, I drop to my knees and shake him. He groans and reaches down to where two six-packs rest on the floor, all without opening his eyes. I grab the boxes and pull them out of reach. Apparently that's the wrong thing to do. When his hands grasp at nothing, Wran's eyes snap open. They're bloodshot and glassy, yet somehow focused. I take a chance, looking away to glance at the floor. Maybe he had some friends over. Maybe he didn't drink all of this. Wran seizes my face and pulls my gaze away from the crumpled cans and back to his face. He lets out a breath and the sickening, stale smell ruins any thought that he didn't do this alone.

Wran's eyes narrow in on me before drifting over to where I have the beers. Without breaking eye contact, he reaches past me and grabs a box. My instincts kick in and I immediately take hold of the box in his grasp. No. He can't drink anymore. The box tumbles out of his hold. Instantly, I grab it along with the other box and scoot away from him to get to my feet. I rush the small distance to our kitchen and start popping cans open. I manage to get one beer halfway down the drain before a hand jerks my arm back, sending the beer flying across the kitchen.

Trembling, I try to ease out of Wran's line of sight. I don't make it far when he notices me easing away and shoots out an arm to stop me. I gulp, staring at him. He stares back. I've never seen a drunk Wran before. Yes, he's probably had drinks at the parties he attended in high school, but he never let it around me. I don't like it. With unsteady movements, Wran's hands slide up both of my arms, feeling like worms slithering up them the entire time. His hands stop at my biceps, fingers curling into my skin.

"Ow!" I shriek as his hold becomes increasingly tighter. "Wran, stop."

He drags me the foot separating us until our chests are touching, and I'm a trembling mess before him. His head falls to the space between my shoulder and neck and he starts peppering my skin with kisses. The smell of alcohol surrounds me, and I try to pull away from him. He doesn't let go. A whimper leaves me just as one of his hands moves up to the base of my neck. Wran curls his hand into my hair there and pulls.

My eyes bug out and I cry out at the pain. "Please, please, stop. I'm sorry, so sorry."

In a flash, he pulls my head up and his mouth crash into mine, sloppy and wet. I push against his chest, but that only makes him hold me tighter. More sobs leave me, and I can feel his mouth hesitating a little before he refocuses, forcing his tongue inside my mouth. I shake my head and push against him some more. This is not what I want. Not like this.

Wran spins us around and shoves me into the edge of the island. Hard. My knees buckle and I fall to the floor. Wran collapses too, landing on me. My vision goes blurry and then Wran's face is three instead of one. With my hand free, I touch the back of my head and feel something slimy and warm. I squeeze my eyes shut and then reopen them. I do that over and over. I need to wake up from this nightmare. This is not Wran. He would never touch me. He would never do this. But then I feel hands making their way up my bare legs. It was a bit warmer today, so I decided a skirt would be fine. I shouldn't have worn this skirt. My breath catches in my lungs and I turn my head, looking at the side of the couch. His fingers reach the edge of my skirt, sending my body into treacherous trembles.

No.

No.

No . . .

I force my eyes to look down to see Wran staring up at me. "Such a beautiful doll."

My eyes widen and I shake my head. I start to crawl backward, but Wran grips one of my ankles. With my free leg, I kick him off me. He falls to the side, letting me go. I leap to my feet but almost fall back down. I steady myself on the island to keep my vision from swimming. I bring a hand to my head and groan. It feels like someone stuffed it with cotton. Wran moves on the floor, and I push myself out of the kitchen and down the hall to my room. Locking the room's door, I move over to my small closet and drop inside, pressing myself underneath hanging jeans.

A loud boom jars me out of my hazy state. I search my pockets for my phone until I have it in hand. With shaky fingers, I send a quick message to Cade. Another bang sounds and then I hear my door slam against the wall. A sharp pain edges into the back of my head, and things blur again. The last thing I see before everything fades away is booted feet coming right toward me.

"James, we're going to be late," a tall woman in an ivory gown states as she hops around, strapping silver open-toed shoes onto her feet.

Arms circle around the woman from behind and she drops the other strappy heel to the floor. She turns around in the man's arms and plants a swift peck on his lips. Tilting my head, I study the woman. She is pretty. Long hair like spun gold hangs loose all the way to her tiny waist, and her skin is as pale as winter snow. When she turns back around, eyes matching my own greet me. She smiles and beckons me forward. I go to her without hesitation, entranced by her beauty.

"You have to leave Mr. Snuggles at home tonight," she utters and takes the rabbit from my hands.

I shake my head. "No, Mommy. I want to keep him."

She runs a hand over my head. "How about for one night, you play with your brother and friends? It'll be fun."

I shake my head again. "They're mean to me. Caden always pulls my hair."

My hands automatically go up to the braid my mommy did earlier tonight. Someone grabs me from behind and I go soaring through the sky. Daddy catches me and swings me around before slowing down.

"You know, my little lost girl, boys only pick on girls because they like them," my daddy says.

I frown at him and shake my head. "Nuh-uh. I saw you and Mommy watching a movie last night and the boy was nice to the girl. He gave her pink flowers."

My daddy smiles and then turns to look at Mommy. I turn around in his hold and look at her too. She has a goofy expression on her pretty face as she puts her other shoe on. When she's done strapping it on, she gets up and comes over to where Daddy and I are. Mommy leans down and kisses my forehead.

"That wasn't a real movie, baby," she says.

I'm confused. "But it was on the TV."

"Yes, it was. How about I let you watch it tomorrow, if you go get in the car with your brother and Caden."

"Do I get ice cream too?" I ask her. "I want ice cream. Chocolate ice cream. With sprinkles!"

Mommy takes me out of my father's arms and sets me down on the floor. "You can have all of that if you go so Daddy can get dressed."

Without another word, I turn and run out of my parents' room and down the stairs. The boys are in the foyer, tossing a football back and forth. I come to a stop in front of them and point to the ball. Daddy is going to be mad; they're not supposed to play with balls in the house. I look back upstairs and then back at the boys. I shake my head at them.

"You're not supposed to do that in the house," I whisper at them, so Daddy doesn't hear.

The last time they played with a ball in here, Daddy got really angry. He yelled at Kiellan and hit him. It was bad. Kiellan was bleeding and Mommy was crying. But Daddy said it was what bad kids get. He's never been mad at me, but I don't like seeing my brother hurt.

"Don't tell him then," Kiellan says, and tosses the ball to Caden again.

I turn to my brother's friend, hoping he will stop this. "Caden, Daddy's coming down. We're all supposed to be in the car."

He looks at me for a second before resting the ball underneath his arm and turning to my brother. "Maybe she's right."

Kiellan stomps across the foyer to where Caden stands and yanks the ball from under his arm. "Don't be such a girl!"

Caden shakes his head at my brother. He walks over to where I stand at the bottom of the staircase. "Come on. Let's go get in the car, kiddo."

"I'm not a kid. And we're the same age."

"You're still a kid."

I stick my tongue out at him and march out the door to the waiting black car. I climb inside and immediately go for my car seat. I don't know why my mommy and daddy make me sit in a car seat and not Kiellan, but I know if I don't, Daddy will get mad. I don't want to make Daddy mad. He'll hurt Kiellan if he does. Caden slides across the seat and reaches over to get my seat belt. He secures it around me and smiles.

"Your dress is pretty today," Caden says to me.

"You really like it?"

He nods. "It's the same color as your eyes."

"My eyes are ugly. A girl at school says they look like clown eyes."

"They're the prettiest clown eyes I've ever seen."

"You're going to get cooties!" I hear my brother yell from over Caden's shoulder.

Caden's face turns pink and he slides away from me, putting on his seat belt beside my brother. Moments later my parents come get in the car. Daddy drives off so fast I have to grip the sides of my car seat. He doesn't turn on the music, but he never does. I glance over at Caden and my brother and they are playing some game, not making a noise. I look up front to my parents and they are just as quiet as my brother.

We drive for a long time until Daddy stops. He's not at a light, so I lift a little from my seat to see what's going on. Daddy's eyes meet mine in the mirror and they narrow at me. I sink back down in my seat and wait for us to start moving again.

My mommy says something up front and my ears perk up. I don't hear what she says though. Daddy's hand slams down on the wheel and I jump. Caden grabs my hand and holds it tightly.

"Dammit, Lora! Shut up, woman."

My mommy looks back at us and smiles, but it's wrong. All wrong. She has lines on her head, and she looks too tense. She turns back to Daddy and says something else. She makes sure not to let us hear, knowing we all want to know what she's saying. Daddy takes a drink out of a shiny rectangle jar and then shoves it into my mommy's open hand. The car starts moving again and everything falls back into silence. I squeeze Caden's hand and look down at him. He doesn't look at me though. Instead, my brother looks over at me. His eyes drop to Caden's and my linked hands. I can feel Caden tense as he pulls his hand away from mine.

I stick my tongue out at my brother and he does the same back. Reaching over, I take the game from his hand.

"Hey!" he screams without meaning to. His eyes dart to the front of the car and I bite down on my lip.

Please don't yell.

Please don't yell.

But there's no time to yell for anyone. There's a loud sound and my body jerks forward and then back when the seat belt doesn't stretch anymore. Everything seems to start moving in slow motion. And then suddenly there's no silence; there's noise everywhere. I yell for my mommy as she turns upside down and then back upright and over again. I shake my head, not understanding why she's not staying still. My eyes move over to my brother and Caden. My brother's eyes are closed and there is blood on the side of his face. Caden grabs hold of my hand and seat belt, holding it tight against my seat.

Caden says something, but the noise outside drowns out his words. I shake my head at him and use my free hand to reach for my seat belt. I want out of this seat. He grabs hold of my hand, pulling it away from the button, as he slides forward in his seat. His head slams against the center compartment, and he doesn't move. I scream and watch as Mommy turns over again. Then everything stops.

Daddy moves in the front seat and reaches over to Mommy. He shakes her, but she doesn't move. He shakes her harder. When she doesn't move again, Daddy yells out.

"Daddy," I cry out. "Daddy!"

"Shut up. Just shut up."

A loud wee woo, wee woo sounds outside, followed by police cars. I nudge Caden to let him know we're going to be okay, but he doesn't move. I kick him again, only to get the same result. I frantically shake my head, screaming his name over and over. He doesn't move. Moments later, someone pull me from my car seat. The world turns back upright. A man dressed in black baggy clothes pulls Caden from the car next and rushes away with him. My gaze follows the man with my friend, only to see them put him on a small white bed.

I turn back to the car. It's all broken and sitting upside down. My brother is pulled from the car next. Instead of putting him on the white bed thingy, they lay him on the ground. They do the same with my mommy. My father is the last to get out of the car. When he's finally free, he shoves the man in the baggy clothes away and races over to where my mommy lies. He shakes her and shakes her and shakes her. She does not move. Daddy's head falls back as if he is looking up at the sky before searching the crowd. His eyes land on me and then he frowns. He jumps up from the ground super-fast and comes at me.

He grabs my hair and pulls me away from the police officer.

"Your fault!" he yells. "You couldn't be fucking quiet!"

Two men pull him from me, but he shoves them away. "Do you know who the fuck I am? You will all lose your jobs for touching me!"

I get up from the ground and run over to where I saw them take Caden. Climbing inside the truck, I fall to my knees beside him. I shake him a little to see if he'll wake. When he doesn't, I go to shake him again, but hands clamp around mine and I look up to see a woman in a white coat.

"He'll be okay," she says. "How are you?"

I shake my head at her but say nothing. I look down at Caden again and grab his hand.

CHAPTER 22

WRAN

My eyes follow Cade as he paces back and forth in front of the bed Rox is lying on. It's been a day since I . . . did what I did. I can't even fucking believe it. I let my head fall into my hands. Of all things I could have done, I did that. I took advantage of my Rox. I'm never fucking drinking again. I don't know why I thought beer and whiskey would take the edge off finding out that Rox had been pregnant three years ago. Nothing else seemed to work, and I had spent the few days prior to yesterday pounding guys' faces in at the gym. She kept moving through the week as if nothing had happened. School, work. School, work. I needed some form of release. Pretty boy here showing up after she decided to ditch school yesterday only made it worse.

That's no excuse for what I did. I know that.

God, I probably deserve to take up residence in her father's now vacant cell.

When Cade came barging into the apartment yesterday, I was half out of it. Hell, I don't even remember him punching me. Apparently he did. He made a point of informing me this morning when I woke up in a bed not my own, barely able to open my right eye. I can't believe I let some punk teenager get the best of me.

I run my hand over my swollen eye and lift my head just in time to see Cade glaring down at me. He grins when he notices my eye. It's undoubtedly purple by now. Rising from the floor, I step up to him. I have Cade by a good two inches, so in order to keep glaring he has to look up at me. See me as his superior. He doesn't though. The dumb punk just turns around and goes over to Rox. I take the side opposite of him and sink down on the bed as well. My fingers trace up to the bruising handprints on her upper arm. I suck in a breath and glance away. I hurt her.

Dammit!

I've done some stupid shit to her, but this. . .

I have never physically done anything to her. Yeah, I wanted her to feel my pain when we were younger, but when I decided to come back here, that was no longer my goal. I wanted her back. I wanted her to be mine. But I never, never wanted to turn into her father. I can't even imagine how she's going to look at me when she wakes up. Or what she'll do.

I get up from the bed and start pacing. She's been unconscious since yesterday. Cade told me she's been that way since he took her from the apartment. She hasn't moved once since I came into this room this morning. What if Rox doesn't wake up? I'm not going to pretend to know the human brain, but is there really a reason for her to wake up? Me? Ha! I hurt her. I fuckin' hurt her. Not to mention she has no one besides the dickwad next to her.

I wouldn't want to wake up for this life either.

"Dude! You're creating a draft," Cade calls over to me, but I don't stop pacing.

I glance over my shoulder at him. "Says the dickwad that was doing the same thing an hour ago."

He doesn't say anything to that. My phone buzzes and I pull it from my back pocket to see my brother's name splashed across the screen. I press the ignore button. Not even a minute later a text appears on my phone from him as well.

> **JOSH:** Answer your damn phone!

The phone rings again and I answer it. "What?"

Cade shushes me and I walk out of the room into a hallway with pictures of his childhood gracing a shit-green wall. If a family can afford to live on this side of town in a house that can accommodate at least twenty overnight visitors, they should be able to hire someone to change the color of these walls. It makes no sense for the outside of this place to look like the Property Brothers did the works and the inside to look like a log cabin, adorned with stuffed ducks and bucks.

"Are you listening?" Josh yells over the phone.

"No," I admit, and walk down the staircase. "What did you say?"

"I went over to your apartment to pick up Rox. There was blood on your kitchen floor."

I nod and make my way into the family room. "Yeah. There was an incident."

"Wran, what the hell did you do?" he shouts through the phone.

"What makes you think I did anything?" I yell back at him.

"You've been off your shit since you found out. You think no one's noticed your behavior?"

I roll my eyes at his assumptions. No, I know no one's noticed nothin'. I haven't exactly put a sticker on my damn forehead stating that I got my now eighteen-year-old girl-friend knocked up three years ago and now I can't deal with shit. Besides, the only people that have seen me since Josh let the cat out the bag are the guys at the gym (that probably need face surgery) and Janice. I know she hasn't said anything to Josh.

"She hit her head, okay? She'll be fine." I hope. "Did you really call me for that? You know I'm not gonna let anything happen to Roxy."

"No. That's not why I called. I found something in her room."

Her room? He was in her fucking room. "Going through her panty drawer, you sick fuck?"

"Ha! That's your job."

There's a pregnant pause, and I make my way over to some ancient-appearing couch with curved armrests in an angel print material.

"I was following the blood drops and they led me to her closet. Wran, I found letters in there. Sick, twisted letters. One was crumpled up and the others looked fresh, like she'd just gotten them."

I sit up straight on the brick-hard couch. Blinking, I take in what he's just said. Letters. "From who?"

There's an intake of breath on Josh's end of the line. "You're not gonna like it."

"Just tell me!" I shout into the phone.

"All the letters end with 'Love Daddy.'"

Fuck! I get up from the couch and march back up the stairs. Rox has been getting fucking letters from that sick fuck and she hasn't told anyone. No wonder she hasn't been sleeping well and the nightmares are back. Why wouldn't she tell someone? She's with Josh every Saturday. He's the sheriff for crying out loud! Someone could have handled him.

"I take it you've already handled this," I say into the phone as I reenter Roxy's room.

Cade looks over from where he is perched beside Rox and his brow wrinkles.

"No. It's not like I can just pop by wherever he's at and arrest him," Josh says defensively.

"Why the hell not? You're the sheriff."

"Roxy hasn't said a word about this. For all intents and purposes, we shouldn't know."

"What the hell do these letters say?"

"I'm not telling you that."

"Why the hell not?" I yell a little too loud. I turn to look at Rox and frown when I see that had no effect on her. She's still lying there, a real-life Snow White. Maybe I should kiss her. That'll wake her up. I shake my head. She wakes up to that, she might very well go back under.

"I'm not bailing my little brother out of fucking jail for a piece of ass."

"A piece of ass! You know very damn well she's more than that."

"I'm only informing you about the letters because I need you to get her to confess to them. Anything so we can get a restraining order."

"Can't you do that without her?" I ask him. I've never needed to know how to get a restraining order, so I don't know how the process works. Peeking over at Rox's unmoving form, I frown. If he needs her, then we're out of luck.

"A month ago, yes, but she's eighteen now."

Fucking eighteen.

I suck in a deep breath and run my free hand over my head. This damn weekend couldn't get any worse. "Then we have a problem. Rox is unconscious."

"What?" Josh shrieks. "Get her out of Kingston and don't take her to Arlington. I'm gonna see what I can do."

Cade gets up from Rox's side and comes over to me. He holds his hand out for my phone, and I gladly place it in his hand. Josh acts like I don't know how serious this is. Letters. Fucking letters. I sit down on the edge of Roxy's bed and stare down at her face. Leaning down I place a peck on her forehead.

"Please, wake up," I mutter into her soft skin. "I won't hurt you again. I promise."

I feel a huff of air on my chest and I rise to look at Rox. She's still asleep. First I hurt her, and now my fucking imagination is playing games on me. I could have sworn I felt her breathe on me. Leaning back down, I give her another peck on her forehead before returning to Cade. He hands me my phone and points out the door. I march out ahead of him and he follows. He closes the door to Rox's room and then we head down the stairs of his creepy house.

This morning when I woke up here, I had no clue where I was. I didn't handle that well. I freaked out like a little bitch. If I had been in a cell somewhere, I probably would have been fine. That sounds more like me than waking up here. For a moment I thought I fucked someone else and was at her house. Thought I fell asleep or somethin', but then the door to the room flew open and he came in, causing the pounding in my head to multiply like rabbits. Flashes of my hands on Rox surfaced through my mind. Cade took my moment of loss for weakness and landed another punch to my ribs. Hell, I still feel it.

Cade walks through the bottom floor until we reach a circular sitting area with rows upon rows of leather-bound books on the outskirts of the room. A desk, two brown leather chairs, and a coffee table with an ongoing game of chess rest in the center of the room. The burgundy walls, with the sconces illuminating small patches of them, give this room less of a cabin feel, but the deer above the desk still reminds me that we are still very much in Kingston.

Rich pricks.

Cade sits down in one of the chairs and I take the other. He folds one leg over the other and slumps forward. "I told your brother that I would take Rox to my parents' vacation home in Aspen. He thinks it's a good idea."

"Like hell." There's no way he's taking her away from me. I may not have some fancy fucking vacation home a few states away, but I do know how to protect her. I doubt a preppy, pretty prick could do the job.

"She's already agreed. We were going to leave for spring break tomorrow," he says as if it's nothing.

I scowl at him. "You asked my girlfriend to go on vacation with you?"

"I highly doubt she's your girlfriend. Besides, do I need to remind you what I walked in on last night? Blood on your hands. Rox unconscious in a damn closet. You drunk and blabbing about a baby."

Digging my nails into the smooth leather, most likely Italian or some other luxury type, I inwardly cringe. Last night was bad. Worst night of my life, and this prick can't seem to get enough of reminding me. Does he really think telling me what I did is going to make Rox care for him the way she cares for me? No. He'll always be just a friend. And I'll always be the guy that saved her that fateful day. Cade might have a past with Roxy, but she doesn't remember it. And I'll be damned if anyone reminds her of it. She already has nightmares from before; she doesn't need anything else thrown on top of it. Nothing from her past needs to reemerge. Her PTSD doesn't need to worsen.

"I know what I did," I say at last. "I'll regret that forever, but don't think you have any right to swoop in and try to be her white knight. She doesn't need you."

"You don't know—"

His words are cut off when a scream from upstairs erupts throughout the house. I jump from the chair and race through the house until I hit the stairs, taking them two at a time. When I reach Rox's door, I throw it open. Her wide, frantic eyes snap to me and she screams again. I go over to her and she immediately jumps from the bed, putting space between us. She holds up her hands up in a defensive posture, making her seem even smaller than she already is.

"Stay away from me!" she screams, her eyes hysterically taking in the foreign room. Shit. We probably should have expected her to be panicky after last night and then waking up in a place she doesn't know.

My heart falls and I take a step away. Shit. What the hell do I do? I knew she would be upset when she woke up, but I never thought I'd see fear in her eyes. I take another step back and raise my hands in a surrendering gesture.

"I'm not going to hurt you," I utter, aiming to soothe her. "You know that."

She shakes her head frantically and then falls to the floor with her back against the wall, cradling her knees to her chest and whispering "stop, stop, stop" over and over again. A second later Cade comes rushing through the open door. He stops by my side and watches Rox's trembling form on the floor. He takes a step forward and I grab his arm to keep him in place. No one is soothing her but me. I did this. I hurt her. I'm gonna be the one to fix this.

Cade shoves my hand away but stays put. He knows his place.

Slowly, I ease across the room and fall to my knees. She doesn't seem to notice. Rox just continues to rock in place. I rest a hand on her shoulder and she stops rocking. Her eyes meet mine and she shakes her head. Tears seem to come from nowhere and she buries her head in her knees. Feet sound from behind us, and I give Cade a stern glare. I don't want him anywhere near her.

"Rox?" I prod. "Talk to me."

She turns her head in her lap so she can see me. Her eyes are red rimmed, and I hate that. I absolutely loathe it. She swipes at the tears as they seem to roll faster down her cheeks. I reach out for her but she scoots away from my hand. My heart breaks a little more, but I can't blame her. I hurt her. I physically hurt her. I did the one thing I told myself I wouldn't do. The one thing that made me better than her wretched father. Now I'm just like him. I broke her. I broke my lost girl.

"Roxy, please. I'm so sorry." I plead with her, not caring if I'm giving the prick behind me ammo to use against me. "I'm sorry. I didn't mean to hurt you. I was drunk. It's no excuse, I know it, but please, don't leave me. I love you. I'll do anything to make it up to you. Name it and it's yours."

The only part of Rox that gives any acknowledgment to my declaration is her gorgeous eyes. They flick across my face, searching me. Knowing her, she's picking apart everything I just said. I broke her trust and she's looking for a reason not to trust me. She's not going to find one though. I've never been more real with her than now. Everything I said is true. Even if she can find it in herself to somehow forgive me now, it'll be a while before I can truly trust myself again. I hurt her. She bled by my hands. That's something words will never fix.

"W–why didn't you answer my calls?" she asks me with a shaky voice.

It takes me a moment to figure out what she's talking about. I've answered every single call she's sent me since coming back home. But she's asking about three years ago. I run a hand over my hair that has grown some since returning to Kingston. Slumping down, I lean back against the wall and study her more. Her pale skin is even more ashen than normal, her lips cracked and chapping. She looks so tired. One look in her eyes, though, and I know she can handle the truth of that question. They're bright, even if glassy. Strong. Eyes of a survivor.

"Truthfully, I didn't want to hear your voice, because I hated you. Everything about you reminded me of what I had lost. My life. My father. My brother. My childhood. But your voice was also the one thing that could have had me running back home. It's my kryptonite. Always has been. Always will be."

Her face wrinkles up and more tears leave her eyes. "Why do you hate me?"

I shake my head at her. "I don't. I love you more than anything."

Rox lifts her head and looks past me. Her eyes widen, and I turn to see what caught her sight. She's staring at Cade. I glance between them. Her eyes roam over him, and I do my best not to show any jealousy. I just bared my heart, and now she's checking out the likes of him. Rox gets to her feet and bypasses me, only stopping when she gets to him. My hands flex into fists when she brings her hand up to his cheek.

"Caden," is all she says, loud enough for me to hear.

His eyes widen as he glances over at me and then back to her. "You remember?"

Rox slowly nods as she brings a hand to the back of her head.

I cross the distance separating the three of us. When I bring my hand up to cup her face, Rox flinches but doesn't pull away. She looks at me, hesitating before she pulls her amethyst gaze away from him. I need to know that I still have her. She knows who he is now. She knows that he was once her friend. Her brother's friend. But I need to know she's still mine. That she's still my little lost girl, and I'm still her Peter Pan.

"Roxanna?" Her full name leaves my lips all choked up, and I hate that I'm showing this dickwad so much of me.

Roxy's small hand comes up to mine resting on her cheek. She closes her eyes and nudges her head into my palm. I let out a sigh and pull her to me, wrapping my arms around her like I haven't seen her in years. Hell, I might never let her go.

"I'll give you two some privacy, I guess." I can clearly hear the disappointment in Cade's tone, but I don't care. Roxanna Raine was always meant to be mine. It's time he knows that nothing is going to break us. He might have known her as a kid, but he never really knew her. He didn't see the pain she endured. He didn't bring the light back to her eyes.

Suddenly, Rox pulls from my arms and glances around the room. She then pats herself down frantically. Her panicked eyes snap back to me. "What day is it?"

"It's Saturday night." I pull my phone from my pocket and flash it at her.

She shakes her head and backs up from me until the backs of her legs hit the bed. She slumps down and more tears leave her eyes. I go over to her and squat down so I'm looking up at her. I take her shaking hands in my own, running circles across her soft skin.

"What's wrong, babe?" I probe.

She shakes her head again. "I can't tell you."

Like hell. "Yes, you can. You can tell me anything, Roxy."

Wiping at the tears, she exhales and looks me straight in the eyes. "Three years ago, I tried to call you because I was pregnant, Wran."

I nod at her, already knowing as much. Still, I don't see what that has to do with why she's freaking out about today being Saturday. "I'm sorry I wasn't here for that. I'm even more sorry you had to go through a miscarriage alone. Hating me for that is completely understandable. Hell, I hate me for that."

Her nose wrinkles up and she shakes her head. "I didn't have a miscarriage."

What? I let go of her hand and stand, confused. Josh clearly told me she lost the baby. "I don't understand."

"When you left, I was in a bad place. Stressed out. Depressed. I turned to pills that would make me sleep so I wouldn't have to feel. The doctor said taking them wouldn't harm the baby. But one night I must have taken the wrong thing or mixed it with something else, I don't know. I don't remember. Josh said that he found me at a bar in Arlington, passed out from an overdose. He had to rush me to the hospital, and they did an emergency C-section."

I glance down at her stomach. I remember seeing the small scar on her lower stomach the night I first arrived home, but didn't think much of it. She has many scars. "Okay. Was the baby stillborn?"

Rox shakes her head, lowering it so her eyes don't meet mine. "The next morning my doctor reported that I had overdosed from cocaine and that the alcohol in my system was way above limit. Child protective services came and took her."

My heart literally stops beating as the significance of her words hits me. I have a kid in the world. I have a little girl. I get to my feet, moving away from her. She shakes her head at me, tears making rivers down her cheeks. I so desperately want to tell her not to cry—she's done enough crying—but I can't. All I can think about is the fact that my brother, my own flesh and blood, lied to me about something this damn important. He straight up told me that Rox lost the baby. He knew though. He knew she didn't. He knew that the baby was taken away. He knew three fucking years ago and didn't even have the decency to give me a damn call and tell me to get my ass home.

At that thought, I curse myself. He didn't call because he knew there was nothing I could do. I stare at the weeping girl on the bed, shaking and hurting. Rox would have been almost sixteen by the time she gave birth to my daughter.

Almost, but not. I would have been in handcuffs so fast. . . The bastard was protecting me.

I scoff.

He should have been protecting her.

I go back over to Roxy and sit next to her on the bed. I pull her over to me, hugging her head to my chest. This still makes no sense to me. Why are Saturdays so important to her?

"Saturdays?" I ask, my voice dead.

"That's the only day I get to see her," she replies into my chest.

I suck in a breath and pull back to look at Rox. "You get to see her?"

She nods. "I was supposed to get custody back on my eighteenth birthday, but they're prolonging it. And the social worker made it perfectly clear that they are watching me. Any mistake and I could lose Harley forever."

Harley? My baby's name is Harley. "Can I see her?"

"No."

I don't have time to ask her why the hell not before my phone starts ringing. My brother's name flashes across the screen and I'm tempted to throw the phone across the room. He fucking lied to me about my damn daughter.

I swipe the answer button a little too aggressively. "What the hell do you want?"

Rox flinches beside me and I do my best to calm down. I don't want to freak her out.

"Have y'all left yet?" he questions.

"No. We're packing now."

"Good. Let me know when you make it to the cabin."

As if. "Bye."

"Packing?" Rox ask me.

I nod at her. "We're going on a little vacation, babe."

CHAPTER 23

ROX

I stare at Wran as if he's lost his freaking mind. I just gave him the answers he's been asking since he stepped foot back into that apartment, and now he's trying to whoosh me away on some vacation. Nuh-uh. Not going to happen. I missed the meeting today because of him, and that's going to have dire consequences. Going away on vacation with Wran, one of the three guys Lynn thinks fathered my baby. . . I might as well give up all hope of custody.

"I'm not leaving this town," I say, deadpan.

"You must!" comes from over Wran's shoulder.

My eyes dart to Caden and I can't help but look him over again, a grimace on my face. All these years we've been at the same school and he said nothing. Absolutely fucking nothing. I turn away from him, disregarding him entirely. When I came to, I was shocked that he was who he was. Memories of that day flooded back and start mixing with things that my father had declared as truth. I was confused. I'm not confused now. Caden can kiss my butt for all I care, and dine with Hades in hell. He lied to me. Out of everyone, he lied to me.

"I'm not going away," I state again.

"Yes you are, and it's non-negotiable." Wran shuts down my argument.

I jump from the bed a bit fast and black spots dance into my vision. A sharp pain hits the back of my head, and my hand immediately flies to it. I run my finger over a large patch and inhale.

It hurts like hell.

Glancing between Cade and Wran, I ask, "What happened to my head? Why does it hurt?"

"I'll go find you some pain meds," Cade says and rushes from the room.

"Fucking pansy," Wran mumbles, and I narrow my eyes on him. He runs his hands down the front of his jeans. "You sorta fell and hit your head."

I cross my arms over my chest. "So it wasn't enough for you to grope and abuse me? You had to injure me too?"

My words come out way sharper than I intend. I honestly don't know where the courage is coming from. This isn't me. I don't talk back. Maybe sometimes but most certainly not like this. But I want him to hurt—them both to hurt—because I hurt. Something is telling me that I've lost my daughter. That I've lost my only friend. And I have a feeling I'm going to lose more.

"Rox, we are leaving Kingston tonight. Josh found the letters." His tone is serious and flat, and I know no matter what I say, he's going to get me out of this area. I should have thrown those letters away. They did nothing but torment me and keep me awake at night with new nightmares of my father coming after me and Harley. I tried to work more hours, so I wouldn't have to think about them stashed away in my closet. Tried focusing on school and relationships and being normal. Doing normal things. I supposed I thought everything would just stop, but . . . I got away from my father once; I highly doubt he's going to let me go a second time. Not when he's made it perfectly clear in those letters that I've been less than pleasing.

With reluctance, I nod. "I need to call Lynn."

Wran looks at his phone. "It's damn near midnight."

I don't care. She needs to understand that today was not my doing. I need her to let me explain not showing up today. Yeah, I've missed meetings with Harley in the past, but only on rare occasions. And I always let her know ahead of time. I can't have any of them thinking I'm neglectful.

"This is my baby," I whisper to him.

He drops the phone into my hands. "Can I at least stay in the room?"

Nodding, I quickly enter the number for Lynn, which I've memorized over the years. The line rings and rings and rings. For a moment I don't think she's going to pick up, but then the ringing cuts off and there's a click on the line.

"Hello?" Lynn answers, sounding well awake.

"Umm, Mrs. Adams?" I speak into the phone. "It's me, Roxanna."

"Roxy! Oh, thank God," she says frantically. "Are you all right, dear? Everyone's been trying to contact you all day."

Ohmygod. She sounds freaking terrified. I sit back down on the bed. "I'm fine. There was a bit of an accident."

"You've heard?"

"Heard what?" I ask, getting a bit nervous. This doesn't sound good. I glance up at Wran as Cade comes back into the room with two small white pills and a bottle of water. I really shouldn't be taking pills with my past, but my head hurts. Cade hands them over.

"She's gone!" Lynn blurts into the phone at the same time I take a drink of the water.

"What?" I shout, and sputter on the water, coughing it up. I get up from the bed and start pacing the floor. "W-what do you mean gone?"

"She was taken last night from the home. There was a note in her bed—said 'Daddy warned you.' What does that mean, Roxanna?"

Everything around me stops at her words. The phone in my hand falls to the floor and every single breath leaves my lungs. I stagger back until my knees hit the back of something and my body collapses down to the floor. This isn't happening. This isn't happening. Heart-wrenching cries leave me, and both Cade and Wran cross the room to me. They yell something—my name, I think—but I can't answer. I literally can't bring myself to respond. Images of my father with Harley flash before my very eyes. He's going to hurt her. Ohmygod. Ohmygod. Ohmygod! I shake my head to ward off the images of him trying to drown her. Of him beating her. Of him placing a hot-pressing iron on her back until her flesh bubbles and peels away. All the things he did to me.

I cry out again and begin rocking back and forth. This can't happen. This can't happen. Ohmygod, this can't happen. Everything around me blurs into visions of my father. Long tendrils snake up my neck and wrap around it, cutting my oxygen supply to none. My hands fly to my neck and I gasp for air. Frantically, I claw at the hands around my throat. More hands start shaking me. My tears flow more, and I can't stop them. I don't want to stop them. I deserve them. I'm a horrible mother. I let him take her. I knew something would happen. I knew it!

Someone grabs my hands and pins them away from my neck. I shake my head. I need to breathe. I need air. I inhale a huge gulp of oxygen but it's like a balloon is lodged in my throat. I feel something expand, but I still can't breathe. My head swims, and black blotches creep into my line of vision. I do my best to force them away. I can't go under. I have to breathe. I have to get to Harley.

Something cold splashes on my face, and suddenly air is filling my lungs. It's almost too much as I blink back the liquid.

"Jesus," Cade exclaims. He bends down and pulls me against him. "Are you okay?

A choking sob leaves my lips. "My baby."

Cade runs his hands in a circular motion on my back, trying to pacify me. It doesn't work though, and I pull away. "We'll find her. I promise."

"How do you plan on doing that?" I snap at him. Because if he has a clue how to find a man that seems to move in shadows, I would love to know so I can gut him myself.

"Do you believe Wran or I am going to let him get away with taking Harley?" Cade pulls me to my feet, and I don't answer him. I don't know what either of them will do, or can do, for that matter. Cade's been lying to me, walking the halls of Kingston High knowing who I am yet treating me like a stranger until it suited him. And well, Wran is Wran. He's more likely to go into a blind rage and not think instead of thinking reasonably. Besides, my dad is crazy. Prison made him lose a few screws. Sure, he was abusive, but this? I don't know what the letters and kidnapping is. It's not the man I knew.

"I hope your silence means you have faith in us."

I arch a brow at him. "You want me to lie like you?"

"Ouch. I've never lied to you," he replies as he leads me out of the room. "I just didn't interfere with your life. Figured if you had no memories of me, we could start over."

I roll my eyes at him. Sure, he might not have deliberately lied, but he still withheld the truth. He still used the fact that I didn't remember him to thrust his way into my life. That's lying to me.

As we walk down the stairs, I can hear Wran yelling at someone. I pause on the stairs, remembering that I was on the phone with Lynn. Darnit. I really hope he isn't yelling at her. I don't need any more on my plate. I peek up at Cade with my unanswered question. His brows pull together and his lips fall at the corner. Oh no. Wran's yelling at Lynn. I pull my hand free of Cade and bolt down the remaining stairs. My head throbs for a second, making everything spin. I grab the railing and make my way down.

I follow Wran's voice all the way to a room with burgundy walls. He doesn't notice me coming until I'm snatching the phone from his hand and looking at the screen to see who's on the other end. When I see Josh's name on the screen, I exhale. Wran is really trying to kill me. Cade finally makes it into the room, and Wran sends him a pointed grimace before snatching the phone away from me.

"I'll call you back," he sneers and then marches over to Cade. "I gave you one damn order! Get her out of here!"

"No!" I shout over at him. He's not making me leave. I'm not going to some freaking cabin to hide out like a scared little girl. "It's my dad and my daughter. I'm not leaving her survival in your hands."

Wran stomps over to me and grabs my upper arms just like he did the other night. I wince at the shot of pain that surges up my arms at his touch. It's like I've been injected with liquid nitrogen and my blood is slowly freezing. I hate it.

"Hey!" Cade yells at him.

"She's my daughter too, or did you fuck someone else?" Wran says as his eyes run up and down my body.

I pull my arm from him and my palm lands on the side of his face. The sound echoes off the walls and I see Cade slowly inching his way over to us, glaring at Wran. He's probably expecting Wran to retaliate or do something like he did last night. I don't move, though, and Cade shouldn't feel the need to protect me. Wran has never done anything like he did last night. It's the only reason I'm even talking to him now. Anyone can have a bad night. That doesn't mean I'm going to forgive him right away.

"You have no right to call Harley that. She's not your daughter. You only just found out about her."

"And whose fault is that?" Wran takes a step in my direction, fire in his eyes. "You've had weeks to inform me about her. Instead, you just kept sneaking away to Arlington with Josh. Fucking Josh! Of all people!"

Cade grabs my hand, pulling me out of Wran's line of fire. "We don't have time for this! Rox, you're coming with me." Cade shoves a piece of paper into Wran's chest. "We'll meet you in Aspen."

Cade drags me out of the room. I struggle to get away from him. There's no way I'm leaving. My daughter is here, so I'm going to be here. When we make it around the front to the stairs, I grab hold of the railing to keep him from dragging me any farther. It doesn't matter though. Cade pries my fingers from the rail and throws me over his shoulder. I pound my fist into his back.

"Let me go, you fucker!" I yell into his back, clawing at the white polo he's wearing.

Cade slaps my butt, and I can feel the heat rising to my cheeks. He did not just slap my butt.

"Wran is going to kill you for that."

"What Wran doesn't know won't hurt." He pulls a set of keys from his pocket, and I attempt to look around him. I don't see anything other than headlights shining back. A beeping sound, and then the next thing I know I'm being tossed into the back seat of a car. The. Back. Seat. Cade slams the door on me as I scurry for the handle. I pull, but it doesn't budge. He gets into the driver's seat and immediately pulls the car out of the circle drive. He catches my glare in the mirror and smirks at me.

Fucking idiot.

"Child lock," he mutters.

"Why are you doing this?" The anger is very palpable in my voice. "I'm going to get loose, and you and Wran better hope nothing happens to my baby. You think my father can be crazy, but you both haven't seen crazy."

He slams on the brakes, and I brace myself for the impact. "Rox, I've known you since you were three years old. Three! I've been in love with you since I was six years old. Do you honestly think I would do anything to you or your kid—no matter who the damn father is?"

I stare at the back of Cade's head and shake mine. I know he wouldn't, but still. . . this is my daughter we're talking about. They expect me to just run. I ran from my father as a kid. I don't want to run from my daughter. I'm already in deep crap. If anyone gives me custody after this, they are idiots. And if I'm not getting Harley back, I at least want to go down fighting. I don't want her to remember this and wonder why everyone else came to her rescue but her mother. She probably won't remember, but if she does. . .

I'm supposed to be her hero.

No one else.

"She's my daughter, Caden."

"I know, but what good are you to her if you get killed? You were unconscious thirty minutes ago. What good are you to her in your current condition? Do you have some superhuman strength to fight James?"

I don't say anything to his assumptions. They're right. I can't beat my father. Not alone. I would probably crumble the moment I laid eyes on what he's done to my sweet, sweet baby. Instead of saying anything, I sit back in my seat and buckle the belt. If anyone can get my daughter back, it'll be Wran. He's insane enough to do anything. And he made it perfectly clear how he felt about my dad. I hope he kills him. I just wish I could watch.

"Are we good?" Cade asks and begins driving again.

I nod even though it's a lie. I'm not good. I'm far, far from good. I don't think I'll ever be good again after this. And if something happens to Harley, I hope my father does find me. I hope he does kill me. There's no world I want to live in without my baby. It would only be a constant reminder of how terrible of a person I am.

"Good, we have a long drive ahead of us."

"Drive? Didn't you give Wran a ticket?"

"Yeah, but I'd be insane to take you to an airport."

I let out a huff and cross my arms like a toddler. This is ridiculous. The amount of time it will take us to get to Aspen could be spent searching for my father. What makes them think he's not going to follow us anyways? He's obviously been keeping a close eye on me since he was released. How, I don't know, but if he can sneak letters into my locker and under my bed and in other places he shouldn't be able to get to, he can figure out we're fleeing like cowards to Aspen. I mean, come on. We did have a vacation home there too.

My heart stops in my chest for the nth time tonight since waking up. My eyes find Cade's in the mirror again. "My father has a vacation home in Aspen next to your father's."

Cade nods. "Yeah, I know."

I shake my head, completely confused. Why would he be taking me to the one place my father can get easy access to? It makes no sense. "I don't understand."

"You're bait." Cade doesn't hesitate in saying this. "And he's dead. This is Wran's plan."

I gulp back and try not to freak out. This is going to go horribly, horribly wrong.

CHAPTER 24

WRAN

I step out of the cab, hitching my duffel over my shoulder and rubbing my palms together. I blow a hot breath into them to warm them. It's freezing here, but then again, it's Aspen. Supposed I should have worn something other than jeans and a long-sleeved T-shirt. Shutting the cab's door, I look up at the massive stone cabin flanked by trees on all sides. The place looks like something out of some Disney movie with the icicles twinkling like diamonds from the towering cabin. I glance over at the snow-covered trees, half expecting to see singing chipmunks or something come prancing out of the woods with a girl singing and dancing around in a dress that's in no way, shape, or form suitable for negative twenty-degree weather. When nothing happens, I pull the keys Cade gave me from my pocket and go up the stone path to the cabin. It is obvious Cade's parents have this place kept up, from the lack of snow on the pathway.

Rich. People.

If Cade listens and doesn't make any stops except for gas and piss breaks, they should arrive later tomorrow. That's a day to track down a hardware shop and lure that fucker out here. If I'm lucky, I won't need Rox as bait, but if I have to use her, I will. Fucker has my daughter. He signed his own death certificate.

I stride inside the massive cabin, not taking it in, and head up the stairs. All the spare bedrooms are supposed to be on this floor. I need some sleep. While I don't want to shut my eyes until I have Harley back. I need to be well rested to deal with James fucking Raine. I haven't slept since yesterday morning, and there's no way I'm putting Rox and our child in danger due to lack of sleep. A smart man would have just slept on the plane ride, but I was far too busy researching ways to dismember a human body in the most torturous ways ever. And trust me, I found some pretty gruesome ways to make him pay. Man's gonna wish he never murdered that nanny and ruined my life. . . or took my child.

I open the first door I get to and frown at the all-white interior. If the decorator was going for a winter wonderland feel, they achieved their goal. Too bad it's unlivable. One foot inside that room and my boots would turn this snow-white setting into a sloshy snow setting. Something tells me Cade's parents would be less than pleased to vacation here if their room looks like the day after fresh snowfall. Then again, I'm pretty sure they have a cleaning service come and make the cabin all cozy.

I close the door and keep on walking until I find another room. It's better than the last. I go inside, slamming the heavy door behind me. It doesn't even make a click upon closing. Shaking my head, I go over to the oak dresser and lay my duffel on top, unzipping it. I pull out a set of knives and arrange them on the dresser top. Following that, I take out a gun. I never thought I'd have to use a gun before going into the military. My fists were always my friends. The one thing my father taught me before our lives went to shit was that real men use their fists. If you have to settle for other ways of solving your problems, you're nothing more than a fucking pansy. I guess I'm a pansy. James Raine needs to be dealt with permanently, and unfortunately handling him like a real man isn't going to get the job done. If prison didn't change him, I highly doubt duking it out like grown men will. Besides, he has my daughter.

My.

Fucking.

Daughter.

There's no way I'm playing fair.

Yanking out the black pants and hoodie I brought as a change of clothes, I shove them in one of the drawers. I have a daughter. The idea of that still hasn't dawned on me. Yeah, for nearly a week I used booze to mourn a child lost, but I never actually thought that I had one. Alive. Breathing. Living.

I let myself truly think about everything Rox told me before leaving. Suddenly my mouth is very dry, and I can't keep myself from clenching my jaw. I take a step away from the dresser, and then another and another, until the backs of my legs hit the bed frame. Rounding the bed, I collapse back onto the mattress and bring my hands up to cover my face. Rox lost our child. Rox didn't even tell me I had a fucking child. None of the messages she left me during the months after my departure even remotely sounded like her secret was this monumental.

Wran, I know you don't want to talk to me, but I need you. S–something happened. I did something bad. I–I don't know what to do. I'm scared. Please, please call me. Text me. Anything, please. I just need to hear you.

How the hell am I supposed to know she's pregnant from that shit? Rox doing something bad could have meant she used purple instead of blue to paint a sky. I know saying "I'm pregnant" over the phone is no way to tell anyone such news, but I was gone. G–O–N–E! In a different state. Those words would have at least made me think differently. AWOL or no AWOL, I would have found a way to come back for her if I had only known.

"Fuck!" I yell at nothing in particular.

She let our child get taken by family services.

And now she won't even let me see Harley.

This isn't happening. Rox isn't keeping my own child from me. I have no idea what I did to make her want to keep Harley from me, but it's not happening. I will fight her tooth and nail if I have to. I don't want to, but . . . I want my daughter. I want a little girl that looks like Rox. Minus the short blue pixie hair. God, I bet she's adorable. I wonder if she has Rox's eyes. I hope so. Rox has the most gorgeous eyes.

I inhale and sit up on the bed. Why the hell am I thinking about this shit? Family services have legal custody of her. They have Harley. I doubt getting her back is going to be as easy as Rox following orders. Hell, her birthday was last month and still no Harley. Maybe there's something I could do. I don't know what. This is something I would need to hire a lawyer for. One thing's for certain: I'm getting our daughter back—and I'm getting my girl too. We'll be a family. A real family. One of those damn Stepford families with white picket fences and family dinners every night. I will make Rox's Neverland a reality if it's the last thing I accomplish.

With a yawn, I lie back on the bed and let my mind drift back to the little girl with big purple eyes and long brunette hair, skin so fair it could be painted on as a canvas. I smile at that image and yawn again. I have a daughter. James might have her, but Daddy is coming.

"I promise," I mutter as my vision slowly fades to black.

When I wake, half the day is gone. The sky has faded from a bright blue to a pinkish orange and the temperature has dropped dramatically. As much as I want to stay in this cabin and not face the outdoors of Aspen, I need supplies. I can't very well kill a man with my bare hands without suffering imprisonment. No, I need supplies. I pat my pockets down for my phone, but when I don't feel it, I get up and head over to the dresser. It's lying on top, next to my empty duffel. Grabbing the phone, I inhale at the number of messages left from Josh, Rox, and even that fucker Cade. I guess I was more tired than I thought.

I input my code and reply to a few of the messages, assuring everyone that I made it to Aspen in one piece. Truthfully, unless the plane had crashed, I was probably safer than them driving up snow-covered ice mountains. I don't wait for anyone to respond to the messages before I have the browser open and am searching for the closest hardware store. There's one a few miles from here—farther than I would consider close, but this isn't Kingston. I can't expect everything to be at my fingertips.

Calling a cab, I give them the address and wait. It doesn't take any time at all for the cab to pull up to the stone pathway. I stomp out of the huge house, arms wound tightly around my T-shirt-and-jean-clad body, and march up to the cab just as a pudgy, balding man rushes out and rounds the car to the backside. He looks up at the massive cabin that belongs on the cover of some magazine and then at me with a wide-ass grin. If he thinks I'm tipping him because I just so happen to be at a cabin that could belong to Tom fucking Cruise, he's sorely mistaken.

The guy opens the back door for me, the grin not slipping from his crusty lips, and I hop inside the car. At least it's warm. The driver wobbles back around to the driver's seat and gets inside as well. He turns around to face me. I frown at him.

"Where to, sir?" he asks, turning back around when he finally gets the hint that I'm not in the mood for his overly pleasing personality.

"Closest hardware store, and then somewhere to get a coat." I really should have brought a damn coat. Who travels to Aspen and forgets to grab a coat?

"Of course, sir!"

I shake my head at the man, but he doesn't notice. Wonder if he knew I didn't own this cabin would he still be cheesing and calling me sir? Ha, hell no. He probably wouldn't even be talking to me.

The twenty-minute drive to the hardware store is the most unbearable thing I have ever experienced while in the back of a car. The man asks more questions than a toddler hyped up on sugar sticks. For the most part I didn't say anything to him, but then he asked why I was there and I told him the truth. I was here to kill a man. Of course he thought I was joking. I wish I was joking. Premeditated murder. What's that? Life in prison? Hell, it would be worth it, but if this is done right and if Josh has my back as he claims, everything should go smoothly.

I walk around the hardware store until an assistant comes my way. She's petite with long blond hair and bright brown eyes. She's wearing a polo with the store name on it across her modest chest. Another time and place, I would have been all over her. She's just my type: not Rox. Now, the sight of her proves just how pussy-whipped I really am. My mind heads to Rox, and I frown. The girl comes to a stop in front of me and her cheery demeanor dwarfs when she sees the grimace on my face.

"Can I help you?" she questions, trying to make her tone as approachable as possible, even though her body is literally craning away from me.

Doing my damnedest, I force a tiny smile out for the girl. "Yeah, I need supplies."

She relaxes a little, but not much. I can still see the wary way her eyes search my face, never leaving. Most women examine me from head to toe. That's not me being a cocky douche, but it's the truth. This girl is not doing that. At least she is smart. At the moment, I'm no one anyone should be checking out.

"What kind of supplies?"

"A hammer, saw, zip ties, duct tape, and if you sell lye, I need that as well." I honestly don't know what I plan on doing to James Raine at this point. Although I'm pretty sure I could have some fun with the lye.

"Doing some spring cleaning?"

I give her a grin and shake my head. "Nope."

Her fake-as-fuck tan goes as white as the snow outside, and that makes me want to grin again. I probably should have said yeah. She turns away from me and heads down aisle eight. I follow her as she points to the zip ties. The duct tape is in the same aisle. We then pick up the hammer and saw. She comes to a stop at aisle fifteen and turns toward me. Her eyes stay trained on the floor.

"I'll have to get a manager to get the . . . um lye. Do you need anything else?"

I shake my head. The girl doesn't even glance up at me before she sprints away. I could have nodded yeah, but oh well. I probably would be trying to get the fuck away too if someone came asking for the items I'm asking for. I guess it's good I didn't ask for sulfuric acid. Research said that it breaks down bones and teeth, but I don't think I'll be going that far.

Blondie comes back in a matter of minutes with a tall, lanky guy in a light blue shirt with the company's name on it. He gives me a smile; then his eyes drop to the items in my cart. He surveys them and then smiles again.

"Miss Jamison here said you were in need of some lye?" His statement comes out sounding like a question. Understandable, but if he really wants to know what I need with lye and a saw and a hammer and duct tape and fucking zip ties, all he has to do is ask. I won't give him the correct answer, but at least it would show that he has a set of balls—no matter how small.

"I do." I glance over the guy's shoulder to the girl and give her a smirk. She shrinks farther behind the man. If only they knew what kind of people were really in this world, they wouldn't be asking me if I'm one of them. Sure, I want vengeance, but I'm not a bad man. James fucking Raine is who they should fear.

"Normal people don't come in here asking for that. May I ask what you plan to do with it?"

I stare the man straight in the eyes, not giving him a reason to think I have nefarious means in mind. "My girl makes soap. Lye is a main ingredient."

"There's a craft store not far from here."

I laugh. Sucker thinks I'm a sucker. "Heard you sell it by the pound. She has a big order." I honestly don't know if they sell it by the pound, but it sounds like a decent argument.

The manager narrows his eyes on me and tilts his head to the items in my cart. "What's with all that?"

I grab the zip ties out of the small cart. "My girl has a kinky side." If I could, I would laugh. There's no way Rox would let anyone tie her up. Make her helpless. I take the saw out. "I'm staying at a cabin close to the resort. We need wood for the fireplace. Now can I buy the lye or not?"

The man lets out a deep breath and gives me a jerky nod. Of course he's going to sell me the stuff. I would have been more surprised if he had turned me away. He turns and marches to the back of the building; I follow. He goes inside a door and then comes out with a big white bag. He has on blue rubber gloves.

"How much do you need?"

I have no clue. Enough to harm a grown man, but not enough to do serious damage. I want to do that personally. "Three pounds."

Yeah, that should be enough. Probably too much for what I plan to use it for, but at least I have some if I ever need it again. I doubt I will. I'm not this man. Or rather, I don't think I'm this man. I don't want to kill people. I never thought I could be a murderer, but something needs to be done with Roxy's father. Someone needs to show him that he can't harm people and get away with it. Someone needs to punish him for kidnapping my daughter and hurting my girl. For giving her nightmares and marring her beautiful skin. Now's my chance to do what I vowed as a child. If I get rid of James Raine, all the things Rox suffered at my hands will seem so insignificant when she finds out. And she will find out. I can't jump back into a relationship without letting her know everything. Not now that I know we have Harley.

The man hands me a carefully sealed bag with white powder inside of it. A wave of guilt washes over me at the sight of it. This is happening. This is really fuckin' happening. I place the bag in the cart and head to the checkout counter. I look over my shoulder to the manager, whose eyes don't leave me. I suppose some part of me was hoping on some level that the dude would turn me away. That he would say he didn't have any lye, and I could leave the store being the same man that entered. But he didn't, and I'm not. I have the shit and now there's nothing keeping me from finishing the job when the time comes. Nothing but the fact that some part of me doesn't want to be a damn killer. How is Rox going to love someone like that? How can she love a murderer?

Once checked out, I head back out to the cab and get inside. The chatty driver doesn't utter a word as he drives off and heads somewhere to get me a coat. My phone buzzes in my jeans pocket. Rox's name flashes across the screen, and I can't help but look down at the blue bag with my purchases. She can't know. She's most likely just checking in again, although I have no clue why. If I were her, I wouldn't want to speak to me for a while. Not after I hurt her. But she is calling me. That's good. Maybe my apology back at Cade's place helped the situation.

I slide the call button to the right. "Rox?"

"Wran," she says back.

"You okay?" I probe when she says nothing more. "Fucker didn't wreck the car, did he?"

"Caden can drive just fine," she hisses into the phone.

Caden? Jesus. She's calling him that now.

Fuck!

It doesn't mean anything. She's still mine. "Okay, what's up then?"

"Just wanted to let you know that we are pulling into a motel for the rest of the night."

I pull my phone from my ear and look at it. It's not even that late. Cade still has plenty of time to drive. "Put Cade on."

"No. He's getting us a room."

A room? As in singular? "No! If he lays one finger on you—"

"If he lays a finger on me it will be because I want him to. Not because you tell him he can't." She cuts me off, and I have no words. If he so much as runs a finger through her hair, I will cut his hand off.

"You are mine, Roxanna. Mine. Your child is mine. Your body is mine. Your heart is mine. You know it, and I know it. You might be upset at me right now, but it will fuckin' pass. Don't use him to hurt me."

"It's not fair." Her voice is barely a whisper over the phone.

"What's not fair?"

"I remember how I felt for Caden, but now I have all the memories of us, and I hate it. We could have been something great, but the memories of a five-year-old hold nothing to ours. I feel like I'm betraying him, Wran."

"You were a kid, Rox. And yeah, you and Cade could have been something great. You weren't. You're not betraying him, and he can't hold a childhood crush against you. You will only be betraying yourself if you go down that road out of obligation."

There's a sniffle on the line, and I hate that I can't soothe her. I roll my eyes shut and slump forward in the seat, my seatbelt restraining me a little. I run my hand through my short hair.

"And us?" she whispers. "I'm just supposed to forget three years of pain?"

I shake my head, until I realize she can't see me. I don't want her to forget I hurt her. I don't want her to be one of those girls that go right back to a guy just because he showed back up, even if that's what I'm basically asking her to do. "No, Roxanna. I don't want you to forget that I hurt you, because I did. That doesn't change the fact that we were always meant to be together. You're my lost girl, and I'm always goin' to be your Peter Pan. Don't forget, but remember why we're so good together."

Her sniffling has turned into full-on sobs. "I love you," she confesses through her sobs. "I love you so, so much."

"And I love you." The cab comes to a stop in front of an outlet mall, and I let out a sigh. "I have to go, but we'll talk more tomorrow. I promise."

"Okay."

She doesn't hang up the phone, so I end the call. Fuck! I hate this shit. I should have fought to ride in the car with them rather than take a damn plane. The cab driver turns around and looks at me, that stupid grin back on his face. I so wish I could punch it off, but he's my ride back to the cabin.

"Your girl, I take it?" he asks.

I frown at the fucker. "It's not polite to listen in on people's conver-fuckin'-sations."

"Oh! I just wanted to let you know that we're here. But hey, as long as I'm on the clock, I get paid."

I shake my head at the fucker and get out of the cab. The sooner I get some clothes and get back to the cabin, the sooner the night will be over, and I will be back with Rox.

CHAPTER 25

ROX

Cade strides back over to the car, holding out a key. Neither one of us thought it would be a good idea to drive throughout the night like Wran planned for Cade to do. He opens the car door, finally letting me out, and smirks at me. I grab the key from his hand and read the room number. After playing Sleeping Beauty, I don't really want to go to bed. Cade, however, could probably use some sleep.

Walking up behind me, Cade drapes an arm over my shoulder and pulls me close. I look up at him, and I can't help the grin that spreads across my lips. I can't believe I ever forgot him. Caden was my brother's friend, but all three of us were inseparable. We were the three musketeers if there ever were any.

"How are you feeling?" Cade asks, taking the key from my hand as we stop in front of a red door with peeling paint.

We step inside, and I visibly relax when I see two beds. Sharing a bed with Cade wouldn't be a terrible idea, but I meant what I told Wran on the phone. I do love him. And I do love Cade—or rather the Caden from my childhood memories. Nothing is making much sense to me. While I can believe the boy I knew could turn into the guy that's standing before me now, I can't believe that the boy I knew would think it was okay to mess with my feelings. If that's even what's been going on.

"I'm fine," I tell him as I look around the crappy motel room. It has old, stained wallpaper that looks like it's been here since the seventies. There's no TV, which I was kind of hoping for. It's Sunday, and I don't really want to miss my share of reality TV. Other people's drama keeps me from worrying about my own.

"Are you really?" He glances down at me tucked underneath his arm. "You can talk to me about anything."

I look up at him, his messy blond hair looking even more disheveled. "I don't know if I can. I mean, yesterday you were Cade, and now you are Caden."

"They're the same person, Roxy."

I shake my head. To him they are the same people. To me . . . I don't know. It feels different. Pulling away from him, I go over to the bed that's farthest from the door. I hesitate a moment about sitting down before I finally do. With everything that's going on in my life, sitting on a crappy mattress in a crappy motel is the least of my problems. Cade comes over and sits in front of me on his bed. He takes my hand and entwines our fingers. I immediately pull our hands free.

"I can't hold your hand now?" he asks me, disappointed. The last thing I want is to disappoint him, but I don't know how to be his friend now that I know the truth. Now that I'm putting the truths together in my head and nothing is making any sense. My father told me that my mom and brother died in a plane crash, but I clearly remember them dying in a car accident with me in the car. Unless I'm re-membering it wrong or something. And Caden is missing from my memories for the entire year afterward. I don't know what to believe, even if he did tell me everything.

"I think it means something different to you than it does to me," I mutter to him. I know it means more to him. And I don't want to feel guilty for not feeling the way he wants me to feel.

"You're right. It does mean more to me. You have your memories back. That means you remember what we were like. I'm hoping that means we can move forward."

I shake my head at him, thinking back to when we were five. We did everything together, to my brother's dislike. He was always so sweet to me when my brother wasn't around, always complimenting the dresses and giving me candy and touching my hair. It was all so . . . sweet, but we were five and it didn't matter. "Caden . . . we were kids."

He shakes his own head. "Don't do that. Don't disregard what I know you know we felt for each other. Yes, we were kids, but kids love too."

"I'm in love with Wran. I will always be in love with Wran. He's my daughter's father." I try to make myself as clear as possible. I don't want to hurt Cade, but we are not kids anymore. He's not pulling my hair and then apologizing behind my brother's back.

"You don't think I know that he's Harley's father? That doesn't mean you have to be with him. You made a mistake, you can—"

A mistake?

I spring up from the bed, hands on my hips. "Harley is not a fucking mistake!"

His eyes get wide as he gets to his feet as well, running his hands over his already mussed hair. "That's not what I meant and you know it."

"I had sex with a guy I love. That's not a mistake either. I will never consider being with Wran a mistake," I shout at him, letting my frustration out. "Why are we even having this conversation?"

"Because I love you!"

I look away from him, not wanting to hear this. I don't need to hear that he loves me. It won't change anything. I love Wran. I'm going to be with Wran. Maybe not right away. Let's face it, we both have crap to figure out, but one day, Wran will be my end. He and I will have a happy, normal, safe life with our daughter.

"I love you," Cade says again, calmer. "I know you have feelings for me too. If he hadn't come back, we would be together right now. You said so yourself. Just because he's

Harley's father doesn't mean you have to be with him. I can be her father. I will love her like she's mine. I will give you anything you want. I will protect you, Roxanna. I messed up when we were kids. I let your father hurt you and I let mine pull me away after the crash, but I will never allow that again."

I gape at him, eyes wide with shock. Of course I knew his feelings ran deep, but not this deep. That's intense. It's too much. I step away from him, bumping into the cheap metal bedframe, but he eliminates all the space between us. Cade takes hold of my hips and pulls me to him, kissing the top of my head.

"Give me tonight. Let me prove that I'm the right man for you and the right father for Harley."

I shake my head against his chest. Even if I wanted to consider his words, I wouldn't. We're freaking teenagers, for crying out loud. He shouldn't be talking about being a father to another man's child. He has his whole life ahead of him. He has his football scholarship to some big school where he can study whatever he wants. My future might have been decided for me when I was fifteen, but I would never wish this on my worst enemy. God knows I would do just about anything to make Claire suffer, but this is too much for any person.

"No," I whisper into his chest. "I don't want you in that way. I'm sorry, Cade."

His hands fall from my hips, and I can feel the dejection running throughout him. I hate myself for this, but he needed to hear it. I had no choice but to be as blunt as possible. If I would have said yes, what type of life would he have had? Being with a girl that clearly wants someone else? Raising a child that is not his own—given I get her back once this mess is over? He would grow to resent me. I would rather hurt him a little now than for him to resent me forever. He will understand one day. I know it.

"We should probably get some sleep. We have a long drive in the morning," he utters, voice free of any emotions. Without waiting for an answer, he turns from me and drops to the bed, facing the only window in the room so he doesn't have to face me. He doesn't even bother to turn off the light. Going over to the light switch, I flick it off and submerge us into darkness and then return to my bed. I sink down onto the uncomfortable mattress and close my eyes in order to force sleep to come.

"I told you not to go out that damn door!" Daddy screams down at me. He grabs my arm and yanks me hard to him. "Look at you! Look at you! Filthy brat!"

Tears stream down my face and I can't stop them this time. I know if I cry it will be worse, but I can't help it. "Sorry, Daddy. I won't go outside anymore."

I didn't try to get my dress dirty. I just wanted to see my brother again. Daddy said I will, but he won't take me to see him. Daddy yanks at the sleeves of my dress and a loud ripping sound echoes around me. I pull the sleeves back up, but my hands are yanked away. Daddy glares at me with mean eyes and I stop touching the sleeves. He shoves me around and unzips the back of the dress. It falls to the floor and I cry some more. I really, really like that dress. Mommy gave it to me last year for my birthday. Daddy looks down at me in my underwear. My legs are covered in mud from the puddles outside. My hair is wet. I know Daddy doesn't like when my hair is wet. The last time it got wet, he said I looked like a rat and should be treated like one. He put me in the cage with Lillie. Ms. Wells got me out when Daddy went to sleep, and she let me cry all night.

"You look just like your mother," he whispers in my ear. "I hope you look like her when you're older."

"Mommy was pretty," I tell him, my tears drying up at his compliment. Daddy hasn't talked about Mommy since the accident. He says it's bad to talk about the dead. We should only focus on the living.

"Your mommy was really pretty." He grips my arm again. "Too bad you killed her."

He yanks my arm harder and starts pulling me toward the downstairs bathroom that Ms. Wells uses when she stays here. He turns on the water, and I know it's hot from the steam coming off it. I shake my head at him. I want to tell him no, but the words won't leave my mouth. Speaking out of turn will make it worse. When the tub is full of water, he turns it off and stands up. He glares down at me.

Then he's grabbing me.

I scream as soon as my feet touch the hot water, but then I can't scream anymore. Daddy shoves my head under the water, and I cough and cough and cough and I claw at my daddy's hand. He pulls me up from the water and I gasp for air. I don't take in enough before Daddy is pushing me back under the water again. Over and over and over he punishes me.

"Stop that fucking crying, you little cunt!" he screams when he brings me back up for air.

"I'm sorry, I'm sorry, I'm sorry," I weep, clutching onto the sleeve of his black suit jacket. "Please don't do that again."

"Are you going to go outside in the rain again?" he asks me.

I shake my head.

"Are you going to get dirty like a boy again?"

I shake my head again.

"Good." He pulls me out of the hot water and wraps a big fluffy towel around me. "Now give Daddy a kiss and go to your room."

I stare at my daddy for a long time, scared to move. I don't want to go back in the water. When his smile starts to leave his mouth, I lean forward and give Daddy a kiss on his mouth like Mommy used to do. Like Daddy taught me to do after Mommy died. I pull back and Daddy smiles at me before kissing the top of my head like he used to do before the accident.

"Now be a good girl and go to sleep."

I nod and race out of the bathroom and up the stairs to my room. I close the door and head toward my closet. I don't know why I go there, but I do. I crawl behind the rows of pretty dresses and close my eyes. Things will get better when I get a new mommy. That's what Ms. Wells says. All Daddy needs is a new mommy to make things better.

Shouting erupts around me, and I'm violently pulled awake. I blink away the sleep to focus on Cade's panicked face. His brows pull together as he says something. I watch his mouth, but his words aren't entering my ears.

Cade shakes me again. "Breathe, Rox. Breathe!"

I shake my head at him, not understanding. I am breathing.

"Inhale, Rox. Inhale. Please," he shouts at me, and I do as he asks. He nods, but his face doesn't relax. "Dammit, Rox! I thought you were dying."

"I–I'm fine," I hoarsely whisper. My hand goes to my throat, and memories of my father shoving me under boiling water come rushing back to me. He did that to me. He really did that to me. I have no clue why I remember some things and others are just now coming back to me, but this . . . I don't want to remember this.

"What were you dreaming about?" Cade runs a hand over my hair and pulls me to him when I don't answer. I don't want him to know. I don't want anyone to know the horrid things that man did to me. I don't want anyone to look at me like I'm some broken girl. My father being a murderer is bad enough. Lynn said so. Wran even said so. No one needs to know he did things . . . things that no father should do to a child.

I shake my head at Cade and lie back down on the bed. He lies beside me and pulls my head to his chest. This wonderful, wonderful boy.

"You don't have to tell me." Cade whispers and rubs soothing circles on my back. "He will pay for everything he's ever done to you."

I tilt my head up to see his face, but he's not looking at me. His gaze is on the stained ceiling. Pulling my eyes away from him, I bring my knees up. Sleep isn't going to come again tonight. At least not for me. I start to rise from the bed, but Cade's arms tighten around me and he holds me in place.

"Stay. I know I'm not Wran, but . . ."

He trails off, but he doesn't need to say more. He will be here for me in any way I need. The problem is that I don't know what I need. I feel like I don't know anything anymore. My eyes lift to him again, and this time he's staring at me. There's nothing in his eyes though. No hope. No faith. Nothing. They're just blank. Like someone came and destroyed everything that made Cade Cade. Those aren't the eyes I've become used to. Those aren't the eyes of my Cade, and I hate myself for stealing all his passion away.

Rising up on my elbow, I push all thoughts of the dreams and resurfacing memories to the back of my mind. "I'm sorry."

He frowns at me. "Don't be. Never be sorry for anything, Rox."

I lean down so that our faces are so close. I feel his peppermint breath against my cheeks. My eyes flick across his face, telling myself that this is right. If it will bring back the light to his eyes, it can't be bad. Even if it feels like someone is taking a saw to my heart and cutting it into pieces. Wran will never have to know that I'm doing this. And Cade will be happy again. My eyes flick down to his mouth, and I tilt my head forward. Cade's eyes go to my mouth as well, and I can see the debate on his face. He wants this. I know he does. My mouth barely brushes his before bile rushes up my throat. I sit up and shake my head. I can't do this. I can't betray Wran. Not even to make my friend feel better.

Tears stream down my cheeks and I don't wipe them away. I don't want to pretend to be strong anymore. I've been pretending since I was fifteen, and I'm tired. I'm so, so tired. Sobs rip from my throat, and this time, I let everything out. I let the pain of watching Wran walk away from me surface. I let the agony of watching Lynn take my baby away come forth. I let the ache of everything my father did to me show. I can't hide it anymore. I can't hold it in any longer.

Cade wraps a blanket around me and pulls me to his chest, letting me cry into him. "It's okay, Roxanna. It's okay. You don't have to be so strong. You don't have to do anything you don't want to do. I'm here for you in whatever way you need me. And if you only want a friend, then you have a friend."

That only makes me wail harder into him. I don't deserve him. I've done nothing but hurt him tonight after he's done nothing but help. I cry and cry and cry until I fall into a deep, dreamless sleep.

CHAPTER 26

ROX

It's super early when we check out in the morning. Cade only gives me enough time to shower before we're in the lobby and turning in the key. The entire drive, neither one of us mention the prior night. We just sit in the car in silence and listen to the radio. We make one stop to fill up the tank and for me to call Lynn. She hasn't heard anything about Harley's whereabouts, but she assures me that the cops are keeping an eye out for my father. That does nothing to relieve me. If my father doesn't want to be found, he won't be. That's the flaw I see in this so-called plan Wran has come up with. My father is not stupid. He owned one of the top firms in the state, getting criminals that would normally be convicted for heinous crimes off scot-free. I'm sure he's figured out I'm not in Kingston anymore. When he sees that Cade and Wran are also gone, he's going to put things together, and he's not going to like it.

We make it to the cabin in record time, even with our impromptu night at the motel. Wran walks out of the front door in a huge puffer coat just as the car comes to a stop. I don't wait a second before opening the door and running up to him. He circles his arms around me, and I swear he sniffs my hair. I don't care. I throw my arms around his neck, clinging to him with all my strength. I don't think I told him I forgave him before he left Cade's house Saturday night. But I do. I forgive him.

Wran's hands make their way up to my cheeks and his eyes search my face. "I missed you."

I grin up at him. "I missed you too. And I'm sorry, for yelling at you Saturday night. I'm so, so sorry."

"Don't apologize. I understand. I might not like it, but I understand."

A car door shuts behind us and I turn around to see Cade standing by the car glaring at Wran. His eyes fall to mine and that same hollowness I saw in his eyes last night is back. I pull out of Wran's arms and curse myself for not thinking. Cade comes over to us and looks back and forth between Wran and me before settling on Wran.

"You win," he states. Cade doesn't wait on a response from Wran and goes inside the cabin.

A small smile plays on Wran's lips and he folds his arms back around me, dragging me up the stone pathway with him. "What happened in that motel?"

"I kissed him," I admit. "Then I cried myself to sleep in his arms."

"Then why is he giving up so easily?"

I stop walking and wait on him to turn to me. When he does, I take hold of his gloved hands. "Because it didn't matter. I love him, Wran. I do. But the love I feel for him doesn't compare to the love I hold for you. I realized that last night after we talked. He knows it too."

With a grin on his perfect face, Wran pulls me flush against him. My mind goes back to Friday night, but I shove that moment out of my head. That wasn't my Wran. His mouth comes down against mine, and he's kissing me. Once, twice, three times. It's so gentle. Almost as if he's not kissing me at all, but the scorching heat rising inside reassures me that this isn't a trick of the mind. He's kissing me. And it's the most amazing thing ever. I've kissed Wran plenty of times in the past, but it has never felt like this. Like he's drawing something out of me. Like we fit together with precision. I rise to my toes and open my mouth fully to him, taking in everything. The feel of stubble on his chin. The smell of salt and fresh linen. His scent. His everything.

Wran pulls from the kiss, eyes trained solely on mine. "I'm never leaving you again. I promise. You're my forever."

"And you're my Neverland."

A throat clears and we both turn to find Cade watching us with a stone-cold expression. If glares could kill, I'm sure I would be six feet under right now. I squeeze my eyes shut and exhale. Cade will get over this. Over me. And when he does, he will realize that we were never going to work. Not because my love for Wran is stronger, but because Wran and

I know what to expect from each other. Cade isn't the boy I once knew. I'm not the girl he once knew.

"Don't you have a plan to start executing?" Cade scoffs at Wran.

A shiver runs through me at the icy tone of Cade's voice. He's definitely going to need some time to get over this. "Cade?"

I take a step in his direction, but he holds up a hand to stop me. "Don't, Roxy. I'm fine. I know where the line has been drawn. Just give me time."

I nod and he marches back inside his cabin. The air around me and Wran whooshes, and I wrap my arms around my body. We didn't bring much with us, but I'm starting to think the coat I'm wearing isn't enough for the Aspen weather. Wran takes off his coat and drapes it over my shoulders. It's about four sizes too big and it's heavy. The coat's warm though.

Wran places a hand on the small of my back and ushers me inside the cabin. I glance around, highly expecting to see more stuffed animals hanging on the walls, but there are none. Taking my hand, Wran pulls me up the stairs and into a room. Nothing about his room screams lived in besides the duffel on a dresser and bags on the floor. Wran shuts the door and locks it, returning to me.

"I've been waiting forever to have you again. I'm not letting some jealous fuck come between us."

He grips me by my waist and pulls me up against him. My legs coil around him as his mouth slams against mine.

This kiss is nothing like the one we shared moments ago. No, it's urgent and thirsty. Wran's kissing me like he's been walking a desert for three years and now he's finally made it to a lake where he can quench his thirst. I kiss him back with just as much hunger. Honestly, I've been waiting for this. Even when I hated him with a passion, Wran was still the only person I ever thought about doing this with. Cade . . . Cade was a crush. This . . . ohmygod, this is love. Or lust. I don't care. I just want him so, so much.

Wran turns us around, and we go falling to the bed. A squeal leaves me, but it quickly turns into something else when Wran's mouth explores more of me. I can't keep the sounds inside, and I'm hating that. Cade is in this cabin. I'm pretty sure he can hear, and that sucks.

"Wran," I say around the pleasurable sounds echoing throughout the room. "We have to stop."

His hands snakes underneath my sweater, and I gasp out. "I don't want to stop."

Neither do I, but we have to. "Cade is downstairs."

Wran's hand stills on my skin. It's almost unbearable. "Fuck Cade. Let him hear. It's the best he's gonna get."

I shake my head at Wran and push him back. "He's my friend. Besides, we're not here for this."

A loud, unpleasurable sound leaves Wran's lips, and it makes me smile. He gets up from the bed, putting me at eye level with his, um, friend, and I blush. I have suffered childbirth, yet even thinking about this makes me feel like the most inexperienced person alive. I'm not, but still. My eyes travel up Wran's toned torso, only to find him smirking at me. He's gorgeous. I'm not going to pretend I don't think so. I just wish he wouldn't smile at me like that.

I get up from the bed and grab his hand, pulling him behind me. We make our way down the stairs. My phone dings in my pocket and I stop on the last stair to check. It could be Lynn with an update. Surely, she must know something by now. It's Monday and my daughter has been missing since Saturday. It isn't a text from Lynn, though. It's a number I don't know. I click on the message and a picture of my daughter appears. She's smiling and playing with dolls in a pink room. She has on a cutesy yellow dress with matching bows in her hair. The picture would look so normal if the man in the photo didn't bring my nightmares to the forefront of my mind.

He looks different from what I remember. Older. More tired. Yet at the same time he looks as ageless as ever. The only sign that he's even aged is the gray hair along his temples and peppered throughout a beard. My legs start to wobble, and I use the railing to ease myself down on the step. He has her. He really has my baby. A letter is one thing. The cops not being able to find her is one thing. Seeing her in a picture with the man that made me run away from everything is a whole other thing. And he's smiling. Ohmygod, he's smiling. Like having her is some sick joke or something.

Wran yanks the phone from my hand and looks down at the photo. He looks at me for a long moment and then at the photo again. This is not how I wanted him to see Harley for the first time. Sure, the photo could be worse. My father could have sent a photo of her arm broken or her dress ripped open or a number of things, but he chose to send one of her happy and smiling and playing. I don't know which is worse.

Pressing a button, Wran brings the phone to his ear. "Where the fuck is she?" he growls into the phone, and I'm so glad I'm not on the receiving end of the line.

Cade comes rushing over to us from wherever he was before and stares down at me. He starts to ease down beside me, but I shake my head. I'm fine. I'm completely fine. I'm not going to break down. Not this time. I get up from my seat on the stairs and reach my hand out for the phone. This is my father. I should be the one dealing with this crap.

Wran turns his back to me and continues listening to whatever my father is saying. I round him to get a better view. If I can't hear my father's end of the conversation, at least I can read Wran's face.

His nostrils flare. "You will never speak to her again."

Okay, so he's asking for me? I hold out my hand again. If he wants me, then I will talk. I will do whatever he wants to get Harley back.

"You touch a fucking hair on her head, and I will make your death even more painful than I already planned!"

My dad must have found that funny because I can clearly hear laughing coming from the phone. Wran's hand clenches against the phone as the laughter comes to a stop.

His jaw clenches shut and then there is another ding on my phone. Wran pulls it from his ear and glances down at the new photo on the screen. I gasp when I see my father's tongue pressed into the side of Harley's neck. Vomit rises, and this time, it comes. I barf all over the wood floors. When nothing more than dry heaves leave me, I glance up at Wran, my phone no longer in his hand. I glance to where his eyes remain on the wall across from us, my phone in pieces. How are we supposed to contact him now? Or Lynn? Or anyone?

"Why did you do that?" I scream at him. "That was proof! You should have let me talk to him!"

Wran's glare moves to me. "You will never speak to that man again."

"How the hell am I supposed to get my daughter back now?"

"I will get our daughter back. Don't you worry," Wran says.

"How?"

Wran looks over my shoulder to where Cade stands. "He says Roxy will know where to find him, which leads me to believe he's not at the cabin. That would be too obvious. Where else here in Aspen would he be?"

Cade shrugs his shoulders. He only spent time at the cabin with us. He doesn't know my family as well as Wran seems to think. Our families were close, but not that close. There's only one other place here in Aspen that would hold a pink room and some of my toddler clothes, and I'm not telling Wran. He's too manic. If my dad wants to talk to me, he will get me. I swipe my hand across my mouth, still feeling remnants of the vomit, and walk away from the guys. I need my daughter back. I need to put an end to all of this mess.

"I'm going for a walk," I announce, and step aside the vomit.

Wran grabs hold of my arm and pulls me back.

"Dude!" Cade yells at him. "You don't have to be so rough."

Wran ignores him and glares at me. "You're not going anywhere by yourself." He turns to Cade and shoves me in his direction. "Take her to a room and lock her inside."

"I thought she was bait. Isn't that why we're here?" Cade asks him, holding me close to his body.

"The plan has changed. I'm not letting Rox anywhere near that fucker."

Cade nods like an obedient dog and I want to say it. I don't know why he's following Wran's orders. This is his cabin. He doesn't have to listen to a thing that comes out of Wran's mouth! Cade drags me around the mess on the floor and down a hall to a room. He opens the door and pushes me inside. I start for the door but he steps in with me, locking it and standing in my way.

"You can't do this!" I shout at him. This isn't right. I have rights. If I want to give myself to that man to save the one person that means the most to me, I can. I can save my child. "Please don't do this, Caden."

"Don't call me that. I'm Cade, remember? They are two different people to you."

I cross my arms and stomp my feet like a toddler, but it does nothing but make him laugh at me. My hand shoots out and lands a blow against the side of his face. None of this is funny. The grin falls from his face, and he stares at me with his mouth hanging open. At least a slap isn't coffee.

"If you meant for that to change my mind about locking you in here, you're wrong." Cade steps up to me and bends his head so that I can feel his breath against my face. "But it was hot."

My cheeks heat at his statement and I step aside, out of reach of him. I don't need him thinking anything about me is hot. Maybe a month ago, my blush would have meant something else entirely, but now . . . I shake my head and then bring my eyes back to him.

"Don't say stuff like that to me."

"You remember that first day we reunited? You were eating lunch in the common area alone."

I give him a stern nod. Of course I remember that. It also happens to be the same day that Wran came home. And the day that he brought Claire and her goons to terrorize me at work. I'm not likely to forget that day anytime soon.

"You were wearing paint-splattered jeans and a cute little ruffled sweater. Your hair was in two small pigtails. That day you reminded me of the Rox I used to know, and I couldn't help but finally talk to you. If I remember correctly,

I told you that I like my girls a little dirty, and you blushed then too."

"What's your point?" I ask him. None of that matters. I don't understand why he keeps bringing up stuff that happened in a different lifetime. The pre-Wran lifetime.

"My point is that I still affect you, whether you were just screwing him upstairs or not."

"I wasn't—"

"I can hear just fine, Roxanna. Stay here, please. I will come back for you when he calms down. I just don't like you around him when he's like that. Reminds me too much of your father."

"Wran's nothing like my father. He wouldn't intentionally hurt me." I believe that one hundred percent.

"Intentionally or not, your boy is unstable when provoked. I don't like it. Just stay."

I cross my arms again and growl at him. "Woof, woof."

He grins. "Good girl!"

I'm surprised he didn't try to pat my head.

Cade leaves the room and I immediately lunge for the handle. I twist it and shove, but it doesn't budge. What the...? Frustrated, I turn back around and survey the room—or rather office. There's a big window behind the desk and a landline sitting on it. I don't know who uses landlines anymore, but I'm glad there's one here. I go over to the phone and pick it up. It has a dial tone. Yes! I look at the window. The cabin my father owns is just like this one and all the windows have a lock on them. I head to the window to see if this one has a latch on it, and to my luck it does. So much for them trying to keep me in here. I sit down in the black leather office chair and flip open the phonebook next to the landline. I'm not really sure how to use a phonebook, so I just start flipping until I see ads on yellow pages. There's a number for a cab and I call it.

I'm getting Harley back.

This ends today.

CHAPTER 27

WRAN

With the knife in my back pocket and the gun securely tucked into my boot, I race back downstairs only to find Cade standing at the cabin's entrance with his brows drawn down and mouth hanging open. He points out the door, but I don't need him to tell me why. I already knew she would sneak out.

"Did you know—?" he begins, and I swiftly cut him off.

"Yup." I zip up my coat. "We're following her."

"I thought you changed your mind about using our girl as bait."

"My girl," I growl at him. "She's my girl."

"If you say so, but she loves me too," he taunts.

I really wish I could knock his pretty-boy teeth out for the provoking, but the truth is that he's fuckin' right. My girl does love him, and I'll be damned if I give her any reason to choose that ass-wipe over me. If that means holding back when my instinct tells me to put a hurtin' on someone, oh well. She's worth it. She's worth everything.

"You may be right, but I'm the one she wants to fuck," I tease him right on back.

Cade grumbles something under his breath and stomps out the door. With a chuckle, I hurry behind him.

Me, one.

Cade, zilch.

In all honesty, I feel sorry for the guy. Must be hard walking around with perpetual blue balls. I wouldn't wish that on any man.

Cade pulls the door closed and locks it. Without waiting for him, I walk down the pathway and search in both directions for Rox's tiny footprints. When I see prints the size of fairy shoes, I head to my right and keep on walking. I come to a stop when I see her standing at the corner. She doesn't seem to have noticed me, so I quickly reverse my steps and try not to make any noise in the snow. Cade walks straight into my back, and I shush him and shove him around a bush when Rox jerks her head in our direction. I duck down, peeking at her through leaves. Her eyes refocus on the road just as a taxi pulls up and she gets inside.

Fuck!

She called a taxi?

The car speeds off down the road and I hop up from my crouched position.

"Go get your car, and fast!" I yell at Cade.

Dammit! I can't believe she thought of that and I didn't. Of course she's not gonna walk in the freezing fuckin' snow to wherever her dad is waiting on her.

Cade sprints back down the path, but it's fuckin' useless. The cab makes a left at the next stop sign and then Rox is gone. She's fuckin' gone. And I have no way of finding her now without her phone. The phone that I threw against a wall.

Fuck!

Fuckin'!

Fuck!

Cade's all-American car pulls up next to me and I hop inside.

"Where to?"

I run my hands over my head, pulling at the hairs at my temples. I have no fuckin' clue where to. She's gone. My Rox is gone to that man. Shaking my head, I slam my fist into the dashboard over and over and over again. This is all bullshit! I should have never suggested this plan to Cade. It was ill thought out. She was never supposed to go to him alone. I was supposed to be by her side. Protecting her.

"I don't know. I fucked up." My girls are goin' to get hurt, all because of me.

"We can always head to her dad's cabin to see if we can find a clue to where she could be going."

I turn around in my seat and give him a piercing look. Is he stupid or somethin'? We don't have time for this. The more time we spend sitting and searching, the closer Rox gets to James Raine, and the closer he gets to having his hands on my girl. He's already touched my daughter, which he will suffer for; I can't handle him touching Rox too. Not when he's already done so much to her.

"Do we look like Scooby-Doo and the gang?"

He looks at me and then out the window. "No, but that's the best we got."

Cade pulls from the stop sign and makes a right. At this rate, we're going to be too late. I'm going to lose her. I'm going to lose Harley. Leaning my forehead against the cold, frosting window, my throat starts to close up and hot tears start to fill my eyes. This is all my fault. If I had been a man and fought for Rox three years ago, none of this would be happening. My child wouldn't have been in state custody, where Rox's deranged father could get to her so easily. Hell, Rox wouldn't have even lost her in the first place. We would be a proper family right now, and Rox would be my . . . I would be getting ready to make an honest woman out of her.

I watch my reflection in the window and the tears finally spill over, flowing down my cheeks like water breaking from a dam. I deserve this. I deserve to lose them both. I wasn't there when either of them needed me, and now this is my punishment. I'm destined to watch the people that mean the most die. I watched my mom die. I watched as my father drank himself into a stupor. And I watched as my brother gave up his childhood to take care of me and then Rox. I watched it all without caring, and now that I do care, I can't do a damn thing to change it.

The car comes to a stop in front of a cabin that looks similar to Cade's family cabin. Except this one doesn't look anywhere near as well kept. There are piles upon piles of snow covering the walkway. If it wasn't for the overhanging arch, the door would be snowed in. Limbs and pine needles clutter the yard. The place looks awful.

Clearing my throat and blinking back the tears, I question, "How do you know there is anything here that will help me find her?"

"We stopped coming here after the accident, but before, I remember Rox's mom loving to take pictures. This cabin was full of them. If there's another place that family spent time at, her mom would have it documented in an album."

That's somethin', I suppose. I'm still not going to count on that. If the outside of this thing looks like it belongs on one of those fixer-upper shows, the inside of it has to be a million times worse. If there's anything inside, though, I'm goin' to find it.

Not waiting for Cade to cut the engine, I jump out of the car and march through the snow to the door. I don't even consider the doorknob, just smash the heel of my foot against the door. It wouldn't have been open anyway. The door slams open with a deafening bang and I walk in. I stop immediately, what smells like gas invading my nose. Covering my mouth, I continue inside.

There's an entryway table covered in plastic and a staircase just like at the other cabin. I pull at the plastic and it comes off with ease. I'm not expecting to find a picture of a family sitting on this table. Picking it up, I wipe at the dust covering the majority of the photo. There's a woman that looks just like Rox except with long, flowing blond hair. She's holding a toddler with a head full of brunette hair and wide purple eyes. Rox. Even as a baby, Rox was beautiful. Next to her is a man that needs no introduction. He hasn't changed at all. He has a sinister look on his face as he glares at the woman holding Rox, like he's unhappy with something. I bet that was one tragic marriage. In front of them both is a boy. He looks around Rox's age—three, maybe four—and he has a baseball in his hand. His hair is just as blond as the woman's.

"I knew they weren't a happy family, but that was something I was used to. No one I knew had a happy family. If I had only known how bad it was, I could have told some-one," Cade says from over my shoulder.

I set the picture back down, disregarding his comment. He was a kid himself. There's nothing he or anyone could have done. I know people with money. For a long time, my family was one of them. If a situation doesn't concern them, they look the other way. Josh and I learned that the hard way when we lost everything. Besides, I'm not here for him to reminisce and ask what ifs. I don't care about the past right now. I care about the damn present and the future. If Roxy wants to see this stuff, I'll bring her here when this is all done and over and I have her back.

Walking deeper into the cabin, I pull more plastic off things, examining every photo I see. None of them have a picture of a pink room in them. At this point I'm about ready to leave. This is going to get us nowhere. It's only going to waste the precious time we could be using to find her. As we move closer to the back of the cabin, Cade taps me on my shoulder and points to something. I turn in the direction he's pointing and see a mirror. It's uncovered, which is strange since everything else has been covered up. It's dusty but in two spots. Two large handprints are imprinted into the dust on either side of a yellow piece of paper that is taped to the mirror. I glance at Cade, terrified to take a step forward. Yeah, I'm fucking terrified. He's been here. He left one thing in this ruined cabin uncovered and with a note on it. That can only mean that he knew we would come here. He's one step ahead, and I don't like it.

Cade steps into the space and I step up behind him. With a frown firmly placed on my face, I grab the note and read it.

One might be the daddy,

And the other the toy,

But remember, boys,

Roxanna has always been my doll.

Stay away or she'll suffer more.

Sincerely,

Father Dearest

He knew!

He fucking knew!

This is all just some wild goose chase, and we're all the fuckin' geese. How did I not see this? He's been sending Rox letters for a while. That can only mean he's been watching her for a while. Or having someone watch her. Hell, he could have been watching her for years. He probably knows her just as well as I do, which means he knew what she would do. He knew what I would fucking do. I ball the note up and throw it at the wall. It's not enough though. I grab the mirror and throw it as well. It shatters into a million pieces and I crumple to the dirty floor.

It's over.

That fucker won.

He has my girls, and I'm not getting them back.

"Dude, look!" Cade yells at me.

I climb to my feet and exhale, composing myself. Losing my shit isn't going to help anyone. Cade points to a picture that was hidden behind the mirror. It's just another family portrait.

"It's just another family picture," I mutter.

"Yeah, but look. This one's different. It has an elderly woman in it. And they're standing outside in the snow."

"So what? It's probably her grandmother."

"I think that's her mother's mother. I met her once, I think. That's not the point. Look at the background." Cade points to a yellow house in the background. It's cute, with a white picket fence surrounding the place. Rox is sitting in the snow, crying. The boy from the earlier picture is pulling her pigtail and laughing.

"I'm guessing that's her brother?" I ask Cade. I know the answer. He's in all the pictures I've seen so far.

"Yeah, that's Kiellan."

"Do you know where that house is at?"

Cade stares at the picture for a long time before nodding his answer. "Yeah, I do."

"Good."

CHAPTER 28

ROX

I step out of the cab and look at the old yellow house with peeling paint that looks more black than yellow. I never thought I'd be back here. Grandma died when I was four, a year before my mother, and this place became abandoned. I don't remember a whole lot from then, but I do remember that I loved coming here. Grandma always did my hair and dressed me in doll clothes. Maybe that's why my father decided to give me dresses as apologies after his punishments.

With great hesitation, I hand over the credit card Wran gave me upon his departure three years ago. The driver swipes it, hands it back to me, and drives off without asking if I needed him to stay. I wish I could go with him, but I can't. My daughter is in that house, and no one's coming for her but me. Wrapping my arms around myself, I step through the broken white fence and head up the slushy pathway to the front door. It opens, so I walk inside and head straight toward the pink room. My room. The floor creaks under the pressure of my feet, letting my father know I've arrived, and I don't like it. I wanted to come, snatch, and run. It's wishful thinking, but that's all that's keeping me sane right now: the hope that he will just hand her over and let me be.

Stopping in front of a bright pink door that looks out of place with the rest of the blue walls, I can hear giggles coming from inside. A hushed response has me taking steps back until I'm standing against the opposite door. My body trembles as if it's going through the aftershocks of an earthquake, and I can't make myself stop.

"Papi!" my daughter shrieks from the other side of the door just as I hear heavy feet walking and floors starting to squeak.

My head bolts to the side, trying to find somewhere to hide. Both sides of the hall are empty. I turn around and turn the knob for the bathroom, but it's locked. My heartbeat picks up and my breathing becomes very labored as I shove on the door, yanking and twisting at the knob. I'm not ready yet. I need more time to prepare myself to see him. No matter what, this door doesn't budge. That doesn't stop the one behind me from opening though. My heart stops and my body freezes, keeping me in place and my eyes away from the person standing in the doorway on the other side of the hall.

I hear his heavy feet take a step past the threshold, and then another and another and another. He stops right behind me and I can feel his body heat through my thick winter sweater dress. My body starts to quiver, my legs getting shaky. My head spins, knowing he's behind me, and my grip on the door handle tightens. I can feel bits and pieces of the paint chipping away in my hand.

Large hands come down on my shoulders and then continue down my arms until they reach my hands. Hot breath explores the back of my neck as if he's moved in even closer. I slam my eyelids shut and start reciting the words to my Peter Pan book in my head. Peter Pan will come. He will save me. He will find me no matter how impossible it may be. I'm his lost girl and no lost boy is ever left behind.

"Roxanna, Roxanna."

My eyes fly open at the sound of him chanting my name.

"You cut your gorgeous hair."

I don't say anything to him. Just keep my mouth shut. If I learned anything as a child, it's never to antagonize this man. Anything at all could set him off, and it's not safe to do that right now with my daughter here. I hear small pitter-patters coming our way and I force myself to turn around. When Harley sees me, her eyes get wide and her little pitters turn into a full-on run.

"Mommy!" she shouts.

I shove past my father and reach for her, towing her up into my arms. "Baby."

My hands roam all over her, making sure he hasn't left any marks or anything on my child. When I'm sure she's fine, I bury my face in her soft hair and hold her tight. She's okay. Ohmygod, she's okay.

"Aww," my father lets out, sending a cold chill down my spine. He places a hand on the small of my back. "Isn't this wonderful? A family reunion."

I jerk away from him and shift Harley to my side. I spin around so I'm facing him, and he can see just how unfamiliar we really are. We are not family. He is a disease that I want nothing more than to get rid of.

"Don't touch me," I tell him through gritted teeth.

"Mommy?" Harley asks. Her small hand comes up to my face, but I can't take my eyes off this man. If I do, he will strike.

The grin on my father's face falls. He takes a step forward, and I take a step away. We repeat the motion. But then the door to the pink room slams, and I realize this is exactly where he wants me. Harley wiggles her way down my side and runs across the room. I only give her a quick glance, but that's all my father needs. He reaches out and yanks me to him, pinning my arms behind my back with one hand and the other spread across my abdomen.

"You've been a very naughty girl, Roxanna," he fusses in my ear. "Sleeping with men you shouldn't. Having a baby. Tsk. Tsk. Tsk. Only whores spread their legs so willingly. Didn't I teach you anything?"

I don't correct him. I've only ever slept with one man, on one occasion. I'm not apologizing to anyone for that either.

Not to Lynn. Not to Cade. And most certainly not to a man who has done far worse.

My dad's hand moves up my torso and over my shoulder to my hair. He flicks the strands and a low growl only meant for my ears leaves him. "And this hair. You know Daddy don't like little girls with short hair—much less blue."

I flinch at his words about my hair. They remind me of Wran's comments on it the first night he came home. Wran was only teasing, but I still don't like that my father is basically mimicking his reaction to my hair. It's just hair. The dye has already started to fade, and my roots are very prominent now.

"Dad, please," I try to reason with him. "Why are you doing this?"

My father lets go of my arms, but my body refuses to relax. He goes over to where Harley sits on the floor with a doll and a pink castle. I think it used to be mine. I start in the direction of them, but my father holds up a hand to stop me and I do. He picks Harley up off the floor, running a hand up and down her arm. He bounces her a little, just like a father should do a daughter. But then he turns his leer to me. There's nothing fatherly or grandfatherly or anything in it. It just looks sick and twisted.

"We're going to be a family," he says. "A little happy family. You took the one I had, my dear, dear Roxanna. And now you're going to give me one back."

I shake my head at him. "We are never going to be a family."

"Tsk. Tsk. Tsk." He walks over to me, Harley still in his arms. With his free hand, he wraps it around the back of my neck and pulls me forward. My breath catches but I do everything to keep my reaction under control. I don't want to startle Harley. "That's the wrong answer. Little Harley here needs a good mother and father."

I look at my daughter, completely innocent and unaware of what's going on around her. I turn back to my father. "She already has a good mother and a wonderful father."

My dad bursts into laughter. "Wran? You think he's a good man. You poor unfortunate soul. If only you knew half the things that boy has done to make your life miserable. It's humorous. He truly does love you, but at the same time he hates your guts."

"Because of you."

He sucks in air. "Yeah, I suppose I did screw everyone over. But I'm not the one who paid people to start rumors about you in seventh grade. Ever wonder why that Clairey girl hates you so much? You should probably sit down and ask your dear Wran."

Frantically, I shake my head at him. Wran wouldn't do those things. We fought, and yes, I know he did some terrible things to get under my skin, but he wouldn't have my entire class tease me for things. He wouldn't drive away the only person in my class that I considered a friend. Yeah, I said some things to Claire about her crush on Wran, but everyone had a crush on Wran.

"You're lying!" I break. "He wouldn't do that."

"Mommy," Harley calls out. I instantly reach for her, but my father pulls her back. She tries to wiggle out of my father's hold, but he just holds her tighter. I reach for my daughter again. This time my father shoves me backward. I trip over one of the toys lying on the floor and fall, clipping my elbow on the rotting wooden frame of the twin-sized bed. Harley erupts into screams.

Dad holds her out away from his side and seethes. "Shut up!"

Harley screams even louder and kicks out her little feet, trying to get down. When she doesn't obey him, he shakes her violently.

"Daddy, please!" I plead with him.

"You want me to let her go?" he asks me, and I nod viciously. He stomps over to a window and punches out the glass. His hand comes back bloody. I freeze when he dangles Harley out the window. "You want me to let her go like I was forced to let your mother go?"

I shake my head. "Daddy! Daddy, no!"

"Make up your mind!" he shouts at me.

I shake my head.

He yanks Harley back inside the window and my heart literally stops when a piece of ridged glass slices at her leg. She wails, but my father makes no movement to try to see why. He tosses her on the floor by the castle, and I make a move for her. I don't make it across the small distance before my father is in front of me. He grabs my forearms and starts dragging me to the door. I pull and pull but he's strong—too strong for a forty-six-year-old man that's been in prison for twelve years.

I feel something sharp digging through my sweater and I stop fighting him.

"You either come with me the easy way and take your punishment like a good girl, or the hard way."

I point to Harley on the floor, crying and leg bloodied. I break out into a sob. "She's hurt."

"It's a scratch. She'll be fine. But you won't be if I have to say it again."

Ohmygod, ohmygod, I'm going to die.

My father shoves me out of the pink room, and I stumble a little over the threshold. He slams the door, and the loud wailing from inside is the only thing echoing in my mind. Without thinking, I reach for the door, for my baby, but my father slaps my hand away. He brings out the sharp piece of glass and holds it out toward me. He repeats "she's fine" and points down the narrow hall to another room. The green room. My grandmother had a fixation with making each room a theme. At least the green door is more suited to the blue walls.

Obeying him, I walk down the hall to the green door. I don't remember what this room was used for when I was four, but I doubt my father is going to use it for anything good. Punishment. He wants to punish me, which means this room could be filled with anything. Images of him submerging me underwater over and over again flash to the forefront of my mind. I don't want to go through that. I look over my shoulder at him looming over me. He points to the door and I push it open. I gasp when I see the medical room setup, complete with a hospital bed, an IV, and monitors.

I turn to face him, trembling like crazy. I have no idea what he intends to do to me, but it must be worse than nearly drowning me repeatedly if he needs hospital equipment.

"Please. I didn't do anything wrong," I cry to him.

My father cups the side of my face, and I let him. He sighs. "My dear child, you've done everything wrong. You ran."

I shake my head.

"You let another man touch you."

I shake my head again.

"You did drugs. You got pregnant at fifteen. Good girls don't do those things."

His hand drops from my cheek and I let my head fall in shame. I did all of those things. Every. . . single. . .thing he's accusing me of. And on top of all that, I almost killed myself and Harley. Good girls don't do that. Maybe I do need to be punished. Taking a chance, I peep up at my father and the glass in his hand. I don't need his form of punishment.

I shake my head at him. "I've been punished already."

"You think losing her is punishment? You think weekend visitations is punishment? You think going to school and shopping and to the mall is adequate punishment for all the things you've done, Roxanna?"

I nod my head. Yeah, I do. That's all my punishment. I might have those things, but this man has no clue what I have had to give up to get them. Freedom. College. Friendships. Art. Wran. My peace of mind. Everything I have done for the past three years has been my punishment. I'm just now learning that I can have some things back, and I won't stand for him telling me that I shouldn't have them at all.

"How do you know all of this?" I ask him.

"I was the best criminal lawyer in the state. Do you honestly think I didn't have eyes on you from the moment you ran? Now, go lay on the bed."

I shake my head at him. "No. I'm not going to let you hurt me."

His face quickly morphs into one of anger, nostrils flaring like he's about to charge at me, brows dipped and drawn, jaw clenched. He takes a step in my direction and I back up farther into the room. It's not the smart option but it's my only option. I can't very well go charging at a raging bull.

He jabs his hand with the broken glass toward the white mattress. "Get on the fucking bed, Roxanna!"

"No!" I shout back at him. "I am done fearing you. You are nothing more than a miserable, crazy man."

Growling, my father lunges at me and swings the broken glass in my direction. I hop out of range, only to bump into something cold, hard, and obviously metal. He charges at me again and I duck out of the way. I hiss out, though, when I feel something sharp drag across my arm. One of my hands moves to it instinctively. Pulling it back, red tints my normally ashen skin. Too late, I turn around just as my father's hand comes down with the glass, plunging it into my shoulder. I howl out in agony and fall completely to the floor. All I see is blood gushing everywhere as my father pulls the glass piece from my shoulder. He tosses it across the room and grabs my arm, pulling me across the floor. I twist in his hold, but the pain is too much.

"Next time," he hisses out as he stops dragging me, "do as I say, and you won't get hurt."

I whimper at his words. Those are not the words a father should say to his child when she's hurt. He draws me up into his arms as he runs a bloody hand down my hair. He kisses my forehead and I shrink away from him. I don't want him anywhere near me. Picking me up, he lays me across the bed and then walks away, over to the metal tray. He picks up a syringe and my eyes widen when he turns back to me. I shake my head and sob. I try to twist around on the bed, to get away from him, but my arm screams in protest.

My dad steps up to me and takes my arm. "This is for your own good. You'll thank me later."

"No. Don't do this. Please!"

He stabs the needle into my arm just as a loud bang rings throughout the house. I cry out, loud enough so whoever made that noise can hear me.

"Help me," I yell, but it comes out halfheartedly as whatever my father injected me with starts to take effect.

He wraps his hand around my mouth and pulls me up off the bed, holding me to him in a defensive manner. The green door comes slamming open and I see Wran and Cade barge inside. I slump against my father as my body starts to go numb.

"Get your . . . off . . . her," I hear one of the boys say, but I can barely make out what they are saying. They sound so far away even though they are right across the room.

"Well, if it isn't Thing One and Thing Two to the rescue." My father's words come in clearer, but I'm guessing that's because he's right next to me.

I lift my head to look at them, but I feel so heavy. I let my head fall back down to my father's chest. He shoves me aside and I hit something, but I don't feel it. I don't feel anything anymore. Closing my eyes, I lie where I land and listen to the muffled voices around me. There's a ton of yelling and I attempt to look up at everyone, but my head floods, making everything around me fuzzy. I'm only able to make out two figures. Someone left the room. I lay my head back down.

Bang, bang is all I hear before the drug pulls me under entirely.

CHAPTER 29

ROX

A loud, constant beeping rings out, and I crack my eyes open only to close them again. Bright fluorescent light shines down on me, and it feels like my eyes have been sewn shut for a hundred years. Bringing my hands up, I rub at the gunk in my eyes but stop at an annoying pulling in my right shoulder. I moan out and open my eyes fully. I glance over toward where the beeping is coming from to see a heart monitor and IV pump. My eyes widen when I realize where I am.

No.

No.

No!

I start pulling at the IV and the heart machine starts going haywire. I have to get out of here. I have to get away from him. A pair of hands come down on my hand, stopping me from getting the IV out of my wrist. I scream and the hands fall away. I scoot back up on the bed, blinking hysterically and trying to figure out what's going on. I glance away from my wrist and up into a pair of storm-gray eyes. Josh hovers over me with his hands drawn.

A door swings open, and my eyes swing to it. Wran stands in the doorway in black jeans and a black hoodie, eyes wide and mouth open. I look around the room, taking in the large window, ugly paintings on the wall, and the mute TV. A hospital. I'm in a hospital. How did I get to a hospital?

Wran darts inside the room, followed by a doctor and Cade, and Lynn with Harley. Wran comes over to the bed and hesitates before sitting down beside me. The doctor makes her way over to me as well. She gives me a gentle smile that I don't return.

"It's nice to see you awake," she says in an almost too cheery voice. "I'm Dr. Clarke. Do you mind if I check that and draw your blood?" She points to my wrist where the IV is located.

I glance down at the needle and nod my head. When the needle seems securely in place and she has a syringe full of my blood, the doctor excuses herself and leaves the room.

"Mommy!" Harley screams in Lynn's hold, and my eyes drift to my daughter's leg. The last time I saw it, it was bleeding. There's a wrap around it now and she's no longer in the yellow dress.

"I'm so sorry," Wran says, and I force my eyes away from my daughter. His head is down, and his eyes are glassy like he's been crying. That's impossible though. Wran doesn't cry. "I didn't find you in time."

"W–what happened?" I choke out. My throat's so dry it feels like I've been swallowing back cotton balls. "How did I get here?"

"Roxy!" Harley hollers again and runs over to the bed. I reach down for her, ignoring the numb pain in my arm.

I hug her close to me. She's okay. She's okay.

I kiss her forehead and turn to Wran. His eyes are on Harley.

"Can I hold her?" he asks.

My eyes snap up to Lynn. She gives me a weak smile, and I almost break all over again. She knows. She knows that Wran's the father.

She replaces the doctor's previous position and glances at Wran and Harley. "I put the pieces together the moment I saw them together. Everyone else will too."

All I can do is nod. I knew she would put it together. Harley is a carbon copy of Wran. I run a hand down Harley's back and smile at her. I guess there's no time like the present to introduce her to her father.

"Harley?"

She looks up at me and then around at all the faces in the room. I wish it was just me and Wran here, but I know asking everyone to leave is futile. Not after the weekend we've had.

"Harley," I start again. "I want you to meet someone." I point over to Wran. Her eyes follow my finger. There's a bit of a tug on the wire connected to me, but I disregard it. "That's Wran. Your daddy."

"Daaaddy." She strings out the word as if she's trying to get used to saying it. I don't expect her to use it. She knows I'm her mommy, but she hardly ever calls me that. Only when she senses something is wrong. As I pass her over to Wran, she shakes her head. "Poshy!"

Josh takes an immediate step, but I raise a hand to stop him. She has to get used to Wran, and Josh running when she calls isn't going to allow her to get used to another man. Wran takes her from my hands and beams down at her. She's still reaching for Josh. When Josh makes no means to move, she looks back at Wran. I expect waterworks, but they don't come. She just stares at him and vice versa. Studying each other.

"Daaaddy," she says again.

My brows shoot up and I'm a little jealous. It took two years to get her to call me anything other than Roxy.

A grin spread out across Wran's face and he looks up at me. "Did you hear that? She called me daddy."

Yeah, she did.

Just as I turn to Lynn the doctor walks back into the room, smiling at the group. She comes over to me and starts detaching wires. She pulls the IV from my wrist lastly and places a swab and bandage over my wrist.

"Everything checked out," she states, reading from the clipboard in her hand. "And the lorazepam is out of your system. It's a good thing your father didn't give you a large dosage. All your paperwork is ready to be signed at the nurses' station for checkout."

"Lorazepam?" I ask the doctor. It sounds familiar but I'm not sure what type of drug that is.

"It's generally used to treat patients with seizure disorders. Your system showed that you had an immunity built up to it."

I shake my head at her. I've never taken that drug. Not that I can remember anyways.

"She can leave today?" Cade asks her.

She nods. "I'm sure one of you big, strong gentlemen can get her home safely."

With that, the doctor walks out of the room. Lynn reaches across me and takes Harley from Wran. Reluctantly, he lets her go, but I can see the fight on his face. He doesn't want to let Harley go now that he has her. I don't want to let her go either. She was taken from under Lynn's nose. Lynn turns from the bed and starts for the door.

"Wait!" I call after her. "I don't get to keep her?"

Lynn tilts her head to the side and frowns at me. "Roxanna, this doesn't change anything, and now that I have confirmation that Wran Belmont is the father, things are only going to escalate. Keep doing what you are doing and there's still a chance."

I glance around the room at everyone, holding back my tears.

"But we got her back! You guys couldn't even find her!" Cade shouts at Lynn.

She gives us all a sympathetic look. "I know. And that will help your case in the long run. Just not right now. I'm sorry, Roxanna."

Before anyone else has time to object, she walks out of the room, taking Harley with her. You would think that I would be used to walking away from my daughter by now, but I'm not. It doesn't get easier. I knew that after this weekend, things would worsen for my situation, but a part of me also thought that Lynn seeing that I can be there for Harley would change things. It changes nothing. I still don't have her.

Wran scoots over to me and pulls me up against his chest, rubbing circles on my back. "It's okay. We will get her back. I promise. We will have our daughter before this year is over with."

I don't respond to him. There's not really anything anyone in this room can do to get my child back. It was a mistake I made, and I alone will have to deal with that. Wran doesn't even have any rights. At least I think that's how it goes.

"I'm gonna go check you out. Sit tight, all right?"

I nod and watch Wran leave the room. Cade quickly takes his place and Josh moves over by the door, standing awkwardly. I honestly don't know why he's here. Harley's gone, so he should be too. Or according to his logic anyways. Josh points to the door and raises his brow in a questioning manner. I nod and he slips out, leaving me alone with Cade.

Cade scoots back on the bed and drapes an arm across my shoulder. "I thought you were never going to wake up."

"How long have I been here?"

"Only two days, but those two days were torture. You were in and out of it a lot. Screaming in your sleep."

"I'm sorry," I whisper to him. I'm so, so sorry. None of this would have happened if I hadn't sneaked out. Things would have gone according to whatever plan Wran would have undoubtedly come up with.

"Don't be sorry. I'm just happy you're awake."

I lean my head into his chest. "I want to go home."

"We'll be leaving soon."

"Where's my dad?" I noticed no one said a word about him when they were talking. I expected Lynn to be the one to bring it up, but nope.

Cade exhales and I turn to look at him. "He's dead, Rox. Wran shot him."

"Dead dead?"

He nods, and I inhale. I don't know how to feel about that. On one hand, he was my father. Incarceration obviously didn't treat him well. He went loco. Sure, he was always a terrible man, but what I saw was on another level. Maybe he could have been helped. Maybe he just needed someone to give him a chance. On the opposite hand, he hurt me; he's been hurting me. And he hurt Harley. That's not something I'm going to forgive and forget so easily.

"How do you feel about that?" he questions, pressing a kiss into my hair. "Are you okay?"

"I'm fine," I admit. I'm really fine. I don't have to worry about letters anymore. I can sleep at night knowing he's not coming back for me or my kid. I can breathe for the first time in twelve years.

"Good."

The door to my room opens and Wran strolls in with a wheelchair. "All right, sweetheart, let's get you home."

Home?

My eyes shift between the two guys that have become a permanent fixture in my life over the last month. Geez, I can't even believe it has been a month since Wran came back. I don't know why, but I've never really thought of that apartment as home. At least not since Wran's been gone. Some part of me sort of forgot what it was like to have people to depend on—to relent some of the weight on my shoulders. To have someone that isn't just hanging around out of oblig-ation to an adorable two year old. While I appreciate Josh, I don't think he has ever been there for only me. There has always been his brother's welfare and then Harley.

Glancing over my shoulder at Cade still lounging back on the hospital bed like he owns it, I give him a soft smile and reach to squeeze his hand laying lazily across his abdomen as he watches me. His brow twitches, and he squeezes my hand back. He leans forward slightly and gives me a peck on the forehead. Wran let out a low groan in protest, and I pull my gaze away from Cade, turning back to Wran with the wheelchair. Back to the guy that admitted to hating me due to something I had no part in. While that still bugs me and while I still need a ton more answers from him, I know I can't be without him.

Wran is my home.

Wran is my everything.

And while we still need a crap ton of work, I'm willing to work through our issues. He's my Peter Pan after all. My Neverland. And I will forever be his lost girl. Going home sounds good to me.

Acknowledgments

Thank you, thank you, thank you to everyone who put up with me while I wrote this book—but especially to:

Sharon, who is an exceptional sister-in-law and fantastic beta. You gave me great feedback.

To my husband, Curby, who listens to me talk endlessly about these characters and their problems as if they are real, without giving me too many "go-aways" this time around.

To my editor, Amy, you are the best. This book wouldn't be possible without you.

To Quilla, for sharing your story and experiences with me.

And finally, to my mom, you have always been a rock. I know we've gone through some hard times, both in my childhood and not so long ago. You handle them with such elegance and kept me from breaking down. I love you. You truly are the definition of a strong mother.

ALSO BY

T. Marie Alexander

Completed (Kingston City Limits Series)
The Lost and the Scarred (Book 1)
The Saved and the Sorry (Book 2)
The Worthy and the Willful (Book 3)

(Better Than Revenge Duet)
Nothing Sweeter (Book 1)

(Standalones)
Revelations

THE LOST AND THE SCARRED

Follow T. Marie at:
Facebook: @authortmariealexander
Tiktok: @authortmariealexander
Instagram: @authortmariealexander

You can even check out my website:
www.tmariealexander.com